John Cleland's

Fanny Hill

Memoirs of a Woman of Pleasure

The Complete Unexpurgated Edition

Foreword by H. Montgomery Hyde

A Mayflower Paperback

FANNY HILL:
MEMOIRS OF A WOMAN OF PLEASURE
John Cleland

Published in a revised edition 1964
Reprinted many times

First published in this edition by Mayflower Books
1970
Reprinted 1970 (twice)

The Trial of Fanny Hill was written by
Richard Bennett and published by kind permission of
The Sunday Telegraph.

Mayflower Paperbacks are published by
Mayflower Books,
3 Upper James Street, London, W.1.
Made and printed in Great Britain by
Hunt Barnard & Co. Ltd., Aylesbury, Bucks.

FOREWORD

by H. MONTGOMERY HYDE

The Memoirs of a Woman of Pleasure, usually known as *Fanny Hill*, is the most celebrated erotic book in the English language. It is also considered by many critics to be the best written. Although the reader will search in vain for a single dirty or "four-letter" word from the first page to the last, nevertheless it has been described by no less an authority than the *Dictionary of National Biography* as "a scandalously indecent book". Since its original publication over two centuries ago, *Fanny Hill* has been banned in Britain and copies have been seized by the customs and police as an allegedly obscene publication wherever they have been found. Consequently few booksellers have dared to sell it openly, at any rate in its present unexpurgated form.

The book's author John Cleland was a man of scholarly as well as erotic tastes. The son of a civil servant who came to London from Scotland, Cleland was born in 1709 and died in 1790. He was educated at Westminster School, and as a young man he got a job with the East India Company. For a time he acted as British Consul in Smyrna. He later moved to Bombay where he eventually quarrelled with the local directors and left the service with little or no money. For some years he wandered from city to city in Europe, invariably hard up, finally returning to England where he was more than once imprisoned for debt. In fact, it was with the object of satisfying his most pressing creditors that he wrote *Fanny Hill*, the story of which he admitted had been suggested to him many years before by "a young gentleman of the greatest hopes that ever I knew, brother to a nobleman now Ambassador at a Foreign Court". He sold the story for twenty guineas to a book-seller and publisher in St. Paul's Churchyard called Ralph Griffiths, who first published it in two volumes, price 3s., in 1749. It was an immediate success and Griffiths is said to have made £10,000 from the publication.

The book's success attracted the unfavourable attention of several bishops and other church dignitaries who wished the author and publisher to be prosecuted – perhaps because, as Cleland wrote at the time, "more Clergymen bought it, in proportion, than any

5

other distinction of men". However, no prosecution was brought. Instead Cleland was summoned to appear before the Privy Council, and having pleaded poverty as an excuse was merely warned to be more careful with his pen in future. On this occasion he argued so impressively that Lord Granville, one of the members of the council, put him on the government payroll at £100 a year as an information officer, as he would be called today. Cleland wrote several more novels and also plays, as well as a learned work on philology, but henceforward he wisely steered clear of erotica, fervently wishing, as he said, that *Fanny Hill* would be "buried and forgot". Yet *Fanny Hill* is the only one of his works which is remembered today.

Expressed in the elegant language of the period, the book has great historical value in relation to the development of the novel itself and it has similar value in relation to its subject matter in the age in which it was written. Its literary qualities are quite remarkable. The characterisation is good. There is humour in the book – an element of gaiety and lightheartedness – and while it does not rank with the works of Dickens and Scott, it is, in its way, a little masterpiece.

That is what I said in giving evidence for the defence before the Manchester magistrates in April, 1964, when proceedings were brought against the printers of the first unexpurgated edition published by Mayflower Books. In spite of my pleading, *Fanny Hill* was condemned by the Manchester magistrates who made a destruction order, just as the work had been similarly condemned three months earlier by the late Chief Magistrate Sir Robert Blundell at the Bow Street Court in London.

I was the first witness to speak for the defence in Manchester, and I think I was the only one to testify in both trials. The changed climate of opinion during the past five years makes it unlikely that I shall have to appear again in the witness box. This is as it should be. Meanwhile *Fanny Hill* can now be freely bought over instead of under the counter. For this I feel that the public owes a debt of gratitude to the courage and perseverance of Mayflower Books, which notwithstanding two earlier prosecutions has brought out this new and unexpurgated edition of a literary classic.

INTRODUCTION
THE TRIAL OF FANNY HILL

Being an account of her surprise at the outcome of the
sensational Mayflower Fanny Hill trial of 1963, in her
own hand.

Madam,

"I will not conceal from you the gratification, of which I
was fully sensible, that my case was being heard, albeit in
the smallest and meanest court at Bow Street, by no less a
dignitary than Sir Robert Blundell, the Chief Metropolitan
Magistrate, who occupied that rhadamanthine chair, where
I remembered Henry Fielding, the genial author of a bawdy
and liquorish book, 'Tom Jones', which my dear Charles
forbade me to read, and by a prudent parental care withheld
from the eyes of our young son.

"Nor can I deny the hopes with which I was upheld when
I learned that the worthy Sir Robert had been schooled, like
Mr. Cleland, the author who recorded my adventures, at
Westminster, and that he advised the world at large, in the
pages of 'Who's Who', that his recreation is deipnosophism,
or the art of dining.

"I was foolishly filled with the expectation that so rational
a pleasurist, a kindly bachelor of some sixty years, would
view with indulgence the story of the scandalous stages of my
life after my safe coming home to port and the paths of
Virtue.

"I will not weary you with the details of a case encouraging in its progress as it was disappointing in its outcome, save
to express my surprise that I was tried summarily, like a common street player, and not before a judge and jury like Lady
Chatterley, who showed such a want of delicacy in the use of
those vulgar expressions which I was so solicitous to avoid.

"But what woman could not but be flattered by the

approbation of my little work, of its historical interest and its literary merit by witnesses of the highest learning and distinction?

"Under the skilful guidance of my silver-tongued advocate, Mr. Jeremy Hutchinson, they spoke, as one, of the merit of my work. Some passages, indeed, they found as disagreeable to read as they were to experience, but they testified that even these painful incidents had not the power to disaffirm the moral of my little tale: that it is Love and marriage alone which sanctify pleasure. They told Sir Robert of lubricious works lacking all decency and the simplest elements of literary artifice which were everywhere on sale to the common reader.

"None were put out of countenance nor were deflected from their firm conviction that the place of my memoirs was 'in the history of Literature and not in the history of smut,' by the rigorous examination and the withering scorn of the unbending advocate of the Police Commissioner, Mr. Griffith Jones, who could find no witness throughout the length and breadth of the land to speak against me.

"I felt a warm and lively appreciation directed towards me from the journalists and the few members of a curious public, gathered in positions of pinched and cramped discomfort, as Mr. Hutchinson rose to address the magistrate. In a speech in which reasoning vied with eloquence to make an equal match, he seemed to carry all before him: nor did it seem possible, as he argued, that my memoirs, which may be freely read in the American and Canadian colonies, should be proscribed in that very district which was the scene of many of my adventures.

"Judge then of the general amazement and the perturbation into which I was thrown, when the good Sir Robert, with scarcely a minute for reflection, pronounced against me.

"I look to see you soon, and, in the meantime, believe me ever."

MADAM,

Yours, etc., etc.

LETTER THE FIRST

Madam,

I sit down to give you an undeniable proof of my considering your desires as indispensable orders. Ungracious then as the task may be, I shall recall to view those scandalous stages of my life, out of which I emerg'd, at length, to the enjoyment of every blessing in the power of love, health, and fortune to bestow; whilst yet in the flower of youth, and not too late to employ the leisure afforded me by great ease and affluence, to cultivate an understanding, naturally not a despicable one, and which had, even amidst the whirl of loose pleasures I had been tost in, exerted more observation on the characters and manners of the world than what is common to those of my unhappy profession, who looking on all thought or reflection as their capital enemy, keep it at as great a distance as they can, or destroy it without mercy.

Hating, as I mortally do, all long unnecessary prefaces, I shall give you good quarter in this, and use no further apology than to prepare you for seeing the loose part of my life, wrote with the same liberty that I led it.

Truth! stark, naked truth, is the word; and I will not so much as take the pains to bestow the strip of a gauzewrapper on it, but paint situations such as they actually rose to me in nature, careless of violating those laws of decency that were never made for such unreserved intimacies as ours; and you have too much sense, too much knowledge of the ORIGINALS themselves, to sniff prudishly and out of character at the PICTURES of them. The greatest men, those of the first and most leading taste, will not scruple adorning their private closets with nudities, though, in compliance with vulgar prejudices, they may not think them decent decorations of the staircase, or saloon.

This, and enough, premised, I go directly into my personal history. My maiden name was *Frances Hill.* I was born at a small village near *Liverpool*, in *Lancashire*, of parents extremely poor, and, I piously believe, extremely honest.

My father, who had received a maim on his limbs, that disabled him from following the more laborious branches of country-drudgery, got, by making of nets, a scanty subsistence, which was not much enlarg'd by my mother's keeping a little day-school for the girls in her neighbourhood. They had had several children; but none lived to any age except myself, who had received from nature a constitution perfectly healthy.

My education, till past fourteen, was no better than very vulgar; reading, or rather spelling, an illegible scrawl, and a little ordinary plain work composed the whole system of it; and then all my foundation in virtue was no other than a total ignorance of vice, and the shy timidity general to our sex, in the tender stage of life, when objects alarm or frighten more by their novelty than anything else. But then, this is a fear too often cured at the expense of innocence, when Miss, by degrees, begins no longer to look on a man as a creature of prey that will eat her.

My poor mother had divided her time so entirely between her scholars and her little domestic cares that she had spared very little of it to my instruction, having, from her own innocence from all ill, no hint or thought of guarding me against any.

I was now entering on my fifteenth year, when the worst of ills befell me in the loss of my tender fond parents, who were both carried off by the small-pox, within a few days of each other; my father dying first, and thereby hastening the death of my mother: so that I was now left an unhappy friendless orphan (for my father's coming to settle there was accidental, he being originally a *Kentishman*). That cruel distemper which had proved so fatal to them, had indeed seized me, but with such mild and favourable symptoms, that I was presently out of danger, and, what I then did not know the value of, was entirely unmark'd. I skip over here an account of the natural grief and affliction which I felt on this melancholy occasion. A little time, and the giddiness of that age, dissipated too soon my reflections on that irreparable loss; but nothing contributed more to reconcile me to it, than the notions that were immediately put into my head, of going to *London*, and looking out for a service, in which I was promised all assistance and advice from one *Esther Davis*, a young woman that had been down to see her friends, and who, after the stay of a few days, was to return to her place.

As I had now nobody left alive in the village who had concern enough about what should become of me to start any objections to this scheme, and the woman who took care of me after my parents' death rather encouraged me to pursue it, I soon came to a resolution of making this launch into the wide world by repairing to *London*, in order to SEEK MY FORTUNE, a phrase which, by the bye, has ruined more adventurers of both sexes from the country, than ever it made or advanced.

Nor did Esther Davis a little comfort and inspirit me to venture with her, by piquing my childish curiosity with the fine sights that were to be seen in *London*: the Tombs, the Lions, the King, the Royal Family, the fine Plays and Operas, and, in short, all the diversions which fell within her sphere of life to come at; the detail of all which perfectly turns the little head of me.

Nor can I remember, without laughing, the innocent admiration, not without a spice of envy, with which we poor girls, whose church-going clothes did not rise above dowlass shifts and stuff gowns, beheld Esther's scowered satin gowns, caps border'd with an inch of lace, tawdry ribbons, and shoes belaced with silver: all which we imagined grew in London, and entered for a great deal into my determination of trying to come in for my share of them.

The idea however of having the company of a towns-woman with her, was the trivial, and all the motives that engaged Esther to take charge of me during my journey to town, where she told me, after her manner and style, as how several maids out of the country had made themselves and all their kin for ever: that by preserving their VIRTUE, some had taken so with their masters, that they had married them, and kept them coaches, and lived vastly grand and happy; and some, mayhap, came to be Duchesses; luck was all, and why not I, as well as another? with other almanacs to this purpose, which set me a tip-toe to begin this promising journey, and to leave a place which, though my native one, contained no relations that I had reason to regret, and was grown insupportable to me, from the change of the tenderest usage into a cold air of charity, with which I was entertain'd, even at the only friend's house that I had the least expectation of care and protection from. She was, however, so just to me, as to manage the turning into money of the little matters that remained to me after the debts and burial charges were accounted for, and, at my departure, put my whole fortune into my hands; which consisted of a very slender wardrobe, pack'd up in a very portable box, and eight guineas, with seventeen shillings in silver; stowed in a springpouch, which was a greater treasure than ever I had yet seen together, and which I could not conceive there was a possibility of running out; and indeed, I was so entirely taken up with the joy of seeing myself mistress of such an immense sum, that I gave very little attention to a world of good advice which was given me with it.

Places, then, being taken for Esther and me in the London waggon, I pass over a very immaterial scene of leave-taking, at which I dropt a few tears betwixt grief and joy; and, for the same reasons of insignificance, skip over all that happened to me on the road, such as the waggoner's looking liquorish on me, the schemes laid for me by some of the passengers, which were defeated by the vigilance of my guardian Esther; who, to do her justice, took a motherly care of me, at the same time that she taxed me for her protection by making me bear all travelling charges, which I defrayed with the utmost cheerfulness, and thought myself much obliged to her into the bargain.

She took indeed great care that we were not overrated, or imposed on, as well as of managing as frugally as possible; expensiveness was not her vice.

It was pretty late in a summer evening when we reached London-town, in our slow conveyance, though drawn by six at length. As we passed through the greatest streets that led to our inn, the noise of the coaches, the hurry, the crowds of foot passengers, in short, the new scenery of the shops and houses, at once pleased and amazed me.

But guess at my mortification and surprise when we came to the inn, and our things were landed and deliver'd to us, when my fellow traveller and protectress, Esther Davis, who had used me with the utmost tenderness during the journey, and prepared me by no preceding signs for the stunning blow I was to receive, when I say, my only dependence and friend, in this strange place, all of a sudden assumed a strange and cool air towards me, as if she dreaded my becoming a burden to her.

Instead, then, of proffering me the continuance of her assistance and good offices, which I relied upon, and never more wanted, she thought herself, it seems, abundantly acquitted of her engagements to me, by having brought me safe my journey's end; and seeing nothing in her procedure towards me but what was natural and in order, began to embrace me by way of taking leave, whilst I was so confounded, so struck, that I had not spirit or sense enough so much as to mention my hopes or expectations from her experience, and knowledge of the place she had brought me to.

Whilst I stood thus stupid and mute, which she doubtless attributed to nothing more than a concern at parting, this idea procured me perhaps a slight alleviation of it, in the following harangue: That now we were got safe to London, and that she was obliged to go to her place, she advised me by all means to get into one as soon as possible; that I need not fear getting one; there were more places than parish-churches; that she advised me to go to an intelligence office; that if she heard of anything stirring, she would find me out and let me know; that in the meantime, I should take a private lodging, and acquaint her where to send to me; that she wish'd me good luck, and hoped I should always have the grace to keep myself honest, and not bring a disgrace on my parentage. With this, she took her leave of me, and left me, as it were, on my own hands, full as lightly as I had been put into hers.

Left thus alone, absolutely destitute and friendless, I began then to feel most bitterly the severity of this separation the scene of which had passed in a little room in the inn; and no sooner was her back turned, but the affliction I felt at my helpless strange circumstances burst out into a flood of tears, which infinitely relieved the oppression of my heart; though I still remained stupefied, and most perfectly perplex'd how to dispose of myself.

One of the drawers coming in, added yet more to my uncertainty, by asking me, in a short way, if I called for anything? to which I replied innocently: "No." But I wished him to tell me where I might get a lodging for that night. He said he would go and speak to his mistress who, accordingly, came and told me drily, without entering in the least into the distress she saw me in, that I might have a bed for a shilling, and that, as they supposed I had some friends in town (here I fetched a deep sigh in vain!), I might provide for myself in the morning.

'Tis incredible what trifling consolations the human mind will seize in its greatest afflictions. The assurance of nothing more than a bed to lie on that night, calmed my agonies; and being asham'd to acquaint the mistress of the inn that I had no friends to apply to in town, I proposed to myself to proceed, the very next morning, to an intelligence office, to which I was furnish'd with written directions on the back of a ballad Esther had given me. There I counted on getting information of any place that such a country girl as I might be fit for, and where I could get into any sort of being, before my little stock should be consumed; and as to a character, Esther had often repeated to me that I might depend on her managing me one; nor, however affected I was at her leaving me thus, did I entirely cease to rely on her, as I began to think, good-naturedly, that her procedure was all in course, and that it was only my ignorance of life that had made me take it in the light I at first did.

Accordingly, the next morning I dress'd myself as clean and as neat as my rustic wardrobe would permit me; and having left my box, with special recommendation, with the landlady, I ventured out by myself, and without any more difficulty than can be supposed of a young country girl, barely fifteen, and to whom every sign or shop was a gazing trap, I got to the wish'd-for intelligence office.

It was kept by an elderly woman, who sat at the receipt of custom, with a book before her in great form and order, and several scrolls, ready made out, of directions for places.

I made up then to this important personage, without lifting up my eyes or observing any of the people round me, who were attending there on the same errand as myself, and dropping her curtsies nine-deep, just made a shift to stammer out my business to her.

Madam having heard me out, with all the gravity and brow of a petty minister of State, and seeing at one glance over my figure what I was, made me no answer, but to ask me the preliminary shilling, on receipt of which she told me places for women were exceedingly scarce, especially as I seemed too slight built for hard work; but that she would look over her book, and see what was to be done for me, desiring me to stay a little, till she had dispatched some other customers.

On this I drew back a little, most heartily mortified at a declaration which carried with it a killing uncertainty, that my circumstances could not well endure.

Presently, assuming more courage, and seeking some diversion from my uneasy thoughts, I ventured to lift up my head a little, and sent my eyes on a course round the room, wherein they met full tilt with those of a lady (for such my extreme innocence pronounc'd her) sitting in a corner of the room, dress'd in a velvet mantle (*nota bene*, in the midst of summer), with her bonnet off; squab-fat, red-faced, and at least fifty.

She look'd as if she would devour me with her eyes, staring at me from head to foot, without the least regard to the confusion and blushes her eyeing me so fixedly put me to, and which were to her, no doubt, the strongest recommendation and marks of my being fit for her purpose. After a little time, in which my air, person and whole figure had undergone a strict examination, which I had, on my part, tried to render favourable to me, by primming, drawing up my

15

neck, and setting my best looks, she advanced and spoke to me with the greatest demureness:

"Sweetheart, do you want a place?"

"Yes and please you" (with a curtsey down to the ground).

Upon this she acquainted me that she was actually come to the office herself, to look out for a servant; that she believed I might do, with a little of her instructions; that she could take my very looks for a sufficient character; that London was a very wicked, vile place; that she hop'd I would be tractable, and keep out of bad company; in short, she said all to me that an old experienced practitioner in town could think of, and which was much more than was necessary to take in an artless inexperienced country-maid, who was even afraid of becoming a wanderer about the streets, and therefore gladly jump'd at the first offer of a shelter, especially from so grave and matron-like a lady, for such my flattering fancy assured me this new mistress of mine was; I being actually hired under the nose of the good woman that kept the office, whose shrewd smiles and shrugs I could not help observing, and innocently interpreted them as marks of her being pleased at my getting into place so soon: but, as I afterwards came to know, these BELDAMES understood one another very well, and this was a market where *Mrs. Brown*, my mistress, frequently attended, on the watch for any fresh goods that might offer there, for the use of her customers, and her own profit.

Madam was, however, so well pleased with her bargain, that fearing, I presume, lest better advice or some accident might occasion my slipping through her fingers, she would officiously take me in a coach to my inn, where, calling herself for my box, it was, I being present, delivered without the least scruple of explanation as to where I was going.

This being over, she bid the coachman drive to a shop in St. Paul's Churchyard, where she bought a pair of gloves, which she gave me, and thence renewed her directions to the coachman to drive to her house in *** street, who accordingly landed us at her door, after I had been cheer'd up and entertain'd by the way with the most plausible flams, without one syllable from which I could conclude anything

16

but that I was, by the greatest good luck, fallen into the hands of the kindest mistress, not to say friend, that the *varsal* world could afford; and accordingly I enter'd her doors with most complete confidence and exultation, promising myself that, as soon as I should be a little settled, I would acquaint Esther Davis with my rare good fortune.

You may be sure the good opinion of my place was not lessen'd by the appearance of a very handsome back parlour, into which I was led and which seemed to me magnificently furnished, who had never seen better rooms than the ordinary ones in inns upon the road. There were two gilt pierglasses, and a buffet, on which a few pieces of plates, set out to the most show, dazzled, and altogether persuaded me that I must be got into a very reputable family.

Here my mistress first began her part, with telling me that I must have good spirits, and learn to be free with her; that she had not taken me to be a common servant, to do domestic drudgery, but to be a kind of companion to her; and that if I would be a good girl, she would be more than twenty mothers for me; to all which I answered only by the profoundest and the awkwardest curtsies, and a few mono-syllables, such as "yes! no! to be sure!"

Presently my mistress touch'd the bell, and in came a strapping maid-servant, who had let us in. "Here, Martha," said Mrs. Brown – "I have just hir'd this young woman to look after my linen; so step up and shew her her chamber; and I charge you to use her with as much respect as you would myself, for I have taken a prodigious liking to her, and I do not know what I shall do for her."

Martha, who as an arch-jade, and, being used to this decoy, had her cue perfect, made me a kind of half curtsey and asked me to walk up with her; and accordingly shew'd me a neat room, two pair of stairs backwards, in which there was a handsome bed, where Martha told me I was to lie with a young gentlewoman, a cousin of my mistress's, who she was sure would be vastly good to me. Then she ran out into such affected encomiums on her good mistress! her sweet mistress! and how happy I was to light upon her! that I could not have bespoke a better; with other the like gross stuff, such as would itself have started suspicions in any but such an unpractised simpleton, who was perfectly new to life, and who took every word she said in the very sense she laid out for me to take it; but she readily saw what a penetration she had to deal with, and measured me very rightly in her manner of whistling to me, so as to make me pleased with my cage, and blind to the wires.

In the midst of these false explanations of the nature of my future service, we were rung for down again, and I was reintroduced into the same parlour, where there was a table laid with three covers; and my mistress had now got with her one of her favourite girls, a notable manager of her house, and whose business it was to prepare and break such young fillies as I was to the mounting-block; and she was accordingly, in that view, allotted me for a bed-fellow; and, to give her the more authority, she had the title of cousin conferr'd on her by the venerable president of this college.

Here I underwent a second survey, which ended in the full approbation of *Mrs. Phoebe Ayres*, the name of my tutoress elect, to whose care and instructions I was affectionately recommended.

Dinner was now set on table, and in pursuance of treating me as a companion, *Mrs. Brown*, with a tone to cut off all dispute, soon overrul'd my most humble and most confused protestations against sitting down with her LADYSHIP, which my very short breeding just suggested to me could not be right, or in the order of things.

At table, the conversation was chiefly kept up by the two madams, and carried on in double-meaning expressions, interrupted every now and then by kind assurances to me, all tending to confirm and fix my satisfaction with my present condition: augment it they could not, so very a novice was I then.

It was here agreed that I should keep myself up and out of sight for a few days, till such clothes could be procured for me as were fit for the character I was to appear in, of my mistress's companion, observing withal, that on the first impressions of my figure much might depend; and, as they well judged, the prospect of exchanging my country clothes for London finery made the clause of confinement digest perfectly well with me. But the truth was, Mrs. Brown did not care that I should be seen or talked to by any, either of her customers, or her DOES (as they call'd the girls provided for them), till she had secured a good market for my maidenhead, which I had at least all the appearances of having brought into her LADYSHIP's service.

To slip over minutes of no importance to the main of my story, I pass the interval to bed-time, in which I was more and more pleas'd with the views that opened to me, of an easy service under these good people; and after supper being shew'd up to bed, Miss Phoebe, who observed a kind of reluctance in me to strip and go to bed, in my shift, before her, now the maid was withdrawn, came up to me, and beginning with unpinning my handkerchief and gown, soon encouraged me to go on with undressing myself; and, still blushing at now seeing myself naked to my shift, I hurried to get under the bedclothes out of sight. Phoebe laugh'd and it was not long before she placed herself by my side. She was about five and twenty, by her most suspicious account, in which, according to all appearances, she must have sunk at least ten good years: allowance, too, being made for the havoc which a long course of hackneyship and hot waters must have made of her constitution, and which had already brought on, upon the spur, that stale stage in which those of her profession are reduced to think of SHOWING company, instead of SEEING it.

No sooner then was this precious substitute of my mistress's laid down, but she, who was never out of her way when any occasion of lewdness presented itself, turned to me embraced and kiss'd me with great eagerness. This was new, this was odd; but imputing it to nothing but pure kindness, which, for aught I knew, it might be the London way to express in that manner, I was determin'd not to be behind-hand with her, and returned her the kiss and embrace, with all the fervour that perfect innocence knew.

Encouraged by this, her hands became extremely free, and wander'd over my whole body, with touches, squeezes, pressures they either shock'd or alarm'd me.

The flattering praises she intermingled with these invasions contributed also not a little to bribe my passiveness; and, knowing no ill, I feared none, especially from one who had prevented all doubt of her womanhood, by conducting my hands to a pair of breasts that hung loosely down, in a size and volume that full sufficiently distinguished her sex, to me at least, who had never made any other comparison ...

I lay then all tame and passive as she could wish, whilst her freedom raised no other emotions but those of a strange, and, till then, unfelt pleasure. Every part of me was open and exposed to the licentious courses of her hands, which, like a lambent fire, ran over my whole body, and thaw'd all coldness as they went.

My breasts, if it is not bold a figure to call so two hard, firm, rising hillocks that just began to shew themselves, or signify anything to the touch, employ'd and amus'd her hands awhile, till, slipping down lower, over a smooth track, she could just feel the soft silky down, that had but a few months before put forth and garnish'd the mount-pleasant of those parts, and promised to spread a grateful shelter over the seat of the most exquisite sensation, and which had been, till that instant, the seat of the most insensible innocence. Her fingers play'd and strove to twine in the young tendrils of that moss, which nature has contrived at once for use and ornament.

But, not contented with these outer posts, she now attempts the main spot, and began to twitch, to insinuate, and at length to force an introduction of a finger into the quick itself, in such a manner that, had she not proceeded by insensible gradations that inflamed me beyond the power of modesty to oppose its resistance to their progress, I should have jump'd out of bed and cried for help against such strange assaults.

Instead of which, her lascivious touches had lighted up a new fire that wanton'd through all my veins, but fix'd with violence in that centre appointed them by nature, where the first strange hands were now busied in feeling, squeezing, compressing the lips, then opening them again, with a finger between, till an "Oh!" express'd her hurting me, where the narrowness of the unbroken passage refused it entrance to any depth.

In the meantime, the extension of my limbs, languid stretchings, sighs, short heavings, all conspired to assure that experienced wanton that I was more pleased than offended at her proceedings, which she seasoned with repeated kisses and exclamations, such as "Oh! what a charming creature thou art! . . . What a happy man will he be that first makes a woman of you! . . . Oh! that I were a man for your sake! . . . " with the like broken expressions, interrupted by kisses as fierce and fervent, as ever I received from the other sex.

For my part, I was transported, confused, and out of myself; feelings so new were too much for me. My heated and alarm'd senses were in a tumult that robbed me of all liberty of thought; tears of pleasure gush'd from my eyes, and somewhat assuaged the fire that rag'd all over me.

Phoebe, herself, the hackney'd, thorough-bred Phoebe, to whom all modes and devices of pleasure were known and familiar, found, it seems, in this exercise of her art to break young girls, the gratification of one of those arbitrary tastes, for which there is no accounting. Not that she hated men, or did not even prefer them to her own sex; but when she met with such occasions as this was, a satiety of enjoyments in the common road, perhaps too, a secret bias, inclined her to make the most of pleasure, wherever she could find it, without distinction of sexes. In this view, now well assured that she had, by her touches, sufficiently inflamed me for her purpose, she roll'd down the bedclothes gently, and I saw myself stretched nak'd, my shift being turned up to my neck, whilst I had no power or sense to oppose it. Even my glowing blushes expressed more desire than modesty, whilst the candle, left (to be sure not undesignedly) burning, threw a full light on my whole body.

"No!" says Phoebe, "you must not, my sweet girl, think to hide all these treasures from me. My sight must be feasted as well as my touch . . . I must devour with my eyes this springing BOSOM . . . Suffer me to kiss it . . . I have not seen it enough . . . Let me kiss it once more . . . What firm,

smooth, white flesh is here!... How delicately shaped!...
Then this delicious down! Oh! let me view the small, dear,
tender cleft!... This is too much, I cannot bear it!... I
must... I must..." Here she took my hand, and in a
transport carried it where you will easily guess. But what a
difference in the state of the same thing!... A spreading
thicket of bushy curls marked the full-grown, complete
woman. Then the cavity to which she guided my hand
easily received it; and as soon as she felt it within her, she
moved herself to and fro, with so rapid a friction, that I
presently withdrew it, wet and clammy, when instantly
Phoebe grew more composed, after two or three sighs, and
heart-fetched Oh's! and giving me a kiss that seemed to
exhale her soul through her lips, she replaced the bedclothes
over us. What pleasure she had found I will not say; but
this I know, that the first sparks of kindling nature, the
first ideas of pollution, were caught by me that night; and
that the acquaintance and communication with the bad of
our own sex is often as fatal to innocence as all the seductions
of the other. But to go on. When Phoebe was restor'd to that
calm, which I was far from the enjoyment of myself, she
artfully sounded me on all the points necessary to govern the
designs of my virtuous mistress on me, and by my answers,
drawn from pure undissembled nature, she had no reason
but to promise herself all imaginable success, so far as it
depended on my ignorance, easiness, and warmth of
constitution.

After a sufficient length of dialogue, my bedfellow left me
to my rest, and I fell asleep, through pure weariness, from
the violent emotions I had been led into, when nature (which
had been too warmly stir'd and fermented to subside without
allaying by some means or other) relieved me by one of
those luscious dreams, the transports of which are scarce
inferior to those of waking real action.

In the morning I awoke about ten, perfectly gay and
refreshed. Phoebe was up before me, and asked me in the
kindest manner how I did, how I had rested, and if I was
ready for breakfast, carefully, at the same time, avoiding
to increase the confusion she saw I was in, at looking her in

the face, by any hint of the night's bed scene. I told her if she pleased I would get up, and begin any work she would be pleased to set me about. She smil'd; presently the maid brought in the tea-equipage, and I had just huddled my clothes on, when in waddled my mistress. I expected no less than to be told of, if not chid for, my late rising, when I was agreeably disappointed by her compliments on my pure and fresh looks. I was "a bud of beauty" (this was her style), "and how vastly all the fine men would admire me!" to all which my answers did not, I can assure you, wrong my breeding; they were as simple and silly as they could wish, and, no doubt, flattered them infinitely more than had they proved me enlightened by education and a knowledge of the world.

We breakfasted, and the tea things were scarce removed, when in were brought two bundles of linen and wearing apparel: in short, all the necessaries for *rigging me out*, as they termed it, completely.

Imagine to yourself, Madam, how my little coquette heart flutter'd with joy at the sight of a white lute-string, flower'd with silver, scoured indeed, but passed on me for spick-and-span new, a *Brussels* lace cap, braided shoes, and the rest in proportion, all second-hand finery, and procured instantly for the occasion, by the diligence and industry of the good Mrs. Brown, who had already a chapman for me in the house, before whom my charms were to pass in review; for he had not only, in course, insisted on a previous sight of the premises, but also on immediate surrender to him, in case of his agreeing for me; concluding very wisely that such a place as I was in was of the hottest to trust the keeping of such a perishable commodity in as a maidenhead.

The care of dressing, and tricking me out for the market, was then left to Phoebe, who acquitted herself, if not well, at least perfectly to the satisfaction of everything but my impatience of seeing myself dress'd. When it was over, and I view'd myself in the glass, I was, no doubt, too natural, too artless, to hide my childish joy at the change: a change, in the real truth, for much the worse, since I must have much better become the neat easy simplicity of my rustic dress than the awkward, untoward, tawdry finery that I could not conceal my strangeness to.

Phoebe's compliments, however, in which her own share in dressing me was not forgot, did not a little confirm me in the first notions I had ever entertained concerning my person; which, be it said without vanity, was then tolerable to justify a taste for me, and of which it may not be out of place here to sketch you an unflatter'd picture.

I was tall, yet not too tall for my age, which, as I before remark'd, was barely turned of fifteen; my shape perfectly straight, thin-waisted, and light and free, without owing any thing to stays; my hair was a glossy auburn, and as soft as silk flowing down my neck in natural buckles, and did not a little set off the whiteness of a smooth skin; my face was rather too ruddy, though its features were delicate, and the shape was a roundish oval, except where a pit on my chin had far from a disagreeable effect; my eyes were as black as can be imagin'd, and rather languishing than sparkling, except on certain occasions, when I have been told they struck fire fast enough; my teeth, which I ever carefully preserv'd, were small, even and white; my bosom was finely rais'd, and one might then discern rather the promise, than the actual growth, of the round firm breasts, that in a little time made that promise good. In short, all the points of beauty that are most universally in request, I had, or at least my vanity forbade me to appeal from the decision of our sovereign judges the men, who all, that I ever knew at least, gave it thus highly in my favour; and I met with, even in my own sex, some that were above denying me that justice, whilst others praised me yet more unsuspectedly, by endeavouring to detract from me, in points of person and figure that I obviously excelled in. This is, I own, too strong of self-praise; but should I not be ungrateful to nature, and to a form to which I owe such singular blessings of pleasure and fortune, were I to suppress, through an affectation of modesty, the mention of such valuable gifts?

Well then, dress'd I was, and little did it then enter into my head that all this gay attire was no more than decking the victim out for sacrifice, whilst I innocently attributed all to mere friendship and kindness in the sweet good Mrs. Brown; who, I was forgetting to mention, had, under pretence of keeping my money safe, got from me, without the least hesitation, the driblet (so I now call it) which remained to me after the expenses of my journey.

After some little time most agreeably spent before the glass, in scarce self-admiration, since my new dress had by much the greatest share in it, I was sent for down to the parlour, where the old lady saluted me, and wished me joy of my new clothes, which, she was not asham'd to say, fitted me as if I had worn nothing but the finest all my life-time; but what it she could not see me silly enough to swallow. At the same time, she presented me to another cousin of her own creation, an elderly gentleman, who got up, at my entry into the room, and on my dropping a curtsy to him, saluted me, and seemed a little affronted that I had only presented my cheek to him: a mistake, which, if one, he immediately corrected, by gluing his lips to mine, with an ardour which his figure had not at all disposed me to thank him for: his figure, I say, than which nothing could be more shocking or detestable: for ugly, and dis-agreeable were terms too gentle to convey a just idea of it.

Imagine to yourself a man rather past threescore, short and ill-made, with a yellow cadaverous hue, great goggling eyes, that stared as if he was strangled; an out-mouth from two more properly tusks than teeth, livid lips, and breath like a jake's: then he had a peculiar ghastliness in his grin that made him perfectly frightful, if not dangerous to women with child; yet, made as he was thus in mock of man, he was so blind to his own staring deformities as to think himself born for pleasing, and that no woman could see him with impunity: in consequence of which idea he had lavish'd great sums on such wretches as could gain upon themselves to pretend love to his person, whilst to those who had not art or patience to dissemble the horror it inspir'd he behaved even brutally. Impotence, more than necessity, made him seek in variety the provocative that was wanting to raise him to the pitch of enjoyment, which too he often saw himself baulked of, by the failure of his powers: and this always threw him into a fit of rage, which he wreak'd, as far as he durst, on the innocent objects of his fit of momentary desire.

This then was the monster to which my conscientious benefactress, who had long been his purveyor in this way, had doom'd me, and sent for me down purposely for his examination. Accordingly she made me stand up before him, turn'd me round, unpinn'd my handkerchief, remark'd to him the rise and fall, the turn and whiteness of a bosom just beginning to fill; then made me walk, and took even a handle from the rusticity of my gait, to inflame the inventory of my charms: in short, she omitted no point of jockeyship; to which he only answer'd by gracious nods of approbation, whilst he look'd goats and monkies at me: for I sometimes stole a corner glance at him, and encountering his fiery, eager stare, looked another way from pure horror and affright, which he, doubtless in character, attributed to nothing more than maiden modesty, or at least the affectation of it.

However, I was soon dismiss'd, and reconducted to my room by Phoebe, who stuck close to me, not leaving me alone, and at leisure to make such reflections as might naturally rise to any one, not an idiot, on such a scene as I had just gone through; but to my shame be it confess'd, such was my invincible stupidity, or rather portentous innocence, that I did not yet open my eyes to Mrs. Brown's designs, and saw nothing in this titular cousin of hers, but a shocking hideous person, which did not at all concern me, unless that my gratitude for my benefactress made me extend my respect to all her cousinhood.

Phoebe, however, began to sift the state and pulses of my heart towards this monster, asking me how I should approve of such a fine gentleman for a husband? (Fine gentleman, I suppose she called him, from his being daubed with lace.) I answered her very naturally, that I had no thoughts of a husband, but that if I was to choose one, it should be among my own degree, sure! So much had my aversion to that wretch's hideous figure indisposed me to all "fine gentlemen," and confounded my ideas, as if those of that rank had been necessarily cast in the same mould that he was. But Phoebe was not to be beat off so, but went on with her endeavours to melt and soften me for the purposes of my reception into that hospitable house: and whilst she talked of the sex in general, she had no reason to despair of a compliance, which more than one reason shewed her would be easily enough obtained of me; but then she had too much experience not to discover that my particular fix'd aversion to that frightful cousin would be a block not so readily to be removed, as suited the consummation of their bargain, and sale of me.

Mother Brown had in the meantime agreed the terms with this liquorish old goat, which I afterwards understood were to be fifty guineas peremptory for the liberty of attempting me, and a hundred more at the complete gratification of his desires, in the triumph over my virginity: and as for me, I was to be left entirely at the discretion of his liking and generosity. This unrighteous contract being thus settled, he was so eager to be put in possession, that he insisted on being introduc'd to drink tea with me that afternoon, when we were to be left alone; nor would he hearken to the procuress's remonstrances, that I was not sufficiently prepared and ripened for such an attack; that I was too green and untam'd, having been scarce twenty-four hours in the house: it is the character of lust to be impatient, and his vanity arming him against any supposition of other than the common resistance of a maid on those occasions, made him reject all proposals of a delay, and my dreadful trial was thus fix'd, unknown to me, for that very evening.

At dinner, Mrs. Brown and Phoebe did nothing but run riot in praises of this wonderful cousin, and how happy that woman would be that he would favour with his address; in short my two gossips exhausted all their rhetoric to persuade me to accept them: that the gentleman was "violently smitten" with me at first sight . . . that he would make my fortune if I would be a good girl and not stand in my own light . . . that I should trust his honour . . . that I should be made for ever, and have a "chariot to go abroad in . . . ," with all such stuff as was fit to turn the head of such a silly ignorant girl as I then was: but luckily here my aversion had taken already such deep root in me, my heart was so strongly defended from him by my senses, that, wanting the art to mask my sentiments, I gave them no hopes of their employer's succeeding, at least very easily, with me. The glass too march'd pretty quick, with a view, I suppose, to make a friend of the warmth of my constitution, in the minutes of the imminent attack.

Thus they kept me pretty long at table, and at about six in the evening, after I was retired to my own apartment, and the tea board was set, enters my venerable mistress, follow'd close by that satyr, who came in grinning in a way peculiar to him, and by his odious presence confirm'd me in all the sentiments of detestation which his first appearance had given birth to.

He sat down fronting me, and all tea time kept ogling me in a manner that gave me the utmost pain and confusion, all the marks of which he still explained to be my bashfulness, and not being used to see company.

Tea over, the obliging old lady pleaded urgent business (which indeed was true) to go out, and earnestly desir'd me to entertain her cousin kindly till she came back, both for my own sake and hers; and then, with a "Pray, sir, be very good, be very tender of the sweet child," she went out of the room, leaving me staring, with my mouth open, and un-prepar'd, by the suddenness of her departure, to oppose it.

We were now alone; and on that idea a sudden fit of trembling seiz'd me. I was so afraid, without a precise notion of why, and what I had to fear, that I sat on the settee, by the fireside, motionless, and petrified, without life or spirit, not knowing how to look or how to stir.

But long I was not suffered to remain in this state of stupe-faction: the monster squatted down by me on the settee, and without further ceremony or preamble, flings his arms about my neck, and drawing me pretty forcibly towards him, oblig'd me to receive, in spite of my struggles to disengage from him, his pestilential kisses, which quite overcame me. Finding me then next to senseless, and unresisting, he tears off my handkerchief, and laid all open there to his

28

eyes and hands: still I endur'd all without flinching, till embolden'd by my sufferance and silence, for I had not the power to speak or cry out, he attempted to lay me down on the settee, and I felt his hand on the lower part of my naked thighs, which were cross'd, and which he endeavoured to unlock . . . Oh then! I was roused out of my passive endurance, and springing from him with an activity he was not prepar'd for, threw myself at his feet, and begg'd him, in the most moving tone, not to be rude, and that he would not hurt me: – "Hurt you, my dear?" says the brute; "I intend you no harm . . . has not the old lady told you that I love you? . . . that I shall do handsomely by you?" "She has indeed, sir," said I; "but I cannot love you, indeed I cannot! . . . pray let me alone . . . yes! I will love you dearly if you will let me alone, and go away . . ." But I was talking to the wind; for whether my tears, my attitude, or the disorder of my dress prov'd fresh incentives, or whether he was now under the dominion of desires he could not bridle, but snorting and foaming with lust and rage, he renews his attack, seizes me, and again attempts to extend and fix me on the settee: in which he succeeded so far as to lay me along, and even to toss my petticoats over my head, and lay my thighs bare, which I obstinately kept close, nor could he, though he attempted with his knee to force them open, effect it so as to stand fair for being master of the main avenue; he was unbuttoned, both waistcoat and breeches, yet I only felt the weight of his body upon me, whilst I lay struggling with indignation, and dying with terrors; but he stopped all of a sudden, and got off, panting, blowing, cursing, and repeating "old and ugly!" for so I had very naturally called him in the heat of my defence.

The brute had, it seems, as I afterwards understood, brought on, by his eagerness and struggle, the ultimate period of his hot fit of lust, which his power was too short-liv'd to carry him through the full execution of; of which my thighs and linen received the effusion.

When it was over he bid me, with a tone of displeasure, get up, saying that he would not do me the honour to think of me any more . . . that the old bitch might look out for another cully ... that he would not be fool'd so by e'er a country mock modesty in England ... that he supposed I had left my maidenhead with some hobnail in the country, and was come to dispose of my skim-milk in town, with a volley of the like abuse; which I listened to with more pleasure than ever fond woman did to protestations of love receiving any addition to my perfect hatred and aversion to him; I look'd on this railing as my security against his renewing his most odious caresses.

Yet, plain as Mrs. Brown's view were now come out, I had not the heart or spirit to open my eyes to them: still I could not part with my dependence on that beldam, so much did I think myself hers, soul and body: or rather, I sought to deceive myself with the continuation of my good opinion of her, and chose to wait the worst at her hands, sooner than be turn'd out to starve in the streets, without a penny of money or a friend to apply to: these fears were my folly.

Whilst this confusion of ideas was passing in my head, and I sat pensive by the fire, with my eyes brimming with tears, my neck still bare, and my cap fall'n off in the struggle, so that my hair was in the disorder you may guess, the villain's lust began, I suppose, to be again in flow, at the sight of all that bloom of youth which presented itself to his view, a bloom yet unenjoy'd, and of course not yet indifferent to him.

After some pause, he ask'd me, with a tone of voice mightily softened, whether I would make it up with him before the old lady returned and all should be well; he would restore me his affections, at the same time offering to kiss me and feel my breasts. But now my extreme aversion, my fears, my indignation, all acting upon me, gave me a spirit not natural to me, so that breaking loose from him, I ran to the bell, and rang it, before he was aware, with such violence and effect as brought up the maid to know what was the matter, or whether the gentleman wanted anything; and before he could proceed to greater extremities, she bounc'd into the room, and seeing me stretch'd on the floor, my hair all dishevell'd, my nose gushing out blood, which did not a little tragedize the scene, and my odious persecutor still intent of pushing his brutal point, unmoved by all my cries and distress, she was herself confounded and did not know what to say.

As much, however, as Martha might be prepared and hardened to transactions of this sort, all womanhood must have been out of her heart, could she have seen this unmov'd. Besides that, on the face of things, she imagined that matters had gone greater lengths than they really had, and that the courtesy of the house had been actually consummated on me, and flung me into the condition I was in: in this notion she instantly took my part, and advis'd the gentleman to go down and leave me to recover myself, and said that all would be soon over with me . . . that when Mrs. Brown and Phoebe, who were gone out, were return'd, they would take order for everything to his satisfaction . . . that nothing would be lost by a little patience with the poor tender thing . . . that for her part she was frighten'd . . . she could not tell what to say to such doings . . . but that she would stay by me till my mistress came home. As the wench said all this in a resolute tone, and the monster himself began to perceive that things would not mend by his staying, he took his hat and went out of the room, murmuring, and pleating his brows like an old ape, so that I was delivered from the horrors of his detestable presence.

As soon as he was gone, Martha very tenderly offered me her assistance in anything, and would have got me some hartshorn drops, and put me to bed; which last, I at first positively refused, in the fear that the monster might return and take me at that advantage. However, with much persuasion, and assurances that I should not be molested that night she prevailed on me to lie down; and indeed I was so weakened by my struggles, so dejected by my fearful apprehensions, so terror-struck, that I had not power to sit up, or hardly to give answers to the questions with which the curious Martha ply'd and perplex'd me.

Such too, and so cruel was my fate, that I dreaded the sight of Mrs. Brown, as if I had been the criminal, and she the person injur'd; a mistake which you will not think so strange, on distinguishing that neither virtue or principles had the least share in the defence I had made, but only the particular aversion I had conceiv'd against the first brutal and frightful invader of my tender innocence.

I pass'd then the time till Mrs. Brown's return home, under all the agitations of fear and despair that may easily be guessed.

About eleven at night my two ladies came home, and having receiv'd rather a favourable account from Martha, who had run down to let them in, for *Mr. Crofts* (that was the name of my brute) was gone out of the house, after waiting till he had tired his patience for Mrs. Brown's return, they came thundering upstairs, and seeing me pale my face bloody, and all the marks of the most thorough dejection, they employed themselves more to comfort and re-inspirit me, than in making me the reproaches I was weak enough to fear, I who had so many juster and stronger to retort upon them.

Mrs. Brown withdrawn, Phoebe came presently to bed to me, and half with the answers she drew from me, half with her own method of *palpably* satisfying herself, she soon discovered that I had been more frighted than hurt; upon which I suppose, being herself seiz'd with sleep, and reserving her lectures and instructions till the next morning, she left me, properly speaking, to my unrest; for, after tossing and turning the greatest part of the night, and tormenting myself with the falsest notions and apprehensions of things, I fell, through sheer fatigue, into a kind of delirious doze, out of which I waked late in the morning, in a violent fever: a circumstance which was extremely critical to reprieve me, at least for a time, from the attacks of a wretch, infinitely more terrible to me than death itself.

The interested care that was taken of me during my illness, in order to restore me to a condition of making good the bawd's engagements, or of enduring further trials, had however such an effect on my grateful disposition, that I even thought myself oblig'd to my undoers for their attention to promote my recovery; and, above all, for the keeping out of my sight of that brutal ravisher, the author of my disorder, on their finding I was too strongly mov'd at the bare mention of his name.

Youth is soon raised, and a few days were sufficient to conquer the fury of my fever: but what contributed most to my perfect recovery and to my reconciliation with life was the timely news that *Mr. Crofts*, who was a merchant of considerable dealings, was arrested at the King's suit, for near forty thousand pounds, on account of his driving a certain contraband trade, and that his affairs were so desperate, that even were it in his inclination, it would not be in his power to renew his designs upon me: for he was instantly thrown into a prison, which it was not likely he would get out of in haste.

Mrs. Brown, who had touched his fifty guineas, advanc'd to so little purpose, and lost all hopes of the remaining hundred, began to look upon my treatment of him with a more favourable eye; and as they had observ'd my temper to be perfectly tractable and conformable to their views, all the girls that compos'd her flock were suffered to visit me, and had their cue to dispose me, by their conversation, to a perfect resignation of myself to Mrs. Brown's direction.

Accordingly they were let in upon me, and all that frolic and thoughtless gaiety in which those giddy creatures consume their leisure made me envy a condition of which I only saw the fair side; insomuch, that the being one of them became even my ambition: a disposition which they all carefully cultivated; and I wanted now nothing but to restore my health, that I might be able to undergo the ceremony of the initiation.

Conversation, example, all, in short, contributed in that house to corrupt my native purity, which had taken no root in education; whilst now the inflammable principle of pleasure, so easily fired at my age, made strange work within me, and all the modesty I was brought up in the habit, not the instruction of, began to melt away like dew before the sun's heat; not to mention that I made a vice of necessity, from the constant fears I had of being turn'd out to starve.

I was soon pretty well recover'd, and at certain hours allow'd to range all over the house, but cautiously kept from seeing any company till the arrival of *Lord B* . . ., from *Bath*, to whom Mrs. Brown, in respect to his experienced generosity on such occasions, proposed to offer the perusal of that trinket of mine, which bears so great an imaginary value; and his lordship being expected in town in less than a fortnight, Mrs. Brown judged I would be entirely renewed in beauty and freshness by that time, and afford her the chance of a better bargain than she had driven with Mr. Crofts.

In the meantime, I was so thoroughly, as they call it, brought over, so tame to their whistle that, had my cage door been set open, I had no idea that I ought to fly anywhere, sooner then stay where I was; nor had I the least sense of regretting my condition, but waited very quietly for whatever Mrs. Brown should order concerning me; who on her side, by herself and her agents, took more then the necessary precautions to lull and lay asleep all just reflections on my destination.

Preachments of morality over the left shoulder; a life of joy painted in the gayest colours; caresses, promises, indulgent treatment: nothing, in short, was wanting to domesticate me entirely and to prevent my going out anywhere to get better advice. Alas! I dream'd of no such thing.

Hitherto I had been indebted only to the girls of the house for the corruption of my innocence: their luscious talk, in which modesty was far from respected, their description of their engagements with men, had given me a tolerable insight into the nature and mysteries of their profession, at the same time that they highly provok'd an itch of florid warm-spirited blood through every vein: but above all, my bed-fellow Phoebe, whose pupil I more immediately was, exerted her talents in giving me the first tinctures of pleasure: whilst nature, now warm'd and wantoned with discoveries so interesting, piqu'd a curiosity which Phoebe artfully whetted, and leading me from question to question of her own suggestion, explain'd to me all the mysteries of Venus. But I could not long remain in such a house as that, without being an eye-witness of more than I could conceive from her descriptions.

One day, about twelve at noon, being thoroughly recover'd of my fever, I happen'd to be in Mrs. Brown's dark closet, where I had not been half an hour, resting upon the maid's settee-bed, before I heard a rustling in the bed-chamber, separated from the closet only by two sashdoors, before the glasses of which were drawn two yellow damask curtains, but not so close as to exclude the full view of the room from any person in the closet.

I instantly crept softly, and posted myself so, that seeing everything minutely, I could not myself be seen; and who should come in but the venerable mother Abbess herself! handed in by a tall, brawny young Horse-grenadier, moulded in the *Hercules* style: *in fine*, the choice of the most experienced dame, in those *affairs*, in all London.

Oh! how still and hush did I keep at my stand, lest any noise should baulk my curiosity, or bring Madam into the closet!

But I had not much reason to fear either, for she was so entirely taken up with her present great concern, that she had no sense of attention to spare to anything else.

Droll was it to see that clumsy fat figure of hers flop down on the foot of the bed, opposite to the closet-door, so that I had a full front-view of all her charms.

Her paramour sat down by her: he seemed to be a man of very few words, and a great stomach; for proceeding instantly to essentials, he gave her some hearty smacks, and thrusting his hands into her breasts, disengag'd them from her stays, in scorn of whose confinement they broke loose, and swagged down, navel-low at least. A more enormous pair did my eyes never behold, nor of a worse colour, flagging-soft, and most lovingly contiguous: yet such as they were, this neck-beef eater seem'd to paw them with a most uninvitable lust, seeking in vain to confine or cover one of them with a hand scarce less than a shoulder of mutton. After toying with them thus some time, as if they had been worth it, he laid her down pretty briskly, and

35

canting up her petticoats, made barely a mask of them to her broad red face, that blush'd with nothing but brandy.

As he stood on one side, for a minute or so, unbuttoning his waistcoat and breeches, her fat brawny thighs hung down, and the whole greasy landscape lay fairly open to my view; a wide open-mouth'd gap, overshaded with a grizzly bush, seemed held out like a beggar's wallet for its provision.

But I soon had my eyes called off by a more striking object, that entirely engross'd them.

Her sturdy stallion had now unbutton'd, and produced naked, stiff, and erect, that wonderful machine, which I had never seen before, and which, for the interest my own seat of pleasure began to take furiously in it, I star'd at with all the eyes I had: however, my senses were too much flurried, too much concentred in that now burning spot of mine, to observe anything more than in general the make and turn of that instrument, from which the instinct of nature, yet more than all I had heard of it, now strongly informed me I was to expect that supreme pleasure which she had placed in the meeting of those parts so admirably fitted for each other.

Long, however, the young spark did not remain before giving it two or three shakes, by way of brandishing it; he threw himself upon her, and his back being now towards me, I could only take his being ingulph'd for granted, by the directions he mov'd in, and the impossibility of missing so staring a mark; and now the bed shook, the curtains rattled so, that I could scarce hear the sighs and murmurs, the heaves and pantings that accompanied the action, from the beginning to the end; the sound and sight of which thrill'd to the very soul of me, and made every vein of my body circulate liquid fires: the emotion grew so violent that it almost intercepted my respiration.

Prepared then, and disposed as I was by the discourse of my companions, and Phoebe's minute detail of everything, no wonder that such a sight gave the last dying blow to my native innocence.

Whilst they were in the heat of the action, guided by nature only, I stole my hand up my petticoats, and with fingers all on fire, seized, and yet more inflamed that centre of all my senses: my heart palpitated, as if it would force its way through my bosom: I breath'd with pain; I twisted my thighs, squeezed, and compressed the lips of that virgin slit, and following mechanically the example of Phoebe's manual operation on it, as far as I could find admission, brought on at last the critical ecstasy, the melting flow, into which nature, spent with excess of pleasure, dissolves and dies away.

After which, my senses recover'd coolness enough to observe the rest of the transaction between this happy pair.

The young fellow had just dismounted, when the old lady immediately sprung up, with all the vigour of youth, derived, no doubt, from her late refreshment; and making him sit down, began in her turn to kiss him, to pat and pinch his cheeks, and play with his hair: all which he receiv'd with an air of indifference and coolness, that shew'd him to me much altered from what he was when he first went on to the breach.

My pious governess, however, not being above calling in auxiliaries, unlocks a little case of cordials that stood near the bed, and made him pledge her in a very plentiful dram: after which, and a little amorous parley, Madam sat herself down upon the same place, at the bed's foot; and the young fellow standing sideway by her, she, with the greatest effrontery imaginable, unbuttons his breeches, and removing his shirt, draws out his affair, so shrunk and diminish'd that I could not but remember the difference, now crest-fallen, or just faintly lifting its head: but our experienc'd matron very soon, by chaffing it with her hands, brought it to swell to that size and erection I had before seen it up to.

I admired then, upon a fresh account, and which a nicer survey, the texture of that capital part of man: the flaming red head as it stood uncapt, the whiteness of the shaft, and the shrub growth of curling hair that embrowned the roots of it, the roundish bag that dangled down from it, all exacted my eager attention, and renewed my flame. But, as the main affair was now at the point the industrious dame had laboured to bring it to, she was not in the humour to put off the payment of her pains, but laying herself down, drew

37

him gently upon her, and thus they finish'd, in the same manner as before, the old last act.

This over, they both went out lovingly together, the old lady having first made him a present, as near as I could observe, of three or four pieces; he being not only her particular favourite on account of his performances, but a retainer to the house; from whose sight she had taken great care hitherto to secrete me, lest he might not have had patience to wait for my lord's arrival, but have insisted on being the taster, which the old lady was under too much subjection to him to dare dispute with him; for every girl of the house fell to him in course, and the old lady now and then got her turn, in consideration of the maintenance he had, and which he could scarce be accused of not earning from her.

As soon as I heard them go downstairs, I stole up softly to my own room, out of which I had luckily not been miss'd; there I began to breathe freer, and to give loose to those warm emotions which the sight of such an encounter had raised in me. I laid me down on the bed, stretched myself out joining and ardently wishing, and requiring any means to divert or allay the rekindled rage and tumult of my desires, which all pointed strongly to their pole: man. I felt about the bed as if I sought for something that I grasp'd in my waking dream, and not finding it, could have cry'd for vexation; every part of me glowing with stimulating fires. At length, I resorted to the only present remedy, that of vain attempts at digitation, where the smallness of the theatre did not yet afford room enough for action, and where the pain my fingers gave me, in striving for admission, tho' they procured me a slight satisfaction for the present, started an apprehension, which I could not be easy till I had communicated to Phoebe, and received her explanations upon it.

The opportunity, however, did not offer itself till next morning, for Phoebe did not come to bed till long after I was gone to sleep. As soon then as we were both awake, it was but in course to being our ly-a-bed chat to land on the subject of my uneasiness: to which a recital of the love scene I had thus, by chance, been spectatress of, serv'd for a preface.

Phoebe could not hear it to the end without more than one interruption by peals of laughter, and my ingenuous way of relating matters did not a little heighten the joke to her.

But, on her sounding me how the sight had affected me, without mincing or hiding the pleasurable emotions it had inspir'd me with, I told her at the same time that one remark had perplex'd me, and that very considerably. "Aye!" says she, "what was that?" – Why, replied I, "having very curiously and attentively compared the size of that enormous machine, which does not appear, at least to my fearful imagination, less than my wrist, and at least three of my handfuls long, to that of the tender small part of me which was framed to receive it, I can not conceive that it is possible to effect the entrance without dying, perhaps in the greatest pain, since you well know that even a finger thrust in there hurts me beyond bearing . . . As to my mistress's and yours, I can plainly distinguish the different dimensions of them from mine, palpable to the touch, and visible to the eye; so that, in short, great as the promis'd pleasure may be, I am afraid of the pain of the experiment."

Phoebe at this redoubled her laugh, and whilst I expected a very serious solution of my doubts and apprehensions in this matter, only told me that she never heard of a mortal wound being given in those parts by that terrible weapon, and that some she knew, younger, and as delicately made as myself, had outlived the operation; that she believed, at the worst, I should take a great deal of killing; that true it was, there was a great diversity of sizes in those parts, owing to nature, child-bearing, frequent over-stretching with unmerciful machines, but that at a certain age and habit of body even the most experienc'd in those affairs could not well distinguish between the maid and the woman, supposing too an absence of all artifice, and things in their natural situation: but that since chance had thrown in my way one sight of that sort, she would procure me another, that should feast my eyes more delicately, and go a great way in the cure of my fears from that imaginery disproportion.

On this she asked me if I knew *Polly Philips*. "Undoubtedly," say I, "the fair girl which was so tender of me when I was sick, and has been, as you told me, but two months in the house." "The same," says Phoebe. "You must know then, she is kept by a young Genoese merchant, whom his uncle, who is immensely rich, and whose darling he is, sent over here with an English merchant, his friend, on a pretext of settling some accounts, but in reality to humour his inclinations for travelling, and seeing the world. He met casually with this *Polly* once in company, and taking a liking to her, makes it worth her while to keep entirely to him. He comes to her here twice or thrice a week, and she receives him in the light closet up one pair of stairs, where he enjoys her in a taste, I suppose, peculiar to the heat, or perhaps the caprices of his own country. I say no more, but tomorrow being his day, you shall see what passes between them, from a place only known to your mistress and myself."

You may be sure, in the state that I was now in, I had no objection to the proposal, and was rather on tip-toe for its accomplishment.

At five in the evening, next day, Phoebe, punctual to her promise, came to me as I sat alone in my own room, and beckon'd me to follow her.

We went down the back-stairs very softly, and opening the door of a dark closet, where there was some old furniture kept, and some cases of liquor, she drew me in after her, and fastening the door upon us, we had no light but what came through a long crevice in the partition between ours and the light closet, where the scene of action lay; so that sitting on those low cases, we could, with the greatest ease, as well as clearness, see all objects (ourselves unseen), only by applying our eyes close to the crevice, where the moulding of a panel had warped, or started a little on the other side.

The young gentleman was the first person I saw, with his back directly towards me, looking at a print. Polly was not yet come: in less than a minute tho', the door opened, and she came in; and at the noise the door made he turned

40

about, and came to meet her, with an air of the greatest tenderness and satisfaction.

After saluting her, he led her to a couch that fronted us, where they both sat down, and the young Genoese help'd her to a glass of wine, with some Naples biscuit on a salver.

Presently, when they had exchanged a few kisses, and questions in broken English on one side, he began to unbutton, and, in fine, stript to his shirt.

As if this had been the signal agreed on for pulling off all their clothes, a scheme which the heat of the season perfectly favoured, Polly began to draw hei pins, and as she had no stays to unlace, she was in a trice, with her gallant's officious assistance, undress'd to all but her shift.

When he saw this, his breeches were immediately loosen'd, waist and knee bands, and slipped over his ankles, clean off; his shirt collar was unbuttoned too: then, first giving Polly an encouraging kiss, he stole, as it were, the shift off the girl, who being, I suppose, broke and familiariz'd to this humour, blush'd indeed, but less than I did at the apparition of her, now standing stark-naked, just as she came out of the hands of pure nature, with her black hair loose and afloat down her dazzling white neck and shoulders, whilst the deepen'd carnation of her cheeks went off gradually into the hue of glaz'd snow: for such were the blanded tints and polish of her skin.

This girl could not be above eighteen: her face regular and sweet-featur'd, her shape exquisite; nor could I help envying her two ripe enchanting breasts, finely plump'd out in flesh, but withal so round, so firm, that they sustain'd themselves, in scorn of any stay: then their nipples, pointing different ways, mark'd their pleasing separation; beneath them lay the delicious tract of the belly, which terminated in a parting or rift scarce discernable, that modestly seem'd to retire downwards, and seek shelter between two plump fleshy thighs: the curling hair that overspread its delightful front, clothed it with the richest sable fur in the universe: in short, she was evidently a subject for the painter to court her sitting to them for a pattern of female beauty, in all the true pride and pomp of nakedness.

The young Italian (still in his shirt) stood gazing and transported at the sight of beauties that might have fir'd a dying hermit; his eager eyes devour'd her, as she shifted attitudes at his discretion: neither were his hands excluded their share of the high feast, but wander'd, on the hunt of pleasure, over every part and inch of her body, so qualified to afford the most exquisite sense of it.

In the meantime, one could not help observing the swell of his shirt before, that bolster'd out, and shewed the condition of things behind the curtain: but he soon remov'd it, by slipping his shirt over his head; and now, as to nakedness, they had nothing to reproach one another.

The young gentleman, by Phoebe's guess, was about two and twenty; tall and well limb'd. His body was finely form'd, and of a most vigorous make, square-shoulder'd, and broad-chested: his face was not remarkable in any way, but for a nose inclining to the *Roman*, eyes large, black, and sparkling, and a ruddiness in his cheeks that was the more a grace, for his complexion was of the brownest, not of that dusky dun colour which excludes the idea of freshness, but of that clear, olive gloss, which, glowing with life, dazzles perhaps less than fairness, and yet pleases more, when it pleases at all. His hair, being too short to tie, fell no lower than his neck, in short easy curls; and he had a few sprigs about his paps, that garnish'd his chest in a style of strength and manliness. Then his grand movement, which seem'd to rise out of a thicket of curling hair that spread from the root all round thighs and belly up to the navel, stood stiff and upright, but of a size to frighten me, by sympathy, for the small tender part which was the object of its fury, and which now lay expos'd to my fairest view; for he had, immediately on stripping off his shirt, gently push'd her down on the couch, which stood conveniently to break her willing fall. Her thighs were spread out to their utmost extension, and discovered between them the mark of the sex, the red-centred cleft of flesh, whose lips, vermilioning inwards, exprest a small ruby line in sweet miniature, such as *Guido's* touch or colouring could never attain to the life or delicacy of.

Phoebe, at this, gave me a gentle jog, to prepare me for a whispered question: whether I thought my little maidenhead was much less? But my attention was too much engross'd, too much enwrapp'd with all I saw, to be able to give her any answer.

By this time the young gentleman had changed her posture from lying breadth to length-wise on the couch: but her thighs were still spread, and the mark lay fair for him, who, now kneeling between them, display'd to us a side-view of that fierce erect machine of his, which threaten'd no less than splitting the tender victim, who lay smiling at the uplifted stroke, nor seem'd to decline it. He looked upon his weapon himself with some pleasure, and guiding it with his hand to the invisible slit, drew aside the lips, and lodg'd it (after some thrusts, which Polly seem'd even to assist) about half way; but there it stuck, I suppose from its growing thickness: he draws it again, and just wetting it with spittle, re-enters, and with ease sheath'd it now up to the hilt, at which Polly gave a deep sigh, which was quite another tone than one of pain; he thrusts, she heaves, at first gently, and in a regular cadence; but presently the transport began to be too violent to observe any order or measure; their motions were too rapid, their kisses too fierce and fervent for nature to support such fury long: both seem'd to me out of themselves: their eyes darted fires: "Oh! . . . oh! . . . I can't bear it . . . It is too much . . . I die . . . I am going . . ." were Polly's expressions of ecstasy: his joys were more silent; but soon broken murmurs, sighs heart-fetch'd, and at length a dispatching thrust, as if he would have forced himself up her body, and then motionless languor of all his limbs, all shewed that the die-away moment was come upon him; which she gave signs of joining with, by the wild throwing of her hands about, closing her eyes, and giving a deep sob, in which she seemed to expire in an agony of bliss.

When he had finish'd his stroke, and got from off her, she lay still without the last motion, breathless, as it should seem, with pleasure. He replaced her again breadth-wise on the couch, unable to sit up, with her thighs open, between

43

which I could observe a kind of white liquid, like froth, hanging about the outward lips of that recently opened wound, which now glowed with a deeper red. Presently she gets up, and throwing her arms round him, seemed far from undelighted with the trial he had put her to, to judge at least by the fondness with which she ey'd and hung upon him.

For my part, I will not pretend to describe what I felt all over me during this scene; but from that instant, adieu all fears of what man could do unto me; they were now changed into such ardent desires, such ungovernable longings, that I could have pull'd the first of that sex that should present himself, by the sleeve, and offered him the bauble, which I now imagined the loss of would be a gain I could not too soon procure myself.

Phoebe, who had more experience, and to whom such sights were not so new, could not however be unmoved at so warm a scene; and drawing me away softly from the peephole, for fear of being overheard, guided me as near the door as possible, all passive and obedient to her least signal.

Here was no room either to sit or lie, but making me stand with my back towards the door, she lifted up my petticoats, and with her busy fingers fell to visit and explore that part of me, where now the heat and irritations were so violent, that I was perfectly sick and ready to die with desire; the bare touch of her finger, in that critical place, had the effect of a fire to a train, and her hand instantly made her sensible to what a pitch I was wound up, and melted by the sight she had thus procured me. Satisfied then with her success, in allaying a heat that would have made me impatient of seeing the continuation of the transaction between our amorous couple, she brought me again to the crevice, so favourable to our curiosity.

We had certainly been but a few instants away from it, and yet on our return we saw everything in good forwardness for recommencing the tender hostilities.

The young foreigner was sitting down, fronting us, on the couch, with Polly upon one knee, who had her arms round his neck, whilst the extreme whiteness of her skin was not

44

undelightfully contrasted by the smooth glossy brown of her lover's.

But who could count the fierce, unnumber'd kisses given and taken? in which I could often discover their exchanging the velvet thrust, when both their mouths were double tongued, and seemed to favour the mutual insertion with the greatest gusto and delight.

In the meantime, his red-headed champion, that had so lately fled the pit, quell'd and abash'd, was now recover'd to the top of his condition, perk'd and crested up between Polly's thighs, who was not wanting, on her part, to coax and keep it in good humour, stroking it, with her head down, and received even its velvet tip between the lips of not its proper mouth: whether she did this out of any particular pleasure, or whether it was to render ir more glib and easy of entrance, I could not tell; but it had such an effect, that the young gentleman seem'd by his eyes, that sparkled with more excited lustre, and his inflamed countenance, to receive increase of pleasure. He got up, and taking Polly in his arms, embraced her, and said something too softly for me to hear, leading her withal to the foot of the couch, and taking delight to slap her thighs and posterior with that stiff sinew of his, which hit them with a spring that he gave it with his hand, and made them resound again, but hurt her about as much as he meant to hurt her, for she seemed to have as frolic a taste as himself.

But guess my surprise, when I saw the lazy young rogue lie down on his back, and gently pull down Polly upon him, who giving way to his humour, straddled, and with her hands conducted her blind favourite to the right place; and following her impulse, ran directly upon the flaming point of this weapon of pleasure, which she stak'd herself upon, up pierc'd, and infix'd to the extremest hair-breadth of it: thus she sat on him a few instants, enjoying and relishing her situation, whilst he toyed with her provoking breasts. Sometimes she would stop to meet his kiss: but presently the sting of pleasure spurr'd them up to fiercer action; then began the storm of heaves, which, from the undermost combatant, were thrusts at the same time, he crossing his

45

hands over her, and drawing her home to him with a sweet violence: the inverted strokes of anvil over hammer soon brought on the critical period, in which all the signs of a close conspiring ecstasy informed us of the *point* they were at.

For me, I could bear to see no more; I was so overcome, so inflamed at the second part of the same play, that, mad to an intolerable degree, I hugg'd, I clasped Phoebe, as if she had wherewithal to relieve me. Pleased however with, and pitying the taking she could feel me in, she drew me towards the door, and opening it as softly as she could, we both got off undiscover'd, and she reconducted me to my own room, where, unable to keep my legs, in the agitation I was in, I instantly threw myself down on the bed, where I lay transported, though asham'd at what I felt.

Phoebe lay down by me, and ask'd me archly if, now that I had seen the enemy, and fully considered him, I was still afraid of him? or did I think I could venture to come to a close engagement with him? To all which, not a word on my side; I sigh'd, and could scarce breathe. She takes hold of my hand, and having roll'd up her own petticoats, forced it half strivingly towards those parts, where, now grown more knowing, I miss'd the main object of my wishes; and finding not even the shadow of what I wanted, where everything was so flat, or so hollow, in the vexation I was in at it, I should have withdrawn my hand but for fear of disobliging her. Abandoning it then entirely to her management, she made use of it as she thought proper, to procure herself rather the shadow than the substance of any pleasure. For my part, I now pin'd for more solid food, and promis'd tacitly to myself that I would not be put off much longer with this foolery from woman to woman, if Mrs. Brown did not soon provide me with the essential specific. In short, I had all the air of not being able to wait the arrival of my lord B . . ., tho' he was now expected in a very few days: nor did I wait for him, for love itself took charge of the disposal of me, in spite of interest, or gross lust.

It was now two days after the closet-scene, that I got up

46

about six in the morning, and leaving my bed-fellow fast asleep, stole down, with no other thought than of taking a little fresh air in a small garden, which our backparlour open'd into, and from which my confinement debarr'd me, at the times company came to the house; but now sleep and silence reign'd all over it.

I open'd the parlour door, and well surpriz'd was I at seeing, by the side of a fire half-out, a young gentleman in the old lady's elbow chair, with his legs laid upon another, fast asleep, and left there by his thoughtless companions, who had drank him down, and then went off with every one his mistress, whilst he stay'd behind by the courtesy of the old matron, who would not disturb or turn him out in that condition, at one in the morning; and beds, it is more than probable, there were none to spare. On the table still remain'd the punch bowl and glasses, strew'd about in their usual disorder after a drunken revel.

But when I drew nearer, to view the sleeping form, heavens! what a sight! No! no term of years, no turn of fortune could ever erase the lightning-like impression his form made on me ... Yes! dearest object of my earliest passion, I command for ever the remembrance of thy first appearance to my ravish'd eyes ... it calls thee up, present; and I see thee now!

Figure to yourself, Madam, a fair stripling between eighteen and nineteen, with his head reclin'd on one of the sides of the chair, his hair in disorder'd curls, irregularly shading a face, on which all the roseate bloom of youth and all the manly graces conspired to fix my eyes and heart. Even the langour and paleness of his face, in which the momentary triumph of the lily over the rose was owing to the excesses of the night, gave an inexpressible sweetness to the finest features imaginable: his eyes, closed in sleep, displayed the meeting edges of their lids beautifully bordered with long eyelashes; over which no pencil could have described two more regular arches than those that grac'd his forehead, which was high, perfectly white and smooth. Then a pair of vermilion lips, pouting and swelling to the touch, as if a bee had freshly stung them, seem'd to challenge me to get the gloves of this lovely sleeper, had not the modesty and respect, which in both sexes are inseparable from a true passion, check'd my impulses.

But on seeing his shirt-collar unbutton'd, and a bosom whiter than a drift of snow, the pleasure of considering it could not bribe me to lengthen it, at the hazard of a health that began to be my life's concern. Love, that made me timid, taught me to be tender too. With a trembling hand I took hold of one of his, and waking him as gently as possible, he started, and looking, at first a little wildly, said with a voice that sent its harmonious sound to my heart: "Pray, child, what o'clock is it?" I told him, and added that he might catch cold if he slept longer with his breast open in the cool of the morning air. On this he thanked me with a sweetness perfectly agreeing with that of his features and eyes; the last now broad open, and eagerly surveying me, carried the sprightly fires they sparkled with directly to my heart.

It seems that having drank too freely before he came upon the rake with some of his young companions, he had put himself out of a condition to go through all the weapons with them, and crown the night with getting a mistress; so that seeing me in a loose undress, he did not doubt but I was one of the misses of the house, sent in to repair his loss of time; but though he seiz'd that notion, and a very obvious one it was, without hesitation, yet, whether my figure made a more than ordinary impression on him, or whether it was natural politeness, he address'd me in a manner far from rude, tho' still on the foot of one of the house pliers, come to amuse him; and giving me the first kiss that I ever relish'd from man in my life, ask'd me if I could favour him with my company, assuring me that he would make it worth my while: but had not even new-born love, that true refiner of lust, oppos'd so sudden a surrender, the fear of being surpriz'd by the house was a sufficient bar to my compliance.

I told him then, in a tone set me by love itself, that for reasons I had not time to explain to him, I could not stay with him, and might not even ever see him again: with a sigh at these last words, which broke from the bottom of my heart. My conqueror, who, as he afterwards told me, had been struck with my appearance, and lik'd me as much as he could think of liking any one in my suppos'd way of life, ask'd me briskly at once, if I would be kept by him, and that he would take a lodging for me directly, and relieve me from any engagements he presum'd I might be under to the house. Rash, sudden, undigested, and even dangerous as this offer might be from a perfect stranger, and that stranger a giddy boy, the prodigious love I was struck with for him had put a charm into his voice there was no resisting, and blinded me to every objection; I could, at that instant, have died for him: think if I could resist an invitation to live with him! Thus my heart, beating strong to the proposal, dictated my answer, after scarce a minute's pause, that I would accept of his offer, and make my escape to him in what way he pleased, and that I would be entirely at his disposal, let it be good or bad. I have often since wondered that so great a compliance did not disgust him, or make me too cheap in his eyes, but my fate had so appointed it, that in his fears of the hazard of the town, he had been some time looking out for a girl to take into keeping, and my person happening to hit his fancy, it was by one of those miracles reserved to love that we struck the bargain in the instant, which we sealed by an exchange of kisses, that the hopes of a more uninterrupted enjoyment engaged him to content himself with.

Never, however, did dear youth care in his person, more wherewith to justify the turning of a girl's head, and making her set all consequences at defiance, for the sake of following a gallant.

For, besides all the perfections of manly beauty which were assembled in his form, he had an air of neatness and gentility, a certain smartness in the carriage and port of his head that yet more distinguish'd him; his eyes were sprightly and full of meaning; his looks had in them something at once sweet and commanding. His complexion outbloom'd the lovely-colour'd rose, whilst its inimitable tender vivid glow clearly sav'd it from the reproach of wanting-life, of raw and dough-like, which is commonly made to those so extremely fair as he was.

Our little plan was that I should get out about seven the next morning (which I could *readily* promise, as I knew where to get the key of the street door), and he would wait at the end of the street with a coach to convey me safe off; after which, he would send, and clear any debt incurr'd by my stay at Mrs. Brown's, who, he only judged, in gross, might not care to part with one, he thought so fit to draw custom to the house.

I then just hinted to him not to mention in the house his having seen such a person as me, for reasons I would explain to him more at leisure. And then, for fear of miscarrying, by being seen together, I tore myself from him with a bleeding heart, and stole up softly to my room, where I found Phœbe still fast asleep, and hurring off my few clothes, lay down by her, with a mixture of joy and anxiety that may be easier conceived than express'd.

The risks of Mrs. Brown's discovering my purpose, of disappointments, misery, ruin, all vanish'd before this newkindl'd flame. The seeing, the touching, the being, if but for a night, with this idol of my fond virgin-heart, appeared to me a happiness above the purchase of my liberty of life. He might use me ill, let him! he was the master; happy, too happy, even to receive death at so dear a hand.

To this purpose were the reflections of the whole day, of which every minute seem'd to me a little eternity. How often did I visit the clock! nay, was tempted to advance the tedious hand, as if that would have advanc'd the time with it! Had those of the house made the least observations on me, they must have remark'd something extraordinary from the discomposure I could not help betraying; especially when at dinner mention was made of the charmingest youth having been there, and stay'd for breakfast. "Oh! he was such a beauty!. . . . I should have died for him!. . . . they would pull caps for him!. . . ." and the like fooleries, which, however, was throwing oil on a fire I was sorely put to it to smother the blaze of.

The fluctuations of my mind, the whole day, produc'd

one good effect: which was that, through mere fatigue, I slept tolerably well till five in the morning, when I got up, and having dress'd myself, waited, under the double tortures of fear and impatience, for the appointed hour. It came at last, the dear, critical, dangerous hour came; and now, supported only by the courage love lent me, I ventured, on tip-toe, downstairs, leaving my box behind, for fear of being surpriz'd with it in going out.

I got to the street-door, the key whereof was always laid on the chair by our bedside, in trust with Phœbe, who, having not the least suspicion of my entertaining any design to go from them (nor indeed had I but the day before), made no reserve or concealment of it from me. I open'd the door with great ease; love, that embolden'd, protected me too: and now, got safe into the street, I saw my new guardian-angel waiting at a coach-door, ready open. How I got to him I know not: I suppose I flew; but I was in the coach in a trice, and he by the side of me, with his arms clasp'd round me, and giving me the kiss of welcome. The coachman had his orders, and drove to them.

My eyes were instantly fill'd with tears, but tears of the most delicious delight; to find myself in the arms of that beauteous youth was a rapture that my little heart swam in. Past or future were equally out of the question with me. The present was as much as all my powers of life were sufficient to bear the transport of, without fainting. Nor were the most tender embraces, the most soothing expressions wanting on his side, to assure me of his love, and of never giving me cause to repent the bold step I had taken, in throwing myself thus entirely upon his honour and generosity. But, alas! this was no merit in me, for I was driven to it by a passion too impetuous for me to resist, and I did what I did because I could not help it.

In an instant, for time was now annihilated with me, we landed at a public house in *Chelsea*, hospitably commodious for the reception of duet-parties of pleasure, where a breakfast of chocolate was prepared for us.

An old jolly stager, who kept it, and understood life perfectly well, breakfasted with us, and leering archly at me, gave us both joy, and said we were well paired, i' faith! that a great many gentlemen and ladies used his house, but he had never seen a handsomer couple ... he was sure I was a fresh piece ... I look'd so country, so innocent! well my spouse was a lucky man! ... all which common landlord's cant not only pleas'd and sooth'd me, but help'd to divert my confusion at being with my new sovereign, whom, now the minute approach'd, I began to fear to be alone with: a timidity which true love had a greater share in than even maiden bashfulness.

I wish'd, I doat'd, I could have died for him; and yet, I know not how, or why, I dreaded the point which had been the object of my fiercest wishes; my pulses beat fears, amidst a flush of the warmest desires. This struggle of the passions, however, this conflict betwixt modesty and lovesick longings, made me burst again into tears! which he took, as he had done before, only for the remains of concern and emotion at the suddenness of my change of condition, in committing myself to his care; and, in consequence of that idea, did and said all that the thought would most comfort and reinspirit me.

After breakfast, *Charles* (the dear familiar name I must take the liberty henceforward to distinguish my *Adonis* by), with a smile full of meaning, took me gently by the hand, and said: "Come, my dear, I will show you a room that commands a fine prospect over some gardens"; and without waiting for an answer, in which he relieved me extremely, he led me up into a chamber, airy and lightsome, where all seeing of prospects was out of the question, except that of a bed, which had all the air of having recommended the room to him.

Charles had just slipp'd the bolt of the door, and running, caught me in his arms, and lifting me from the ground, with his lips glew'd to mine, bore me, trembling, panting, dying, with soft fears and tender wishes, to the bed; where his impatience would not suffer him to undress me, more than just unpinning my handkerchief and gown, and unlacing my stays.

My bosom was now bare, and, rising in the warmest

throbs, presented to his sight and feeling the firm hard swell of a pair of young breasts, such as may be imagin'd of a girl not sixteen, fresh out of the country, and never before handled; but even their pride, whiteness, fashion, pleasing resistance to the touch, could not bribe his restless hands from roving; but, giving them the loose, my petti-coats and shift were soon taken up, and their stronger centre of attraction laid open to their tender invasion. My fears, however, made me mechanically close my thighs; but the very touch of his hand, insinuated between them, disclosed them and opened a way for the main attack.

In the meantime, I lay fairly exposed to the examination of his eyes and hands, quiet and unresisting; which con-firm'd him the opinion he proceeded so cavalierly upon, that I was no novice in these matters, since he had taken me out of a common bawdy-house, nor had I said one thing to prepossess him of my virginity; and if I had, he would sooner have believ'd that I took him for a cully that would swallow such an improbability, than that I was still mistress of that darling treasure, that hidden mine, so eagerly sought after by the men, and which they never dig for, but to destroy.

Being now too high wound up to bear a delay, he un-button'd, and drawing out the engine of love-assaults, drove it currently, as at a ready-made breach. . . . Then! then! for the first time, did I feel that stiff horn-hard gristle, battering against the tender part; but imagine to yourself his surprise, when he found, after several vigorous pushes, which hurt me extremely, that he made not the least impression.

I complain'd, but tenderly complain'd that I could not bear it . . . indeed he hurt me!. . . . Still he thought no more, than that being so young, the largeness of his machine (for few men could dispute size with him) made all the difficulty; and that possibly I had not been enjoy'd by any so advan-tageously made in that part as himself: for still, that my virgin flower was yet uncrop'd, never enter'd into his head, and he would have thought it idling with time and words to have question'd me upon it.

He tries again, still no admittances, still no penetration; but he had hurt me yet more, whilst my extreme love made me bear extreme pain, almost without a groan. At length, after repeated fruitless trials, he lay down panting by me, kiss'd my falling tears, and ask'd me tenderly what was the meaning of so much complaining? and if I had not borne it better from others than I did from him? I answered, with a simplicity fram'd to persuade, that he was the first man that ever serv'd me so. Truth is powerful, and it is not always that we do not believe what we eagerly wish.

Charles, already dispos'd by the evidence of his senses to think my pretences to virginity not entirely apocryphal, smothers me with kisses, begs me, in the name of love, to have a little patience, and that he will be as tender of hurting me as he would be of himself.

Alas! it was enough I knew his pleasure to submit joy-fully to him, whatever pain I foresaw it would cost me.

He now resumes his attempts once more: first, he put one of the pillows under me, to give the blank of his aim a more favourable elevation, and another under my head, in ease of it; then spreading my thighs, and placing himself standing between them, made them rest upon his hips; applying then the point of his machine to the slit, into which he sought entrance: it was so small, he could scare assure himself of its being rightly pointed. He looks, he feels, and satisfies himself: then driving forward with fury, its prodigious stiffness, thus impacted, wedgelike, breaks the union of those parts, and gain'd him just the insertion of the tip of it, lip-deep; which being sensible of, he improved his advantage, and following well his stroke, in a straight line, forcibly deepens his penetration; but put me to such intolerable pain, from the separation of the sides of that soft passage by a hard thick body, I could have scream'd out; but, as I was unwilling to alarm the house, I held in my breath, and cram'd my petticoat, which was turn'd up over my face, into my mouth, and bit it through in the agony. At length, the tender texture of that tract giving way to such fierce tearing and rending, he pierc'd something further into me: and now, outrageous and no longer his own master, but borne headlong away by the fury and over-mettle of that member, now exerting itself with a kind of native rage, he breaks in, carries all before him, and one violent merciless lunge sent it, imbrew'd, and reeking with virgin blood, up to the very hilt in me ... Then! then all my resolution deserted me: I scream'd out, and fainted away with the sharpness of the pain; and, as he told me afterwards, on his drawing out, when emission was over with him, my thighs were instantly all in a stream of blood, that flow'd from the wounded torn passage.

When I recover'd my senses, I found myself undress'd, and a-bed, in the arms of the sweet relenting murderer of my virginity, who hung mourning tenderly over me, and holding in his hand a cordial, which, coming from the still dear author of so much pain, I could not refuse; my eyes, however, moisten'd with tears and languishingly turn'd upon him, seemed to reproach him with his cruelty, and ask him if such were the rewards of love. But Charles, to whom I was now infinitely endear'd by this complete triumph over a maidenhead, where he so little expected to find one, in tenderness to that pain which he had put me to, in procuring himself the height of pleasure, smother'd his exultation, and employ'd himself with so much sweetness, so much warmth, to soothe, to caress, and comfort me in my soft complainings, which breath'd, indeed, more love than resentment, that I presently drown'd all sense of pain in the pleasure of seeing him, of thinking that I belong'd to him: he who was now the absolute disposer of my happiness, and, in one word, my fate.

The sore was, however, too tender, the wound too bleeding fresh, for Charle's good nature to put my patience presently to another trial; but as I could not stir, or walk across the room, he order'd the dinner to be brought to the bed-side, where it could not be otherwise than my getting down the wing of a fowl, and two or three glasses of wine, since it was my ador'd youth who both serv'd, and urged them on me, with that sweet irresistible authority with which love had invested him over me.

After dinner, and as everything but the wine was taken

away, Charles very impudently asks leave, he might read the grant if in my eyes, to come to bed with me, and accordingly falls to undressing; which I could not see the progress of without strange emotions of fear and pleasure.

He is now in bed with me the first time, and in broad day; but when thrusting up his own shirt and my shift he laid his naked glowing body to mine ... O insupportable delight! O superhuman rapture! what pain could stand before a pleasure so transporting? I felt no more the smart of my wounds below; but, curling round him like the tendril of a vine, as if I fear'd any part of him should be untouch'd or unpress'd by me, I return'd his strenuous embraces and kisses with a fervour and gusto only known to true love, and which mere lust could never rise to.

Yes, even at this time, when all the tyranny of the passions is fully over, and that my veins roll no longer but a cold tranquil stream, the remembrance of those passages that most affected me in my mouth still cheers and refreshes me. Let me proceed then. My beauteous youth was now glew'd to me in all the folds and twists that we could make our bodies meet in; when, no longer able to rein in the fierceness of refresh'd desires, he gives his steed the head, and, gently insinuating his thighs between mine, stopping my mouth with kisses of humid fire, makes a fresh irruption, and renewing his thrusts, pierces, tears, and forces his way up the torn tender folds, that yielded him admission with a pain little less severe that when the breach was first made. I stifled, however, my cries, and bore him with the passive fortitude of a heroine; soon his thrusts, more and more furious, cheeks flush'd with a deeper scarlet, his eyes turn'd up in the fervent fit, some dying signs, and an agonizing shudder, announced the approaches of that ecstatic pleasure, I was yet in too much pain to come in for my share of it.

Nor was it till after a few enjoyments had numb'd and blunted the sense of the pain, and given me to feel the titillating inspersion of balsamic sweets, drew from me the delicious return, and brought down all my passion, that I arrived at excess of pleasure through excess of pain. But when successive engagements had broke and inur'd me, I began to enter into the true unallay'd relish of that pleasure of pleasures, when the warm gush darts through all the ravish'd inwards; what floods of bliss! what melting transports! what agonies of delight! too fierce, too mighty for nature to sustain; well has she therefore, no doubt, provided the relief of a delicious momentary dissolution, the approaches of which are intimated by a dear delirium, a sweet thrill, on the point of emitting those liquid sweets, in which enjoyment itself is drown'd, when one gives the languishing stretch-out, and dies at the discharge.

How often, when the rage and tumult of my senses had subsided after the melting flow, have I, in a tender meditation ask'd myself coolly the question, if it was in nature for any of its creatures to be so happy as I was? Or, what were all fears of the consequence, put in the scale of one night's enjoyment of anything so transcendently the taste of my eyes and heart, as that delicious, fond, matchless youth?

Thus we spent the whole afternoon till supper time, in a continued circle of love delights, kissing, turtlebilling, toying, and all the rest of the feast. At length, supper was serv'd in, before which Charles had, for I do not know what reason, slipt his clothes on; and sitting down by the bedside, we made table and table-cloth of the bed and sheets, whilst he suffer'd nobody to attend or serve but himself. He ate with a very good appetite, and seem'd charm'd to see me eat. For my part, I was so enchanted with my fortune, so transported with the comparison of the delights I now swam in, with the insipidity of all my past scenes of life, that I thought them sufficiently cheap at even the price of my ruin, or the risk of their not lasting. The present possession was all my little head could find room for.

We lay together that night, when, after playing repeated prizes of pleasure, nature, overspent and satisfy'd, gave us up to the arms of sleep: those of my dear youth encircled me, the consciousness of which made even that sleep more delicious.

Late in the morning I wak'd first; and observing my lover slept profoundly, softly disengag'd myself from his arms, scarcely daring to breathe, for fear of shortening his repose; my cap, my hair, my shift, were all in disorder from the rufflings I had undergone; and I took this opportunity to adjust and set them as well as I could: whilst, every now and then, looking at the sleeping youth, with inconceivable fondness and delight, and reflecting on all the pain he had put me to, tacitly own'd that the pleasure had overpaid me for my sufferings.

It was then broad day. I was sitting up in the bed, the clothes of which were all tossed, or rolled off, by the unquietness of our motions, from the sultry heat of the weather; nor could I refuse myself a pleasure that solicited me so irresistibly, as this fair occasion of feasting my sight with all those treasures of youthful beauty I had enjoy'd, and which lay now almost entirely naked, his shirt being truss'd up in a perfect wisp, which the warmth of the room and season made me easy about the consequence of. I hung over him enamour'd indeed! and devoured all his naked charms with only two eyes, when I could have wish'd them at least a hundred, for the fuller enjoyment of the gaze.

Oh! could I paint his figure as I see it now, still present to my transported imagination! a whole length of an all-perfect, manly beauty in full view. Think of a face without a fault, glowing with all the opening bloom and vernal freshness of an age in which beauty is of either sex, and which the first down over his upper lip scarce began to distinguish.

The parting of the double ruby pout of his lips seem'd to exhale an air sweeter and purer than what it drew in: ah! what violence did it not cost me to refrain the so tempted kiss!

Then a neck exquisitely turn'd, grac'd behind and on the sides with his hair, playing freely in natural ringlets, connected his head to a body of the most perfect form, and of the most vigorous contexture, in which all the strength of manhood was conceal'd and soften'd to appearance by the delicacy of his complexion, the smoothness of his skin, and the plumpness of his flesh.

The platform of his snow-white bosom, that was laid out in a manly proportion, presented, on the vermilion summit of each pap, the idea of a rose about to bloom.

Nor did his shirt hinder me from observing that symmetry of his limbs, that exactness of shape, in the fall of it towards the loins, where the waist ends and the rounding swell of the hips commences; where the skin, sleek, smooth, and dazzling white, burnishes on the stretch'over firm, plump, ripe flesh, that crimp'd and ran into dimples at the least pressure, or that the touch could not rest upon, but slid over as on the surface of the most polished ivory.

His thighs, finely fashioned, and with a florid glossy roundness, gradually tapering away to the knees, seem'd pillars worthy to support that beauteous frame; at the bottom of which I could not, without some remains of terror, some tender emotions too, fix my eyes on that terrible machine, which had, not long before, with such fury broke into, torn, and almost ruin'd those soft, tender parts of mine, that had not yet done smarting with the effects of its rage; but behold it now! crest fall'n, reclining its halfcapt vermilion head over one of his thighs, quiet, pliant, and to all appearance incapable of the mischiefs and cruelty it had committed. Then the beautiful growth of the hair, in short and soft curls round its root, its whiteness, branch'd veins, the supple softness of the shaft, as it lay foreshorten'd, roll'd and shrunk up into a squab thickness, languid, and borne up from between his thighs by its globular appendage, that wondrous treasure-bag of nature's sweets, which, rivell'd round, and purs'd up in the only wrinkles that are known to please, perfected the prospect, and all together formed the most interesting moving picture in nature, and surely infinitely superior to those crudities furnish'd by the painters, statuaries, or any art, which are purchas'd at immense prices; whilst the sight of them in actual life is scarce sovereignly tasted by any but the few whom nature has endowed with a fire of imagination, warmly pointed by a truth of judgement to the springhead, the originals of beauty, of nature's unequall'd composition, above all the imitation of art, or the reach of wealth to pay their price.

But everything must have an end. A motion made by this angelic youth, in the listlessness of going off sleep, replac'd his shirt and the bedclothes in a posture that shut up that treasure from longer view.

I lay down then, and carrying my hands to that part of me in which the objects just seen had begun to raise a mutiny, that prevail'd over the smart of them, my fingers now open'd themselves an easy passage; but I had not long time to consider the wide difference *there*, between the maid and the now finish'd woman, before Charles wak'd, and turning towards me, kindly inquir'd how I had rested, and, scarce giving me time to answer, imprinted on my lips one of his burning rapture-kisses, which darted a flame to my heart, that from thence radiated to every part of me; and presently, as if he had proudly meant revenge for the survey I had smuggled of all his naked beauties, he spurns off the bedclothes, and trussing up my shift as high as it would go, took his turn to feast his eyes on all the gifts nature had bestow'd on my person; his busy hands, too, rang'd intemperately over every part of me. The delicious austerity and hardness of my yet unripe budding breasts, the whiteness and firmness of my flesh, the freshness and regularity of my features, the harmony of my limbs, all seem'd to confirm him in his satisfaction with his bargain; but when curious to explore the havoc he had made in the centre of his over-fierce attack, he not only directed his hands there, but, with a pillow put under, placed me favourably for his wanton purpose of inspection. Then, who can express the fire his eyes glisten'd, his hands glow'd with! whilst sighs of pleasure, and tender broken exclamations were all the praises he could utter. By this time his machine, stiffly risen at me, gave me to see it in its highest state and bravery. He feels it himself, seems pleas'd at its condition, and, smiling love and grace, seizes one of my hands, and carries it, with a gentle compulsion, to this pride of nature, and its richest masterpiece.

I, struggling faintly, could not help feeling what I could not grasp, a column of the whitest ivory, beautifully streak'd with blue veins, and carrying, fully uncapt, a head of the liveliest vermilion; no horn could be harder or stiffer; yet no velvet more smooth or delicious to the touch. Presently he guided my hand lower, to that part in which nature and pleasure keep their stores in concert, so aptly fasten'd and hung on to the root of their first instrument and minister, that not improperly he might be stil'd their pursebearer too: there he made me feel distinctly, through their soft cover, the contents, a pair of roundish balls, that seem'd to play within, and elude all pressure but the tenderest, from without.

But now this visit of my soft warm hand in those so sensible parts had put everything into such ungovernable fury that, disdaining all further preluding, and taking advantage of my commodious posture, he made the storm fall where I scarce patiently expected, and where he was sure to lay: presently, then, I felt the stiff insertion between the yielding, divided lips of the wound, now open for life; where the narrowness no longer put me to intolerable pain, and afforded my lover no more difficulty than what heighten'd his pleasure, in the strict embrace of that tender, warm sheath round the instrument it was so delicately adjusted to, and which, now cased home, so gorged me with pleasure that it perfectly suffocated me and took away my breath; then the killing thrusts! the unnumber'd kisses! every one of which was a joy inexpressible; and that joy lost in a crowd of yet greater blisses! But this was a disorder too violent in nature to last long: the vessels, so stirr'd and intensely heated, soon boil'd over, and for that time put out the fire; meanwhile all this dalliance and disport had so far consum'd the morning that it became a kind of necessity to lay breakfast and dinner into one.

In our calmer intervals Charles gave the following account of himself, every word of which was true. He was the only son of a father, who, having a small post in the revenue, rather over-liv'd his income, and had given this young gentleman a very slender education: no profession had he bred him up to, but design'd to provide for him in the army by purchasing him an ensign's commission, that is to say, provided he could raise the money or procure it by interest, either of which clauses was rather to be wish'd than hop'd for by him. On no better a plan, however, had this improvident father suffer'd this youth, a youth of great promise, to run up to the age of manhood, or near it at least, in next to idleness; and had, besides, taken no sort of pains to give him even the common premonitions against the vices of the town, and the dangers of all sorts which await the unexperienc'd and unwary in it. He liv'd at home, and at discretion, with his father, who himself kept a mistress; and for the rest, provided Charles did not ask him for money, he was indolently kind to him: he might lie out when he pleas'd; any excuse would serve, and even his reprimands were so slight that they carried with them rather an air of connivance at the fault than any serious control or constraint. But, to supply his calls for money, Charles, whose mother was dead, had, by her side, a grandmother, who doted upon him. She had a considerable annuity to live on, and very regularly parted with every shilling she could spare to this darling of hers, to the little heart-burn of his father; he was vex'd, not that she by this means fed his son's extravagance, but that she preferr'd Charles to himself; and we shall too soon see what a fatal turn such a mercenary jealousy could operate on the breast of a father.

Charles was, however, by the means of his grandmother's lavish fondness, very sufficiently enabled to keep a mistress so easily contented as my love made me; and my good fortune, for such I must ever call it, threw me in his way, in the manner above related, just as he was on the look-out for one.

As to temper, the even sweetness of it made him seem born for domestic happiness: tender, naturally polite, and gentle-manner'd, it could never be his fault if quarrels or animosities ruffled a calm he was so qualified in every way to maintain or restore. Without those great or shining qualities that constitute a genius, or are fit to make a noise in the world, he had all those humble ones that compose the softer social merit: plain common sense, set off with every grace of modesty and good nature, made him, if not admir'd, what is much happier, universally belov'd and esteem'd. But, as nothing but the beauties of his person had at first attracted my regard and fix'd my passion, neither was I then a judge of that internal merit, which I had afterward full occasion to discover, and which, perhaps, in that season of giddiness and levity, would have touch'd my heart very little, had it been lodg'd in a person less the delight of my eyes and idol of my senses. But to return to our situation.

After dinner, which we ate a-bed in a most voluptuous disorder, Charles got up, and taking a passionate leave of me for a few hours, he went to town where, concerting matters with a young sharp lawyer, they went together to my late venerable mistress's, from whence I had, but the day before, made my elopement, and with whom he was determin'd to settle accounts, in a manner that should cut off all further reckonings from that quarter.

Accordingly they went; but by the way, the Templar, his friend, on thinking over Charles's information, saw reason to give their visit another turn, and, instead of offering satisfaction, to demand it.

On being let in, the girls of the house flock'd round Charles, whom they knew, and from the earliness of my escape, and their perfect ignorance of his ever having so much as seen me, not having the least suspicion of his being an accessory to my flight, they were, in their way, *making up* to him; and as to his companion, they took him probably for a fresh cully. But the Templar soon check'd their forwardness, by inquiring for the old lady, with whom, he said, with a grave judge-like countenance, that he had some business to settle.

Madam was immediately sent down for and, the ladies being desir'd to clear the room, the lawyer ask'd her, severely, if she did know, or had not decoy'd, under pretence of hiring as a servant, a young girl, just come out of the country, called FRANCES or FANNY HILL, describing me withal as particularly as he could from Charles's description.

It is peculiar to vice to tremble at the inquiries of justice; and Mrs. Brown, whose conscience was not entirely clear upon my account, as knowing as she was of the town, as hackney'd as she was in buffing through all the dangers of her vocation, could not help being alarm'd at the question, especially when he went on to talk of a Justice of peace, *Newgate*, the *Old Bailey*, indictments for keeping a disorderly house, pillory, carting, and the whole process of that nature. She, who, it is likely, imagin'd I had lodg'd an information against her house, look'd extremely blank, and began to make a thousand protestations and excuses. However, to abridge, they brought away triumphantly my box of things, which, had she not been under an awe, she might have disputed with them; and not only that, but a clearance and discharge of any demands on the house, at the expense of no more than a bowl of arrack-punch, the treat of which, together with the choice of the house conveniences, was offer'd and not accepted. Charles all the time acted the chance-companion of the lawyer, who had brought him there, as he knew the house, and appear'd in no wise interested in the issue; but he had the collateral pleasure of hearing all that I had told him verified, so far as the bawd's fears would give her leave to enter into my history, which, if one may guess by the composition she so readily came into, were not small.

Phoebe, my kind tutoress Phoebe, was at that time gone out, perhaps in search of me, or their cook'd-up story had not, it is probable, pass'd so smoothly.

This negotiation had, however, taken up some time, which would have appear'd much longer to me, left, as I was, in a strange house, if the landlady, a motherly sort of a woman, to whom Charles had liberally recommended me, had not come up and kept me company. We drank tea, and her chat help'd to pass away the time very agreeably, since he was our theme; but as the evening deepened, and the hour set for his return was elaps'd, I could not dispel the gloom of impatience and tender fears which gathered upon me, and which our timid sex are apt to feel in proportion to their love.

Long, however, I did not suffer: the sight of him overpaid me; and the soft reproach I had prepar'd for him expired before it reach'd my lips.

I was still a-bed, yet unable to use my legs otherwise than awkwardly, and Charles flew to me, catched me in his arms, rais'd and extending mine to meet his dear embrace, and gives me an account, interrupted by many a sweet parenthesis of kisses, of the success of his measures.

I could not help laughing at the fright the old woman had been put into, which my ignorance, and indeed my want of innocence, had far from prepar'd me for bespeaking. She had, it seems, apprehended that I fled for shelter to some relation I had recollected in town, on my dislike of their ways and proceeding towards me, and that this application came from thence; for, as Charles had rightly judg'd, not one neighbour had, at that still hour, seen the circumstance of my escape into the coach, or, at least, notic'd him; neither had any in the house the least hint or clue of suspicion of my having spoke to him, much less of my having clapt up such a sudden bargain with a perfect stranger: thus the greatest improbability is not always what we should most mistrust.

We supped with all the gaiety of two young giddy creatures at the height of their desires; and as I had most joyfully given up to Charles the whole charge of my future happiness, I thought of nothing beyond the exquisite pleasure of possessing him.

He came to bed in due time; and this second night, the pain being pretty well over, I tasted, in full draughts, all the transports of perfect enjoyment: I swam, I bathed in bliss, till both fell fast asleep, through the natural consequences of satisfied desires, and appeas'd flames; nor did we wake but to renew'd raptures.

Thus, making the most of love and life, did we stay in this

lodging in Chelsea about ten days; in which time Charles took care to give his excursions from home a favourable gloss, and to keep his footing with his fond indulgent grandmother, from whom he drew constant and sufficient supplies for the charge I was to him, and which was very trifling, in comparison with his former less regular course of pleasures.

Charles remov'd me then to a private ready furnish'd lodging in *D . . . street, St. James's,* where he paid half a guinea a week for two rooms and a closet on the second floor, which he had been some time looking out for, and was more convenient for the frequency of his visits than where he had at first plac'd me, in a house which I cannot say but I left with regret, as it was infinitely endear'd to me by the first possession of my Charles, and the circumstance of losing, there, that jewel which can never be twice lost. The landlord, however, had no reason to complain of anything, but of a procedure in Charles too liberal not to make him regret the loss of us.

Arrived at our new lodgings, I remember I thought them extremely fine, though ordinary enough, even at that price; but had it been a dungeon that Charles had brought me to, his presence would have made it a little *Versailles.*

The landlady, *Mrs. Jones,* waited on us to our apartment, and with great volubility of tongue explain'd to us all its conveniences – that her own maid should wait on us . . . that the best of quality had lodg'd at her house . . . that her first floor was let to a foreign secretary of an embassy and his lady . . . that I looked like a very good-natur'd lady . . . At the word lady, I blush'd out of flatter'd vanity: this was too strong for a girl of my condition; for though Charles had had the precaution of dressing me in a less tawdry flaunting style than were the clothes I escap'd to him in, and of passing me for his wife, that he had secretly married, and kept private (the old story) on account of his friends, I dare swear this appear'd extremely apocryphal to a woman who knew the town so well as she did; but that was the least of her concern. It was impossible to be less scruple-ridden than she was; and the advantage of letting her rooms being her sole object, the truth itself would have far from scandaliz'd her, or broke her bargain.

A sketch of her picture and personal history will dispose you to account for the part she is to act in my concerns.

She was about forty-six years old, tall, meagre, red-hair'd, with one of those trivial ordinary faces you meet with everywhere, and go about unheeded and unmentioned. In her youth she had been kept by a gentleman who, dying, left her forty pounds a year during her life, in consideration of a daughter he had by her; which daughter, at the age of seventeen, she sold, for not a very considerable sum either, to a gentleman who was going on *Envoy* abroad, and took his purchase with him, where he us'd her with the utmost tenderness, and it is thought, was secretly married to her: but had constantly made a point of her not keeping up the least correspondence with a mother base enough to make a market of her own flesh and blood. However, as she had no nature, nor, indeed, any passion but that of money, this gave her no further uneasiness, than, as she thereby lost a handle of squeezing presents, or other after-advantages, out of the bargain. Indifferent then, by nature of con-stitution, to every other pleasure but that of increasing the lump, by any means whatever, she commenc'd as a kind of private procuress, for which she was not amiss fitted, by her grave, decent appearance, and sometimes did a job in the match-making way; in short, there was nothing that appear'd to her under the shape of gain that she would not have undertaken. She knew most of the ways of the town, having not only herself been upon, but kept up constant intelligences in it, dealing, beside her practice in promoting a harmony between the two sexes, in private pawn-broking, and other profitable secrets. She rented the house she liv'd in, and made the most of it, by letting it out in lodgings; though she was worth at least near three or four thousand pounds, she would not allow herself even the necessaries of life, and pinn'd her subsistence entirely on what she could squeeze out of her lodgers.

When she saw such a young pair come under her roof, her immediate notions, doubtless, were how she should make the most money of us, by every means that money might be made, and which, she rightly judged, our situation and in-experience would soon beget her occasions of.

In this hopeful sanctuary, and under the clutches of this harpy, did we pitch our residence. It will not be mighty material to you, or very pleasant to me, to enter into a detail of all the petty cut-throat ways and means with which she used to fleece us; all which Charles indolently chose to bear with, rather than take the trouble of removing, the dif-ference of expense being scarce attended to by a young gentleman who had no ideas of stint, or even economy, and a raw country girl who knew nothing of the matter.

Here, however, under the wings of my sovereignly belov'd, did I flow the most delicious hours of my life; my Charles I had, and, in him, everything my fond heart could wish or desire. He carried me to plays, operas, masquerades, and every diversion of the town; all which pleas'd me indeed, but pleas'd me infinitely the more for his being with me, and explaining everything to me, and enjoying perhaps, the natural impressions of surprise and admiration which such sights, at the first, never fail to excite in a country girl, new to the delights of them; but to me, they sensibly prov'd the power and full dominion of the sole passion of my heart over me, a passion in which soul and body were concenter'd, and left me no room for any other relish of life but love.

As to the men I saw at those places, or at any other, they suffer'd so much in the comparison my eyes made of them with my all-perfect Adonis, that I had not the infidelity even of one wandering thought to reproach myself with upon his account. He was the universe to me, and all that was not him was nothing to me.

My love, in fine, was so excessive, that it arriv'd at annihilating every suggestion or kindling spark of jealousy; for, one idea only tending that way, gave me such exquisite torment that my self-love, and dread of worse than death, made me for ever renounce and defy it: nor had I, indeed, occasion; for, were I to enter here on the recital of several instances wherein Charles sacrific'd to me women of greater importance than I dare hint (which, considering his form, was no such wonder), I might, indeed, give you full proof of his unshaken constancy to me; but would not you accuse me of warming up again a feast that my vanity ought long ago to have been satisfy'd with?

In our cessations from active pleasure, Charles fram'd himself one, in instructing me, as far as his own lights reach'd, in a great many points of life, that I was, in consequence of my non-education, perfectly ignorant of: nor did I suffer one word to fall in vain from the mouth of my lovely teacher: I hung on every syllable he utter'd, and receiv'd, as oracles, all he said; whilst kisses were all the interruption I could not refuse myself the pleasure of admitting, from lips that breath'd more than Arabian sweetness.

I was in a little time enabled, by the progress I had made, to prove the deep regard I had paid to all that he had said to me: repeating it to him almost word for word; and to shew that I was not entirely the parrot, but that I reflected upon, that I enter'd into it, I join'd my own comments, and ask'd him questions of explanation.

My country accent, and the rusticity of my gait, manners, and deportment, began now sensibly to wear off, so quick was my observation and so efficacious my desire of growing every day worthier of his heart.

As to money, though he brought me constantly all he receiv'd, it was with difficulty he even got me to give it room in my bureau; and what clothes I had, he could prevail on me to accept of on no other foot, than that of pleasing him by the greater neatness in my dress, beyond which I had no ambition. I could have made a pleasure of the greatest toil, and worked my fingers to the bone, with joy, to have supported him: guess, then, if I could harbour any idea of being burdensome to him, and this disinterested turn in me was so unaffected, so much the dictate of my heart, that Charles could not but feel it: and if he did not love me as much as I did him (which was the constant and only matter of sweet contention between us), he manag'd so, at least, as to give me the satisfaction of believing it impossible for man to be more tender, more true, more faithful than he was.

Our landlady, Mrs. Jones, came frequently up to my apartment, from whence I never stirr'd on any pretext without Charles; nor was it long before she worm'd out, without much art, the secret of our having cheated the church of a ceremony, and, in course, of the terms we liv'd together upon; a circumstance which far from displeas'd, considering the designs she had upon me, and which, alas! she will, too soon, have room to carry into execution. But in the meantime, her own experience of life let her see that any attempts, however indirect or disguis'd, to divert or break, at least presently, so strong a cement of hearts as ours was, could only end in losing two lodgers, of whom she made very competent advantages, if either of us came to smoak her commission; for a commission she had from one of her customers, either to debauch, or get me away from my keeper at any rate.

But the barbarity of my fate soon sav'd her the task of disuniting us. I had now been eleven months with this life of my life, which had passed in one continu'd rapid stream of delight: but nothing so violent was ever made to last. I was about three months gone with child by him, a circumstance which would have added to his tenderness, had he ever left me room to believe it could receive an addition, when the mortal, the unexpected blow of separation fell upon us. I shall gallop hastily over the particulars, which I shudder yet to think of, and cannot to this instant reconcile myself, or by what means I could outlive it.

Two life-long days had I linger'd through without hearing from him, I who breath'd, who existed but in him, and had never yet seen twenty-four hours pass without seeing or hearing from him. The third day my impatience was so strong, my alarms had been so severe, that I perfectly sicken'd with them; and being unable to support the shock longer, I sunk upon the bed, and ringing for Mrs. Jones, who had far from comforted me under my anxieties, she came up. I had scarce breath and spirit enough to find words to beg of her, if she would save my life, to fall upon some

70

means of finding out instantly what was become of its only prop and comfort. She pity'd me in a way that rather sharpen'd my affliction than suspended it, and went out upon this commission.

She had not far to go: Charles's father lived but at an easy distance, in one of the streets that run into *Covent Garden*. There she went into a public house, and from thence sent for a maid-servant, whose name I had given her, as the properest to inform her.

The maid readily came, and as readily, when Mrs. Jones inquir'd of her what was become of Mr. Charles, or whether he was gone out of town, acquainted her with the disposal of her master's son, which, the very day after, was no secret to the servants. Such sure measures had he taken, for the most cruel punishment of his child for having more interest with his grandmother than he had, though he made use of a pretense, plausible enough, to get rid of him in this secret and abrupt manner, for fear her fondness should have interpos'd a bar to his leaving England, and proceeding on a voyage he had concerted for him; which pretext was, that it was indispensably necessary to secure a considerable inheritance that devolv'd to him by the death of a rich merchant (his own brother) at one of the factories in the South-Seas, of which he had lately receiv'd advice, together with a copy of the will.

In consequence of which resolution to send away his son, he had, unknown to him, made the necessary preparations for fitting him out, struck a bargain with the captain of a ship, whose punctual execution of his orders he had secured, by his interest with his principal owner and patron; and, in short, concerted his measures so secretly and effectively that, whilst his son thought he was going down the river for a few hours, he was stopt on board a ship, debar'd from writing, and more strictly watch'd than a State criminal.

Thus was the idol of my soul torn from me, and forc'd on a long voyage, without taking of one friend, or receiving one line of comfort, except a dry explanation and instructions, from his father, how to proceed when he should arrive at

his destin'd port, enclosing, withal, some letters of recommendation to someone there: all these particulars I
did not learn minutely till some time after.

The maid, at the same time, added that she was sure this
usage of her sweet young master would be the death of his
grand-mama, as indeed it prov'd true; for the old lady, on
hearing it, did not survive the news a whole month; and as
her fortune consisted in an annuity, out of which she had
laid up no reserves, she left nothing worth mentioning to her
so fatally envied darling, but absolutely refus'd to see his
father before she died.

When Mrs. Jones return'd, and I observ'd her looks, they
seem'd so unconcern'd, and even near to pleas'd, that I half
flatter'd myself she was going to set my tortur'd heart at
ease, by bringing me good news; but this, indeed, was a
cruel delusion of hope: the barbarian, with all the coolness
imaginable, stabb'd me to the heart, in telling me, suc-
cinctly, that he was sent away at least on a four year's
voyage (here she stretch'd maliciously), and that I could not
expect, in reason, ever to see him again: and all this with
such pregnant circumstances, that I could not help giving
them credit, as in general they were, indeed, too true!

She had hardly finish'd her report before I fainted away
and after several successive fits, all the while wild and
senseless, I miscarried of the dear pledge of my Charles's
love: but the wretched never die when it is fittest they should
die, and women are hard-liv'd to a proverb.

The cruel and interested care taken to recover me sav'd
an odious life: which, instead of the happiness and joys it had
overflow'd in, all of a sudden presented no view before me
of anything but the depth of misery, horror and the sharpest
affliction.

Thus I lay six weeks, in the struggles of youth and constitution, against the friendly efforts of death, which I
constantly invoked to my relief and deliverance, but
which proving too weak for my wish, I recovered at
length, tho' into a state of stupefaction and despair, that
threatened me with the loss of my senses and a mad-
house.

Time, however, that great comforter, presently began to assuage the violence of my sufferings, and to numb my feeling of them. My health return'd to me, though I still retain'd an air of grief, dejection, and languor which, taking off the ruddiness of my country complexion, render'd it rather more delicate and affecting.

The landlady had all this while officiously provided, and taken care that I wanted for nothing: and as soon as she saw me retriev'd into a condition of answering her purpose, one day, after we had dined together, she congratulated me on my recovery, the merit of which she took entirely to herself, and all this by way of introduction to a most terrible and scurvy epilogue: "You are now," says she – "Miss Fanny, tolerably well, and you are very welcome to stay in the lodgings as long as you please; you see I have ask'd you for nothing this long time, but truly I have a call to make up a sum of money, which must be answer'd." And with that, presents me with a bill of arrears for rent, diet, apothecary's charges, nurse, etc., sum total twenty-three pounds, seventeen and sixpence: towards discharging of which, I had not in the world (which she well knew) more than seven guineas, left by chance, of my dear Charles's common stock, with me. At the same time, she desir'd me to tell her what course I would take for payment. I burst out into a flood of tears and told her my conditions; adding that I would sell what few clothes I had, and that, for the rest, I would pay her as soon as possible. But my distress, being favourable to her views, only stiffen'd her the more.

She told me, very coolly, that she was indeed sorry for my misfortunes, but that she must do herself justice, though it would go to the very heart of her to send "such a tender young creature to prison . . ." At the word "prison"! every drop of my blood chill'd, and my fright acted so strongly upon me, that, turning as pale and faint as a criminal at the first sight of his place of execution, I was on the point of swooning. My landlady, who wanted only to terrify me to a certain point, and not to throw me into a state of body inconsistent with her designs upon it, began to soothe me again, and told me, in a tone compos'd to more pity and gentleness, that it would be my own fault, if she was forc'd to proceed to such extremities; but she believ'd there was a friend to be found in the world, who would make up matters to both our satisfactions, and that she would bring him to drink tea with us that very afternoon, when she hop'd we would come to a right understanding in our affairs. To all this, not a word of answer; I sat mute, confounded, terrify'd.

Mrs. Jones, however, judging rightly that it was time to strike while the impressions were so strong upon me, left me to myself and to all the terrors of an imagination, wounded to death by the idea of going to a prison, and, from a principle of self-preservation, snatching at every glimpse of redemption from it.

In this situation I sat near half an hour, swallow'd up in grief and despair, when my landlady came in, and observing a death-like dejection in my countenance, still in pursuance of her plan, put on a false pity, and bidding me be of a good heart: Things, she said, would not be so bad as I imagined, if I would be but my own friend; and closed with telling me she had brought a very honourable gentleman to drink tea with me, who would give me the best advice how to get rid of all my troubles. Upon which, without waiting for a reply, she goes out, and returns with this very honourable gentleman, whose very honourable procuress she had been, on this as well as other occasions.

The gentleman, on his entering the room, made me a very civil bow, which I had scarce strength, or presence of mind enough to return a curtsey to; when the landlady, taking upon her to do all the honours of the first interview (for I had never, that I remember'd, seen the gentleman before), sets a chair for him, and another for herself. All this while not a word on either side; a stupid stare was all the face I could put on this strange visit.

The tea was made, and the landlady, unwilling, I suppose, to lose any time, observing my silence and shyness before this entire stranger: "Come, Miss Fanny," says she, in a coarse familiar style, and tone of authority, "hold up your head, child, and do not let sorrow spoil that pretty face of yours. What! Sorrows are only for a time; come, be free, here is a worthy gentleman who has heard of your misfortunes, and is willing to serve you; you must be better acquainted with him; do not you now stand upon your punctilios, and this and that, but make your bargain while you may.''

At this so delicate and eloquent harangue, the gentleman, who saw I look'd frighted and amaz'd, and indeed, incapable of answering, took her up for breaking things in so abrupt a manner, as rather to shock than incline me to an acceptance of the good he intended me; then, addressing himself to me, told me he was perfectly acquainted with my whole story, and every circumstance of my distress which he own'd was a cruel plunge for one of my youth and beauty to fall into; that he had long taken a liking to my person, for which he appeal'd to Mrs. Jones, there present, but finding me so absolutely engag'd to another, he had lost all hopes of succeeding, till he had heard the sudden reverse of fortune that had happen'd to me, on which he had given particular orders to my landlady to see that I should want for nothing; and that, had he not been forc'd abroad to the Hague on affairs he could not refuse himself to, he would himself have attended me during my sickness; that on his return, which was but the day before, he had, on learning my recovery, desir'd my landlady's good offices to introduce him to me, and was as angry, at least, as I was shock'd, at the manner in which she had conducted herself towards obtaining him that happiness; but, that to show me how much he disown'd her procedure, and how far he was from taking any ungenerous advantage of my situation, and from exacting any security for my gratitude, he would before my face, that instant, discharge my debt entirely to my landlady, and give me her receipt in full; after which I should be at liberty either to reject or grant his suit, as he was much above putting any force upon my inclinations.

Whilst he was exposing his sentiments to me, I ventur'd just to look up to him, and observed his figure, which was that of a very sightly gentleman, well made, about forty, dress'd in a suit of plain clothes, with a large diamond ring on one of his fingers, the lustre of which play'd in my eyes, as he wav'd his hand in talking, and rais'd my notions of his importance. In short, he might have pass'd for what is commonly call'd a comely black man, with an air of distinction natural to his birth and condition.

To all his speeches, however, I answer'd only in tears that flow'd plentifully to my relief, and choking up my voice, excus'd me from speaking, very luckily, for I should not have known what to say.

The sight, however, mov'd him, as he afterwards told me, irresistibly, and by way of giving me some reason to be less powerfully affected, he drew out his purse, and calling for pen and ink, which the landlady was prepar'd for, paid her every farthing of her demand, independent of a liberal gratification which was to follow unknown to me; and taking a receipt in full, very tenderly forc'd me to secure it, by guiding my hand, which he had thrust it into, so as to make me passively put it into my pocket.

Still I continued in a state of stupidity, or melancholy despair, as my spirits could not yet recover from the violent shocks they had receiv'd; and the landlady had actually left the room, and me alone with this strange gentleman, before I observ'd it, and then I observ'd it without alarm, for I was now lifeless, and indifferent to everything.

The gentleman, however, no novice in affairs of this sort, drew near me; and, under the pretence of comforting me, first with his handkerchief dried my tears as they ran down my cheeks; presently he ventur'd to kiss me: on my part, neither resistance nor compliance. I sat stock-still; and now looking on myself as bought by the payment that had been transacted before me, I did not care what became of my wretched body: and wanting life, spirits, or courage to oppose the least struggle, even that of the modesty of my sex, I suffer'd, tamely, whatever the gentleman pleased; who, proceeding insensibly from freedom to freedom, insinuated his hand between my handkerchief and bosom, which he handled at discretion: finding thus no repulse, and that everything favour'd, beyond expectation, the completion of his desires, he took me in his arms, and bore me, without life or motion, to the bed, on which laying me gently down, and having me at what advantage he pleas'd, I did not so much as know what he was about, till recovering from a trance of lifeless insensibility, I found him buried in me, whilst I lay passive and innocent of the least sensation of pleasure: a death-cold corpse could scarce have less life or sense in it. As soon as he had thus pacified a passion which had too little respected the condition I was in, he got off, and after recomposing the disorder of my clothes, employ'd himself with the utmost tenderness to calm the transports of remorse and madness at myself, with which I was seized, too late, I confess, for having suffer'd, on that bed, the embraces of an utter stranger. I tore my hair, wrung my hands, and beat my breast like a madwoman. But when my new master, for in that light I then view'd him, applied himself to appease me, as my whole rage was levell'd at myself, no part of which I thought myself permitted to aim at him, I begged of him, with more submission than anger, to leave me alone, that I might, at least, enjoy my affliction in quiet. This he positively refused, for fear, as he pretended, I should do myself a mischief.

Violent passions seldom last long, and those of women least of any. A dead still calm succeeded this storm, which ended in a profuse shower of tears.

Had anyone, but a few instants before, told me that I should have ever known any man but Charles, I would have spit in his face; or had I been offer'd infinitely a greater sum of money than that I saw paid for me, I had spurn'd the proposal in cold blood. But our virtues and our vices depend too much on our circumstances; unexpectedly beset as I was, betray'd by a mind weakened by a long severe affliction, and stunn'd with the terrors of a jail, my defeat will appear the more excusable, since I certainly was not present at, or a party in any sense, to it. However, as the first enjoyment is decisive, and he was now over the bar, I thought I had no longer a right to refuse the caresses of one that had got that advantage over me, no matter how obtain'd; conforming myself to this maxim, I consider'd myself as so much in his power, that I endur'd his kisses and embraces without affecting struggles or anger; not that they, as yet, gave me any pleasure, or prevail'd over the aversion of my soul, to give myself up to any sensation of that sort; what I suffer'd, I suffer'd out of a kind of gratitude, and as a matter of course after what had pass'd.

He was, however, so regardful as not to attempt the renewal of those extremities which had thrown me, just before, into such violent agitations; but, now secure of possession, contented himself with bringing me to temper by degrees, and waiting at the hand of time for those fruits of generosity and courtship, which he since often reproach'd himself with having gather'd much too green, when, yielding to the invitations of my inability to resist him, and overborne by desires, he had wreak'd his passion on a mere lifeless, spiritless body, dead to all purpose of joy, since, taking none, it ought to be suppos'd incapable of giving any. This is, however, certain; my heart never thoroughly forgave him the manner in which I had fallen to him, although, in point of interest, I had reason to be pleas'd that he found, in my person, wherewithal to keep him from leaving me as easily as he had gained me.

The evening was, in the meantime, so far advanc'd, that the maid came in to lay the cloth for supper, when I understood, with joy, that my landlady, whose sight was present poison to me, was not to be with us.

Presently a neat and elegant supper was introduc'd, and a bottle of Burgundy, with the other necessaries, were set on a dumb-waiter.

The maid quitting the room, the gentleman insisted, with a tender warmth, that I should sit up in the elbow chair by the fire, and see him eat, if I could not be prevailed on to eat myself. I obey'd with a heart full of affliction, at the comparison it made between those delicious *tête-à-tête* with my ever dear youth and this forc'd situation, this new awkward scene, impos'd and obtruded on me by cruel necessity.

At supper, after a great many arguments us'd to comfort and reconcile me to my fate, he told me that his name was H . . ., brother to the Earl of L . . . and that having, by the suggestions of my landlady, been led to see me, he had found me perfectly to his taste, and given her a commission to procure me at any price, and that he had at length succeeded, as much to his satisfaction as he passionately wished it might be to mine; adding, withal, some flattering assurances, that I should have no cause to repent my knowledge of him.

I had now got down at most half a partridge, and three or four glasses of wine, which he compelled me to drink by way of restoring nature; but whether there was anything extraordinary put into the wine, or whether there wanted no more to revive the natural warmth of my constitution, and give fire to the old train, I began no longer to look with that constraint, not to say disgust, on Mr. H . . ., which I had hitherto done; but, withal, there was not the least grain of love mix'd with this softening of my sentiments; any other man would have been just the same as me as Mr. H . . ., that stood in the same circumstances, and had done for me, and with me, what he had done.

There are not, on earth at least, eternal griefs; mine were, if not at an end, at least suspended: my heart, which had been so long overloaded with anguish and vexation, began to dilate and open to the least gleam of diversion or amusement. I wept a little, and my tears reliev'd me; I sigh'd, and my sighs seem'd to lighten me of a load that oppress'd me; my countenance grew, if not cheerful, at least more compos'd and free.

Mr. H . . ., who had watched, perhaps brought on this change, knew too well not to seize it: he thrust the table imperceptibly from between us, and bringing his chair to face me, he soon began, after preparing me by all the endearments of assurances and protestations, to lay hold of my hands, to kiss me, and once more to make free with my bosom, which, being at full liberty from the disorder of a loose dishabille, now panted and throbb'd, less with indignation than with fear and bashfulness, at being us'd

79

so familiarly by still a stranger. But he soon gave me greater occasion to exclaim, by stooping down and slipping his hand above my garters: thence he strove to regain the pass, which he had before found so open, and unguarded: but now he could not unlock the twist of my thighs; I gently complained, and begg'd him to let me alone; told him I was not well. However, as he saw there was more form and ceremony in my resistance than good earnest, he made his conditions for desisting from pursuing his point, that I should be put instantly to bed, whilst he gave certain orders to the landlady, and that he would return in an hour, when he hop'd to find me more reconcil'd to his passion for me than I seem'd at present. I neither assented nor deny'd, but my air and manner of receiving this proposal gave him to see that I did not think myself enough my own mistress to refuse it.

Accordingly he went out and left me, when a minute or two after, before I could recover myself into any composure for thinking, the maid came in with her mistress's service, and a small silver porrenger of what she called a bridal posset, and desir'd me to eat it as I went to bed, which consequently I did, and felt immediately a heat, a fire run like a hue-and-cry thro' every part of my body; I burnt, I glow'd, and wanted even little of wishing for any man.

The maid, as soon as I was lain down, took the candle away, and wishing me a good night, went out of the room, and shut the door after her.

She had hardly time to get downstairs, before Mr. H . . . open'd my room door softly, and came in, now undress'd in his night-gown and cap, with two lighted wax candles, and, bolting the door, gave me, tho' I expected him, some sort of alarm. He came on tip-toe to the bedside, and said with a gentle whisper: "Pray, my dear, do not be startled . . . I will be very tender and kind to you." He then hurry'd off his clothes, and leap'd into bed, having given me openings enough, whilst he was stripping, to observe his brawny structure, strong-made limbs, and rough shaggy breast.

The bed shook again when it receiv'd this new load. He lay on the outside, where he kept the candles burning, no doubt for the satisfaction of ev'ry sense; for as soon as he had kiss'd me, he rolled down the bedclothes, and seemed transported with the view of all my person at full length, which he cover'd with a profusion of kisses, sparing no part of me. Then, being on his knees between my legs, he drew up his shirt, and bared all his hairy thighs, and stiff staring truncheon, red topp'd, and rooted into a thicket of curls, which covered his belly to the navel, and gave it the air of a flesh brush; and soon I felt it joining close to mine, when he had drove the nail up to the head, and left no partition, but the intermediate hair on both sides.

I had it now, I felt it now, and, beginning to drive, he soon gave nature such a powerful summons down to her favourite quarters, that she could no longer refuse repairing thither; all my animal spirits then rush'd mechanically to that centre of attraction, and presently, inly warmed, and stirr'd as I was beyond bearing, I lost all restraint, and yielding to the force of the emotion, gave down, as mere woman, those effusions of pleasure, which, in the strictness of still faithful love, I could have wished to have help up.

Yet oh! what an immense difference did I feel between this impression of a pleasure merely animal, and struck out of the collision of the sexes, by a passive bodily effect, from that sweet fury, that rage of active delight which crowns the enjoyments of a mutual love-passion, where two hearts, tenderly and truly united, club to exalt the joy, and give it a spirit and soul that bids defiance to that end which mere momentary desires generally terminate in, when they die of a surfeit of satisfaction!

Mr. H . . ., whom no distinctions of that sort seemed to disturb, scarce gave himself or me breathing time from the last encounter, but, as if he had task'd himself to prove that the appearances of his vigour were not signs hung out in vain, in a few minutes he was in a condition for renewing the onset; to which, preluding with a storm of kisses, he drove the same course as before, with unbated fervour; and thus, in repeated engagements, kept me constantly in exercise, till dawn of morning; in all which time he made me fully sensible to the virtues of his firm texture of limbs, his square shoulders, broad chest, compact hard muscles, in short a system of manliness that might pass for no bad image of our ancient sturdy barons, when they wielded the battle-axe: whose race is now so thoroughly refin'd and frittered away into the more delicate and modern-built frame of our pap-nerv'd softlings, who are as pale, as pretty, and almost as masculine as their sisters.

Mr. H . . ., content, however, with having the day break upon his triumphs, delivered me up to the freshment of a rest we both wanted, and we soon dropped into a profound sleep.

Tho' he was some time awake before me, yet he did not offer to disturb a repose he had given me so much occasion for; but on my first stirring, which was not till past ten o'clock, I was oblig'd to endure one more trial of his manhood.

About eleven, in came Mrs. Jones, with two basins of the richest soup, which her experience in these matters had mov'd her to prepare. I pass over the fulsome compliments, the cant of the decent procuress, with which she saluted us both; but tho' my blood rose at the sight of her, I suppress'd my emotions, and gave all my concern to reflections on what would be the consequence of this new engagement.

But Mr. H . . ., who penetrated my uneasiness, did not long suffer me to languish under it. He acquainted me that, having taken a solid, sincere affection to me, he would begin by giving me one leading mark of it, in removing me out of a house which must, for many reasons, be irksome and disagreeable to me, into convenient lodgings, where he would take all imaginable care of me; and, desiring me not to have any explanations with my landlady, or be impatient till he returned, he dress'd and went out, having left me a purse with two and twenty guineas in it, being all he had about him, as he express'd it, to keep my pocket till further supplies.

As soon as he was gone, I felt the usual consequence of the first launch into vice (for my love-attachment to Charles never appear'd to me in that light). I was instantly borne away down the stream, without making back to the shore. My dreadful necessities, my gratitude, and above all, to say the plain truth, the dissipation and diversion I began to find in this new acquaintance, from the black corroding thoughts my head had been a prey to ever since the absence of my dear Charles, concurr'd to stun all contrary reflections. If I now thought of my first, my only charmer, it was still the tenderness and regret of the fondest love, embitter'd with the consciousness that I was no longer worthy of him. I could have begg'd my bread with him all over the world, but, wretch that I was! I had neither the virtue or courage requisite not to outlive my separation from him.

Yet, had not my heart been thus engaged, Mr. H . . . might probably have been the sole master of it; but the place was full, and the force of conjunctures alone had made him the possessor of my person; the charms of which had, by the bye, been his sole object and passion, and were, of course, no foundation for a love either very delicate or very durable.

He did not return till six in the evening, to take me away to my new lodgings; and my moveables being soon pack'd, and convey'd into a hackney-coach, it cost me but little regret to take my leave of a landlady whom I thought I had so much reason not to be over-pleas'd with; and as for her part, she made no other difference to my staying or going, but what that of the profit created.

We soon got to the house appointed for me, which was that of a plain tradesman, who, on the score of interest, was entirely at Mr. H . . .'s devotion, and who let him the first floor, very genteely furnish'd, for two guineas a week, in which I was installed mistress, with a maid to attend me.

He stayed with me that evening, and we had a supper from a neighbouring tavern, after which, and a gay glass or two, the maid put me to bed. Mr. H . . . soon follow'd, and notwithstanding the fatigues of the preceding night, I found no quarter nor remission from him: he prided himself, as he told me, on doing the honours of my new apartment.

The morning being pretty well advanc'd, we got to break-fast, and the ice now broken, my heart, no longer engross'd by love, began to take ease, and to please itself with such trifles as Mr. H . . .'s liberal liking led him to make his court to the usual vanity of our sex. Silks, laces, earrings, pearl necklace, gold watch, in sort, all the trinkets and articles of dress were lavishly heap'd upon me; the sense of which, if it did not create returns of love, forc'd a kind of grateful fondness, something like love; a distinction it would be spoiling the pleasure of nine tenths of the keepers in the town to make, and is, I suppose, the very good reason why so few of them ever do make it.

I was now establish'd the kept mistress in form, well lodg'd, with a very sufficient allowance, and lighted up with all the lustre of dress.

Mr. H . . . continu'd kind and tender to me; yet, with all this, I was far from happy; for, besides my regret for my dear youth, which, though often suspended or diverted, still return'd upon me in certain melancholic moments with redoubled violences, I wanted more society, more dis-sipation.

As to Mr. H . . ., he was so much my superior in every sense that I felt it too much to the disadvantage of the gratitude I ow'd him. Thus he gain'd my esteem, though he could not raise my taste; I was qualify'd for no sort of conversation with him except one sort, and that is a satisfaction which leaves tiresome intervals, if not fill'd up by love, or other amusements.

Mr. H . . ., so experienc'd, so learned in the ways of women, numbers of whom had passed through his hands, doubtless, soon perceiv'd this uneasiness, and, without approving or liking me the better for it, had the complais-ance to indulge me.

He made suppers at my lodgings, where he brought several companions of his pleasures, with their mistresses; and by this means I got into a circle of acquaintance, that soon stripp'd me of all the remains of bashfulness and modesty which might be yet left of my country education, and were, to a just taste, perhaps the greatest of my charms.

We visited one another in form, and mimic'd, as near as we could, all the miseries, the follies, and impertinences of the women of quality, in the round of which they trifle away their time, without its ever entering into their little heads that on earth there cannot subsist anything more silly, more flat, more insipid and worthless than, generally consider'd, their system of life is: they ought to treat the men as their tyrants, indeed! were they to condemn them to it.

But tho', amongst the kept mistresses (and I was now acquainted with a good many, besides some useful matrons, who live by their connexions with them), I hardly knew one that did not perfectly detest her keeper, and, of course, made little or no scruple of any infidelity she could safely accomplish, I had still no notion of wronging mine: for, besides that no mark of jealousy on his side induced in me the desire or gave me the provocation to play him a trick of that sort, and that his constant generosity, politeness, and tender attention to please me forc'd a regard to him, that, without affecting my heart, insur'd him my fidelity, no object had yet appeared that could overcome the habitual liking I had contracted for him; and I was on the eve of obtaining, from the movements of his own voluntary generosity, a modest provision for life, when an accident happen'd which broke all the measures he had resolv'd upon in my favour.

I had now liv'd near seven months with Mr. H . . ., when one day returning to my lodgings, from a visit in the neighbourhood, where I us'd to stay longer, I found the street door open, and the maid of the house standing at it, talking with some of her acquaintances, so that I came in without knocking; and, as I passed by, she told me Mr. H . . . was above. I stept upstairs into my own bed-chamber, with no other thought than of pulling off my hat, etc., and then to wait upon him in the dining-room, into which my bed-chamber had a door, as is common enough. Whilst I was untying my hat-strings, I fancied I heard my maid *Hannah's* voice and a sort of tussle, which, raising my curiosity, I stole softly to the door, where a knot in the wood had been slipt out, and afforded a very commanding peep-hole to the scene then in agitation, the actors of which had been too earnestly employ'd to hear my opening my own door, from the landing place of the stairs, into my bed-chamber.

The first sight that struck me was Mr. H . . . pulling and hauling this coarse country strammel towards a couch that stood in a corner of the dining-room; to which the girl made only a sort of awkward hoydenish resistance, crying out so loud, that I, who listened at the door, could scarce hear her: "Pray Sir, don't . . . let me alone . . . I am not for your turn . . . You cannot sure, demean yourself with such a poor body as I . . . Lord! Sir, my mistress may come home . . . I must not indeed . . . I will cry out . . ." All which did not hinder her from insensibly suffering herself to be brought to the foot of the couch, upon which a push of no mighty violence serv'd to give her a very easy fall, and my gentleman having got up his hands to the stronghold of her VIRTUE, she, no doubt, thought it was time to give up the argument, and that all further defence would be vain: and he, throwing her petticoats over her face, which was now as red as scarlet, discover'd a pair of stout, plump, substantial thighs, and tolerably white; he mounted them round his hips, and coming out with his drawn weapon, stuck it in the cloven spot, where he seem'd to find a less difficult entrance than perhaps he had flatter'd himself with (for, by the way, this blouze had left her place in the country, for a bastard), and, indeed, all his motions shew'd he was lodg'd pretty much at large. After he had done, his dearie gets up, drops her petticoats down, and smooths her apron and handkerchief. Mr. H . . . look'd a little silly, and taking out some money, gave it her, with an air diffident enough, bidding her be a good-girl, and say nothing.

Had I lov'd this man, it was not in nature for me to have had patience to see the whole scene through: I should have broke in and play'd the jealous princess with a vengeance. But that was not the case, my pride alone was hurt, my heart not, and I could easier win upon myself to see how far he would go, till I had no uncertainty upon my conscience.

The least delicate of all affairs of this sort being now over, I retir'd softly into my closet, where I began to consider what I should do. My first scheme, naturally, was to rush in and upbraid them; this, indeed, flatter'd my present emotions and vexations, as it would have given immediate vent to them; but, on second thoughts, not being so clear as to the consequences to be apprehended from such a step, I began to doubt whether it was not better to dissemble my discovery till a safer season, when Mr. H . . . should have perfected the settlement he had made overtures to me of, and which I was not to think such a violent explanation, as I was indeed not equal to the management of, could possibly forward, and might destroy. On the other hand, the provocation seem'd too gross, too flagrant, not to give me some thoughts of revenge; the very start of which idea restor'd me to perfect composure; and, delighted as I was with the confus'd plan of it in my head, I was easily mistress enough of myself to support the part of ignorance I had prescrib'd to myself; and as all this circle of reflections was instantly over, I stole on tip-toe to the passage door, and opening it with a noise, past for having that moment come home; and after a short pause, as if to pull off my things, I opened the door into the dining-room, where I found the dowdy blowing the fire, and my faithful shepherd walking about the room, and whistling, as cool and unconcern'd as if nothing had happened. I think, however, he had not much to brag of having out-dissembled me: for I kept up, nobly, the character of our sex for art, and went up to him with the same open air of frankness as I had ever receiv'd him. He stayed but a little while, made some excuse for not being able to stay the evening with me, and went out.

As for the wench, she was now spoil'd, at least for my servant; and scarce eight and forty hours were gone round, before her insolence, on what had pass'd between Mr. H . . . and her, gave me so fair an occasion to turn her away, at a minute's warning, that not to have done it would have been the wonder: so that he could neither disapprove it nor find in it the least reason to suspect my original motive. What became of her afterwards, I know not; but generous as Mr. H . . . was, he undoubtedly made her amends: though, I dare answer, that he kept up no further commerce with her of that sort; as his stooping to such a coarse morsel was only a sudden sally of lust, on seeing a wholesome looking, buxom country-wench, and no more strange than hunger, or even a whimsical appetite's making a fling meal of neck-beef, for change of diet.

Had I consider'd this escapade of Mr. H . . . in no more than that light and contented myself with turning away the wench, I had thought and acted right; but, flush'd as I was with imaginary wrongs, I should have held Mr. H . . . to have been cheaply off, if I had not push'd my revenge farther, and repaid him, as exactly as I could for the soul of me, in the same coin.

Nor was this worthy act of justice long delay'd: I had it too much at heart. Mr. H . . . had, about a fortnight before, taken into his service a tenants' son, just come out of the country, a very handsome young lad, scarce turn'd nineteen, fresh as a rose, well shap'd and clever limb'd: in short, a very good excuse for any woman's liking, even tho' revenge had been out of the question; any, woman I say, who was disprejudic'd, and had wit and spirit enough to prefer a point of pleasure to a point of pride.

Mr. H . . . had clapp'd a livery upon him; and his chief employ was, after being shown my lodgings, to bring and carry letters or messages between his master and me; and as the situation of all kept ladies is not the fittest to inspire respect, even to the meanest of mankind, and, perhaps, less of it from the most ignorant, I could not help observing that this lad, who was, I suppose, acquainted with my relation to his master by his fellow-servants, used to eye me in that bashful confus'd way, more expressive, more moving and readier catch'd at by our sex, than any other declarations whatever: my figure had, it seems, struck him, and modest and innocent as he was, he did not himself know that the pleasure he took in looking at me was

88

love, or desire; but his eyes, naturally wanton, and now enflam'd with passion, spoke a great deal more than he durst have imagin'd they did. Hitherto, indeed, I had only taken notice of the comeliness of the youth, but without the least design: my pride alone would have guarded me from a thought that way, had not Mr. H . . .'s condescension with my maid, where there was not half the temptation in point of person, set me a dangerous example; but now I began to look on this stripling as every way a delicious instrument of my design'd retaliation upon Mr. H . . . of an obligation for which I should have made a conscience to die in his debt.

In order then to pave the way for the accomplishment of my scheme, for two or three times that the young fellow came to me with messages, I manag'd so, as without affectation to have him admitted to my bedside, or brought to me at my toilet, where I was dressing; and by carelessly showing or letting him see, as if without meaning or design, sometimes my bosom rather more bare than it should be; sometimes my hair, of which I had a very fine head, in the natural flow of it while combing; sometimes a neat leg, that had unfortunately slipt its garter, which I made no scruple of tying before him, easily gave him the impressions favourable to my purpose, which I could perceive to sparkle in his eyes, and glow in his cheeks: then certain slight squeezes by the hand, as I took letters from him, did his business completely.

When I saw him thus mov'd, and fir'd for my purpose, I inflam'd him yet more, by asking him several leading questions, such as had he a mistress? . . . was she prettier than me? . . . could he love such a one as I was? . . . and the like; to all which the blushing simpleton answer'd to my wish, in a strain of perfect nature, perfect undebauch'd innocence, but with all the awkwardness and simplicity of country breeding.

When I thought I had sufficiently ripen'd him for the laudable point I had in view, one day that I expected him at a particular hour, I took care to have the coast clear for the reception I design'd him; and, as I laid it, he came to the dining-room door, tapped at it, and, on my bidding him come in, he did so, and shut the door after him. I desir'd him, then, to bolt it on the inside, pretending it would not otherwise keep shut.

I was then lying at length upon that very couch, the scene of Mr. H . . .'s polite joys, in an undress, which was with all the art of negligence flowing loose, and in a most tempting disorder: no stays, no hoop, no encumbrance whatever. On the other hand, he stood at a little distance, that gave me a full view of a fine featur'd, shapely, healthy country lad, breathing the sweets of fresh blooming youth; his hair, which was of a perfect shining black, play'd to his face in natural side-curls, and was set out with a smart tuck-up behind; new buckskin breeches, that, clipping close, shew'd the shape of a plump, well made thigh; white stockings, garter-lac'd livery, shoulder-knot, altogether compos'd a figure in which the beauties of pure flesh and blood appeared under no disgrace from the lowness of a dress, to which a certain spruce neatness seems peculiarly fitted.

I bid him come towards me and give me his letter, at the same time throwing down, carelessly, a book I had in my hands. He colour'd, and came within reach of delivering me the letter, which he held out, awkwardly enough, for me to take, with his eyes riveted on my bosom, which was, through the design'd disorder of my blouse, sufficiently bare, and rather shaded than hid.

I, smiling in his face, took the letter, and immediately catching gently hold of his shirt sleeve, drew him towards me, blushing, and almost trembling; for surely his extreme bashfulness, and utter inexperience, call'd for, at least, all the advances to encourage him: his body was now conveniently inclin'd towards me, and, just softly chucking his smooth beardless chin, I asked him if he was afraid of a lady? . . . and with that took, and carrying his hand to my breasts, I prest it tenderly to them. They were now finely furnish'd, and rais'd, in flesh, so that, panting with desire, they rose and fell, in quick heaves, under his touch: at this, the boy's eyes began to lighten with all the fires of inflam'd nature, and his cheeks flush'd with a deep scarlet:

tongue-tied with joy, rapture, and bashfulness, he could not speak, but then his looks, his emotion, sufficiently satisfy'd me that my train had taken, and that I had no disappointment to fear.

My lips, which I threw in his way, so as that he could not escape kissing them, fix'd, fir'd, and embolden'd him: and now, glancing my eyes towards that part of his dress which cover'd the essential object of enjoyment, I plainly discover'd the swell and commotion there; and as I was now too far advanc'd to stop in so fair a way, and was indeed no longer able to contain myself, or wait the slower progress of his maiden bashfulness (for such it seem'd, and really was), I stole my hand upon his thighs, down one of which I could both see and feel a stiff hard body, confin'd by his breeches, that my fingers could discover no end to. Curious then, and eager to unfold so alarming a mystery, playing, as it were, with his buttons, which were bursting ripe from the active force within, those of his waistband and flore-flap flew open at a touch, when out it started; and now, disengag'd from the shirt, I saw, with wonder and surprise, what? not the play-thing of a boy, not the weapon of a man, but a maypole of so enormous a standard, that had proportions been observ'd, it must have belong'd to a young giant. Its prodigious size made me shrink again; yet I could not, without pleasure, behold, and even ventur'd to feel, such a length, such a breadth of animated ivory! perfectly well turn'd and fashion'd, the proud stiffness of which distended its skin, whose smooth polish and velvet softness might vie with that of the most delicate of our sex, and whose exquisite whiteness was not a little set off by a sprout of black curling hair round the root, through the jetty springs of which the fair skin shew'd as in a fine evening you may have remark'd the clear light ether through the branchwork of distant trees overtopping the summit of a hill: then the broad and blueish casted incarnate of the head, and blue serpentines of its veins, altogether compos'd the most striking assemblage of figure and colours in nature. In short, it stood an object of terror and delight.

But what was yet more surprising, the owner of this

natural curiosity, through the want of occasions in the strictness of his home-breeding, and the little time he had been in town not having afforded him one, was hitherto an absolute stranger, in practice at least, to the use of all that manhood he was so nobly stock'd with; and it now fell to my lot to stand his first trial of it, if I could resolve to run the risks of its disproportion to that tender part of me, which such an oversiz'd machine was very fit to lay in ruins.

But it was now much too late to deliberate; for, by this time, the young fellow, overheated with the present objects, and too high mettled to be longer curb'd in by that modesty and awe which had hitherto restrain'd him, ventur'd, under the stronger impulse and instructive promptership of nature alone, to slip his hands, trembling with eager impetuous desires, under my petticoats; and seeing, I suppose, nothing extremely severe in my looks to stop or dash him, he feels out, and seizes, gently, the centre-spot of his ardours. Oh then! the fiery touch of his fingers determines me, and my fears melting away before the glowing intolerable heat, my thighs disclose of themselves, and yield all liberty to his hand: and now, a favourable movement giving my petticoats a toss, the avenue lay too fair, too open to be miss'd. He is now upon me: I had placed myself with a jet under him, as commodious and open as possible to his attempts, which were untoward enough, for his machine, meeting with no inlet, bore and batter'd stiffly against me in random pushes, now above, now below, now beside his point; till, burning with impatience from its irritating touches, I guided gently, with my hand, this furious engine to where my young novice was now to be taught his first lesson of pleasure. Thus be nick'd, at length, the warm and insufficient orifice; but he was made to find no breach impracticable, and mine, tho' so often enter'd, was still far from wide enough to take him easily in.

By my direction, however, the head of his unwieldy machine was so critically pointed, that, feeling him fore-right against the tender opening, a favourable motion from me met his timely thrust, by which the lips of it, strenuously dilated, gave way to his thus assisted impetuosity, so that we might both feel that he had gain'd a lodgement. Pursuing then his point, he soon, by violent, and, to me, most painful piercing thrusts, wedges himself at length so far in, as to be now tolerably secure of his entrance: here he stuck, and I now felt such a mixture of pleasure and pain, as there is no giving a definition of. I dreaded alike his splitting me farther up, or his withdrawing; I could not bear either to keep or part with him. The sense of pain however prevailing, from his prodigious size and stiffness, acting upon me in those continued rapid thrusts, with which he furiously pursu'd his penetration, made me cry out gently: "Oh! my dear, you hurt me!" This was enough to check the tender respectful boy even in his mid-career; and he immediately drew out the sweet cause of my complaint, whilst his eyes eloquently express'd, at once, his grief for hurting me, and his reluctance at dislodging from quarters, of which the warmth and closeness had given him a wave of pleasure that he was now desire-mad to satisfy, and yet too much a novice not to be afraid of my withholding his relief, on account of the pain he had put me to.

But I was, myself, far from being pleas'd with his having too much regarded my tender exclamations; for now, more and more fir'd with the object before me, as it still stood with the fierce erection, unbonnetted, and displaying its broad vermilion head, I first gave the youth a re-encouraging kiss, which he repaid me with a fervour that seem'd at once to thank me, and bribe my farther compliance; and soon replac'd myself in a posture to receive, at all risks, the renewal, which he did not delay an instant: for, being presently remounted, I once more felt the smooth hard gristle forcing an entrance, which he achiev'd rather easier than before. Pain'd, however, as I was, with his efforts of gaining a complete admission, which he was so regardful as to manage by gentle degrees, I took care not to complain. In the meantime, the soft strait passage gradually loosens, yields, and, stretch'd to its utmost bearing, by the stiff, thick, indriven engine, sensible, at once, to the ravishing pleasure of the *feel* and the pain of the distension, let him in about half way, when all the most nervous activity he now exerted, to further his penetration, gain'd him not an inch of his purpose: for, whilst he hesitated there, the crisis of pleasure overtook him, and the close compressure of the warm surrounding fold drew from him the ecstatic gush, even before mine was ready to meet it, kept up by the pain I had endur'd in the course of the engagement, from the insufferable size of his weapon, tho' it was not as yet in above half its length.

I expected then, but without wishing it, that he would draw, but was pleasingly disappointed: for he was not to be let off so. The well breath'd youth, hot-mettled, and flush with genial juices, was now fairly in for making me know my driver. As soon, then, as he had made a short pause, waking, as it were, out of the trance of pleasure (in which every sense seem'd lost for a while, whilst, with his eyes shut, and short quick breathing, he had yielded down his maiden tribute), he still kept his post, yet unsated with enjoyment, and solacing in these so new delights; till his stiffness, which had scarce perceptibly remitted, being thoroughly recovered to him, who had not once unsheath'd, he proceeded afresh to cleave and open to himself an entire entry into me, which was not a little made easy to him by the balsamic injection with which he had just plentifully moisten'd the whole internals of the passage. Redoubling, then, the active energy of his thrusts, favoured by the fervid appetite of my motions, the soft oiled wards can no longer stand so effectual a picklock, but yield, and open him an entrance. And now, with conspiring nature, and my industry, strong to aid him, he pierces, penetrates, and at length, winning his way inch by inch, gets entirely in, and finally a mighty thrust sheathes it up to the guard; on the information of which, from the close jointure of our bodies (insomuch that the hair on both sides perfectly interweav'd and incircl'd together), the eyes of the transported youth sparkl'd with more joyous fires, and all his looks and motions acknowledged excess of pleasure, which I now began to share, for I felt him in my very vitals! I was quite sick with delight, stir'd beyond bearing with its furious agitations within me, and gorged and cramm'd, even to surfeit. Thus I lay gasping, panting under him, till his broken breathings, faltering accents, eyes twinkling with humid fires, lunges more furious, and an increas'd stiffness, gave me to hail the approaches of the second period: it came . . . and the sweet youth, overpower'd with the ecstasy, died away in my arms, melting in a flood that shot in genial warmth into the innermost recesses of my body; every conduit of which, dedicated to that pleasure, was on flow to mix with it. Thus we continued for some instants, lost, breathless, senseless of everything, and in every part but those favourite ones of nature, in which all that we enjoyed of life and sensation was now totally concentred.

When our mutual trance was a little over, and the young fellow had withdrawn that delicious stretcher, with which he had most plentifully drowned all thoughts of revenge in the sense of actual pleasure, the widen'd wounded passage refunded a stream of pearly liquids, which flowed down my thighs, mixed with streaks of blood, the marks of the ravage of that monstrous machine of his, which had now triumph'd over a kind of second maidenhead. I stole, however, my handkerchief to those parts, and wip'd them as dry as I could, whilst he was re-adjusting and buttoning up.

I made him now sit down by me, and as he had gather'd courage from such extreme intimacy, he gave me an after-course of pleasure, in a natural burst of tender gratitude and joy, at the new scenes of bliss I had opened to him: scenes positively new, as he had never before had the least acquaintance with that mysterious mark, the cloven stamp of female distinction, tho' nobody better qualify'd than he to penetrate into its deepest recesses, or do it nobler justice. But when, by certain motions, certain unquietnesses of his hands, that wandered not without design, I found he languish'd for satisfying a curiosity, natural enough, to view and handle those parts which attract and concentre the warmest force of imagination, charmed, as I was, to have any occasion of obliging and humouring his young desires, I suffer'd him to proceed as he pleased, without check or control, to the satisfaction of them.

Easily, then, reading in my eyes the full permission of myself to all his wishes, he scarce pleased himself more than me when, having insinuated his hand under my petticoat and shift, he presently removed those bars to the sight, by slyly lifting them upwards, under favour of a thousand kisses, which he thought, perhaps, necessary to divert my attention from what he was about. All my drapery being now roll'd up to my waist, I threw myself into such a posture upon the couch, as gave up to him, in full view, the whole region of delight, and all the luxurious landscape round it. The transported youth devour'd everything with his eyes, and try'd, with his fingers, to lay more open to his sight the secrets of that dark and delicious deep: he opens the folding lips, the softness of which, yielding entry to anything of a hard body, close round it, and oppose the sight: and feeling further, meets with, and wonders at, a soft fleshy excrescence, which, limber and relaxed after the late enjoyment, now grew, under the touch and examination of his fiery fingers, more and more stiff and considerable, till the titillating ardours of that so sensible part made me sigh, as if he had hurt me; on which he withdrew his curious probing fingers, asking me pardon, as it were, in a kiss that rather increased the flame *there*.

Novelty ever makes the strongest impressions, and in pleasures, especially: no wonder then, that he was swallowed up in raptures of admiration of things so interesting by their nature, and now seen and handled for the first time. On my part, I was richly overpaid for the pleasure I gave him, in that of examining the power of those objects thus abandon'd to him, naked and free to his loosest wish, over the artless, natural stripling: his eyes streaming fire, his cheeks glowing with a florid red, his fervid frequent sighs, whilst his hands convulsively squeez'd, opened, pressed together again the lips and sides of that deep fleshwound, or gently twitched the overgrowing moss; and all proclaimed the excess, the riot of joys, in having his wantonness thus humour'd. But he did not long abuse my patience, for the objects before him had now put him by all his, and, coming out with that formidable machine of his, he lets the fury loose, and pointing it directly to the pouting-lipped mouth, that bid him sweet defiance in dumbshew, squeezes in the head, and, and, driving with refreshed rage, breaks in, and plugs up the whole passage of that soft pleasure-conduit, where he makes all shake again, and put, once more, all within me into such an uproar, as nothing could still, but a fresh inundation from the very engine of those flames, as well as from all the springs with which nature floats that reservoir of joy, when risen to its flood-mark.

I was now so bruised, so batter'd, so spent with this over-match, that I could hardly stir, or raise myself, but lay palpitating, till, the ferment of my sense subsiding by degrees, and the hour striking at which I was oblig'd to dispatch my young man, I tenderly advised him of the necessity there was for parting; which I felt as much displeasure at as he did, who seemed eagerly disposed to keep the field, and to enter on a fresh action. But the danger was too great, and after some hearty kisses of leave, and recommendations of secrecy and discretion, I forc'd myself to send him away, not without assurances of seeing him again, to the same purpose, as soon as possible, and thrust a guinea into his hands: not more, lest, being too flush of money, a suspicion or discovery might arise from thence, having everything to fear from the dangerous indiscretion of that age in which young fellows would be too irresistible, too charming, if we had not that terrible fault to guard against.

Giddy and intoxicated as I was with such satiating draughts of pleasure, I still lay on the couch, supinely stretched out, in a delicious languor diffus'd over all my limbs, hugging myself for being thus revenged to my heart's content, and that in a manner so precisely alike, and on the identical spot in which I had received the supposed injury. No reflections on the consequences ever once perplex'd me, nor did I make myself one single reproach for having, by this step, completely entered of a profession more decry'd than disused. I should have held it ingratitude to the pleasure I had received to have repented of it; and since I was now over the bar, I thought, by plunging over head and ears into the stream I was hurried away by, to drown all sense of shame or reflection.

Whilst I was thus making these laudable dispositions, and whispering to myself a kind of tacit vow of incontinency, enters Mr. H . . . The consciousness of what I had been doing deepen'd yet the glowing of my cheeks, flushed with the warmth of the late action, which, joined to the piquant air of my deshabillé, drew from Mr. H . . . a compliment on my looks, which he was proceeding to back the sincerity of with proofs, and that with so brisk an action, as made me tremble for fear of a discovery from the condition those parts were left in from their late severe handling: the orifice dilated and inflamed, the lips swollen with their uncommon distension, the ringlets pressed down, crushed and un-curl'd with the overflowing moisture that had wet every-thing round it; in short, the different feel and state of things would hardly have passed upon one of Mr. H . . .'s nicety and experience unaccounted for but by the real cause. But here the woman saved me: I pretended a violent disorder of my head, and a feverish heat, that indispos'd me too much to receive his embraces. He gave in to his, and good-naturedly desisted. Soon after, an old lady coming in made a third, very *à-propos* for the confusion I was in, and Mr. H . . ., after bidding me take care of myself, and recom-mending me to my repose, left me much at ease and reliev'd by his absence.

In the close of the evening, I took care to have prepar'd for me a warm bath of aromatics and sweet herbs; in which having fully laved and solaced myself, I came out volupt-uously refresh'd in body and spirit.

The next morning, waking pretty early, after a night's perfect rest and composure, it was not without some dread and uneasiness that I thought of what innovation that tender, soft system of mine might have sustained, from the shock of a machine so sized for its destruction.

Struck with this apprehension, I scarce dared to carry my hand thither, to inform myself of the state and posture of things.

But I was soon agreeably cur'd of my fears.

The silky hair that covered round the borders, now smooth'd and repruned, had resumed its wonted curl and trimness; the fleshy pouting lips that had stood the brunt of the engagement were no longer swollen or moisture-drenched: and neither they, nor the passage into which they opened, that had suffered so great a dilatation, betray'd any the least alteration, outward or inwardly, to the most curious research, notwithstanding also the laxity that naturally follows the warm bath.

This continuation of that grateful stricture which is in us, to the men, the very jet of their pleasure, I ow'd, it seems, to a happy habit of body, juicy, plump and furnished towards the texture of those parts, with a fullness of soft springy flesh, that yielding sufficiently, as it does, to almost any distension soon recovers itself so as to retighten that strict compression of its mantlings and folds, which for the sides of the passage, wherewith it so tenderly embraces and closely clips any foreign body introduc'd into it, such as my exploring finger then was.

Finding then everything in due tone and order, I remember'd my fears, only to make a jest of them to myself. And now, palpably mistress of any size of man, and triumphing in my double achievement of pleasure and revenge, I abandon'd myself entirely to the ideas of all the delight I had swam in. I lay stretching out, glowingly alive all over, and tossing with burning impatience for the renewal of joys that had sinned but in a sweet excess; nor did I loose my longing, for about ten in the morning, according to expectation, *Will*, my new humble sweetheart, came with a message from his master, Mr. H . . ., to know how I did. I had taken care to send my maid on an errand into the city, that I was sure would take up time enough; and, from the people of the house, I had nothing to fear, as they were plain good sort of folks, and wise enough to mind no more other people's business than they could well help.

All dispositions then made, not forgetting that of lying in bed to receive him, when he was entered the door of my bed-chamber, a latch, that I governed by a wire, descended and secur'd it.

I could not but observe that my young minion was as much spruced out as could be expected from one in his condition: a desire of pleasing that could not be indifferent to me, since it prov'd that I pleased him; which, I assure you, was now a point I was not above having in view.

His hair trimly dressed, clean linen, and, above all, a hale, ruddy, wholesome country look, made him out as pretty a piece of woman's meat as you could see, and I should have thought anyone much out of taste that could not have made a hearty meal of such a morsel as nature seemed to have design'd for the highest diet of pleasure.

And why should I here suppress the delight I received from this amiable creature, in remarking each artless look, each motion of pure undissembled nature, betrayed by his wanton eyes; or shewing, transparently, the glow and suffusion of blood through his fresh, clear skin, even his sturdy rustic pressures wanted not their peculiar charm? Oh! but, say you, this was a young fellow of too low a rank of life to deserve so great a display. Maybe so: but was my condition, stricly consider'd one jot more exalted? or, had I really been much above him, did not his capacity of giving such exquisite pleasure sufficiently raise and ennoble him, to *me*, at least? Let who would, for me, cherish, respect, and reward the painter's, the statuary's, the musician's arts, in proportion to the delight taken in them: but at my age, and with my taste for pleasure, a taste strongly constitutional to me, the talent of pleasing, with which nature has endowed a handsome person, form'd to me the greatest of all merits; compared to which, the vulgar prejudices in favour of titles, dignities, honours, and the like, held a very low rank indeed. Nor perhaps would the beauties of the body be so much affected to be held cheap, were they, in their nature, to be bought and delivered. But for me, whose natural philosophy all resided in the favourite centre of sense, and who was rul'd by its powerful instinct in taking pleasure by its right handle, I could scarce have made a choice more to my purpose.

Mr. H . . .'s loftier qualifications of birth, fortune and sense laid me under a sort of subjection and constraint that were far from making harmony in the concert of love; nor had he, perhaps, thought me worth softening that superiority to; but, with this lad, I was more on that level which love delights in.

We may say what we please, but those we can be the easiest and freest with are ever those we like, not to say love, the best.

With this stripling, all whose art of love was the action of it, I could, without check of awe or restraint, give a loose to joy, and execute every scheme of dalliance my fond fancy might put me on, in which he was, in every sense, a most exquisite companion. And now my great pleasure lay in humouring all the petulances, all the wanton frolic of a raw novice just fleshed, and keen on the burning scent of his game, but inbroken to the sport: and, to carry on the figure, who could better THREAD THE WOOD than he, or stand fairer for the HEART OF THE HUNT?

He advanc'd then to my bedside, and whilst he faltered out his message, I could observe his colour rise, and his eyes lighten with joy, in seeing me in a situation as favourable to his loosest wishes, as if he had bespoke the play.

I smiled, and put out my hand towards him, which he kneeled down to (a politeness taught him by love alone, that great master of it) and greedily kiss'd. After exchanging a few confused questions and answers, I ask'd him if he could come to bed to me, for the little time I could venture to detain him. This was like asking a person, dying with hunger, to feast upon the dish on earth the most to his palate. Accordingly, without further reflection, his clothes were off in an instant; when, blushing still more at this new liberty, he got under the bedclothes I held up to receive him, and was now in bed with a woman for the first time in his life.

Here began the usual tender preliminaries, as delicious, perhaps, as the crowning act of enjoyment itself; which they often beget an impatience of, that makes pleasure destructive of itself, by hurrying on the final period, and closing that scene of bliss, in which the actors are generally too well pleas'd with their parts, not to wish them an eternity of duration.

When he had sufficiently graduated his advances towards

the main point, by toying, kissing, clipping, feeling my breasts, now round and plump, feeling that part of me I might call a furnace-mouth, from the prodigious intense heat his fiery touches had rekindled there, my young sportsman, embolden'd by every freedom he could wish, wantonly takes my hand, and carries it to that enormous machine of his, that stood with a stiffness! a hardness! an upward bent of erection! and which, together, with its bottom dependance, the inestimable bulse of lady's jewels, formed a grand show out of goods indeed! Then its dimensions, mocking either grasp or span, almost renew'd my terrors.

I could not conceive how, or by what means I could take, or put such a bulk out of sight. I stroked it gently, on which the mutinous rogue seemed to swell, and gather a new degree of fierceness and insolence; so that finding it grew not to be trifled with any longer, I prepar'd for rubbers in good earnest.

Slipping then a pillow under me, that I might give time the fairest play, I guided officiously with my hand this furious battering ram, whose ruby head, presenting nearest the resemblance of a heart, I applied to its proper mark, which lay as finely elevated as we could wish; my hips being borne up, and my thighs at their utmost extension, the gleamy warmth that shot from it, made him feel that he was at the mouth of the indraught, and driving foreright, the powerfully divided lips of that pleasure-thirsty channel receiv'd him. He hesitated a little; then, settled well in the passage, he made his way up the straits of it, with a difficulty nothing more than pleasing, widening as he went, so as to distend and smooth each soft furrow: our pleasure increasing deliciously, in proportion as our points of mutual touch increas'd in that so vital part of me in which I had now taken him, all indriven, and completely sheathed; and which, crammed as it was, stretched, splitting ripe, gave it so gratefully straight an accommodation! so strict a fold! a suction so fierce! that gave and took unutterable delight. We had now reach'd the closest point of union; but when he backened to come on the fiercer, as if I had been actuated by a fear of losing him, in the height of my fury, I twisted my legs round his naked loins, the flesh of which, so firm, so springy to the touch, quiver'd again under the pressure; and now I had him every way encircled and begirt; and having drawn him home to me, I kept him fast there, as if I had sought to unite bodies with him at that point. This bred a pause of action, a pleasure stop, whilst that delicate glutton, my nethermouth, as full as it could hold, kept palating, with exquisite relish, the morsel that so deliciously engorged it. But nature could not long endure a pleasure that so highly provoked without satisfying it: pursuing then its darling end, the battery recommenc'd with redoubled exertion; nor lay I inactive on my side, but encountring him with all the impetuosity of motion I was mistress of. The downy cloth of our meeting mounts was now of real use to break the violence of the tilt; and soon, too soon indeed! the highwrought agitation, the sweet urgency of this to-and-fro friction, raised the titillation on me to its height; so that finding myself on the point of going, and loathe to leave the tender partner of my joys behind me, I employed all the forwarding motions and arts my experience suggested to me, to promote his keeping me company to our journey's end. I not only then tighten'd the pleasure-girth round my restless inmate, by a secret spring of friction and compression that obeys the will in those parts, but stole my hand softly to that store bag of nature's prime sweets, which is so pleasingly attach'd to its conduit pipe, from which we receive them: there feeling, and most gently indeed, squeezing those tender globular reservoirs, the magic touch took instant effect, quicken'd, and brought on upon the spur the symptoms of that sweet agony, the melting moment of dissolution, when pleasure dies by pleasure, and the mysterious engine of it overcomes the titillation it has rais'd in those parts, by plying them with the stream of a warm liquid, that is itself the highest of all titillations, and which they thirstily express and draw in like the hot-natured leech, which to cool itself, tenaciously attracts all the moisture within its sphere of exsuction. Chiming then to me, with exquisite consent, as I melted away, his oily balsamic injection, mixing deliciously with the sluices in flow from me, sheath'd and blunted all the stings of pleasure, it flung us into an ecstasy that extended us fainting, breathless, entranced. Thus we lay, whilst a voluptuous languor possess'd, and still maintain'd us motionless and fast locked in one another's arms. Alas! that these delights should be no longer-lived! for now the point of pleasure, unedged by enjoyment, and all the brisk sensations flatten'd upon us, resigned us up to the cool cares of insipid life. Disengaging myself then from his embrace, I made him sensible of the reasons there were for his present leaving me; on which, though reluctantly, he put on his clothes, with as little expedition, however, as he could help, wantonly interrupting himself, between whiles, with kisses, touches and embraces I could not refuse myself to. Yet he happily return'd to his master before he was missed; but, at taking leave, I forc'd him (for he had sentiments enough to refuse it) to receive money enough to buy a silver watch, that great article of subaltern finery, which he at length accepted, as a remembrance he was carefully to preserve of my affections.

And here, Madam, I ought, perhaps to make you an apology for this minute detail of things, that dwelt so strongly upon my memory, after so *deep* an impression: but, besides that this intrigue bred one great revolution in my life, which historical truth requires I should not keep from you, may I not presume that so exalted a pleasure ought not to be ungratefully forgotten, or suppress'd by me, because I found it in a character in low life; where, by the bye, it is oftener met with purer, and more unsophisticate, than among the false, ridiculous refinements with which the great suffer themselves to be so grossly cheated by their pride: the great! than whom, there exist few amongst those they call the vulgar, who are more ignorant of, or who cultivate less, the art of living than they do; they, I say, who for ever mistake things the most foreign to the nature of pleasure itself; whose capital favourite object is enjoyment of beauty, wherever that rare invaluable gift is found, without distinction of birth, or station.

As love never had, so now revenge had no longer any share

in my commerce with this handsome youth. The sole pleasures of enjoyment were now the link I held to him by: for though nature had done such great matters for him in his outward form, and especially in that superb piece of furniture she had so liberally enrich'd him with; though he was thus qualify'd to give the senses their richest feast, still there was something more wanting to create in me, and constitute the passion of love. Yet Will had very good qualities too: gentle, tractable, and, above all, grateful; close, and secret, even to a fault: he spoke, at any time, very little, but made it up emphatically with action; and, to do him justice, he never gave me the least reason to complain, either of any tendency to encroach upon me for the liberties I allow'd him, or of his indiscretion in blabbing them. There is, then, a fatality in love, or have loved him I must; for he was really a treasure, a bit for the *bonne bouche* of a duchess; and, to say the truth, my liking for him was so extreme that it was distinguishing very nicely to deny that I loved him.

My happiness with him, however, did not last long, but found an end from my own imprudent neglect. After having taken even superfluous precautions against a discovery, our success in repeated meetings embolden'd me to omit the barely necessary ones. About a month after our first intercourse, one fatal morning (the season Mr. H . . . rarely or never visited me in) I was in my closet, where my toilet stood, in nothing but my shift, a bed gown and underpetticoat. Will was with me, and both ever too well disposed to baulk the opportunity. For my part, a warm whim, a wanton toy had just taken me, and I had challeng'd my man to execute it on the spot, who hesitated not to comply with my humour: I was set in the arm-chair, my shift and petticoat up, my thighs widespread and mounted over the arms of the chair, presenting the fairest mark to Will's drawn weapon, which he stood in act to plunge into me; when, having neglected to secure the chamber door, and that of the closet standing ajar, Mr. H . . . stole in upon us, before either of us was aware, and saw us precisely in these convicting attitudes.

I gave a great scream, and dropp'd my petticoat: the

thunderstruck lad stood tembling and pale, waiting his sentence of death. Mr. H . . . looked sometimes at one, sometimes at the other, with a mixture of indignation and scorn; and, without saying a word, turn'd upon his heel and went out.

As confused as I was, I heard him very distinctly turn the key, and lock the chamber-door upon us, so that there was no escape but through the dining-room, where he himself was walking about with distempered strides, stamping in a great chafe, and doubtless debating what he would do with us.

In the meantime, poor William was frightened out of his senses, and, as much need as I had of spirits to support myself, I was obliged to employ them all to keep his a little up. The misfortune I had now brought upon him, endear'd him the more to me, and I could have joyfully suffered any punishment he had not shared in. I water'd, plentifully, with my tears, the face of the frightened youth, who sat, not having strength to stand, as cold and as lifeless as a statue.

Presently Mr. H . . . comes in to us again, and made us go before him into the dining-room, trembling and dreading the issue. Mr. H . . . sat down on a chair whilst we stood like criminals under examination; and, beginning with me, ask'd me, with an even firmer tone of voice, neither soft nor severe, but cruelly indifferent, what I could say for myself, for having abused him in so unworthy a manner, with his own servant too, and how he had deserv'd this of me?

Without adding to the guilt of my infidelity that of an audacious defence of it, in the old style of a common kept miss, my answer was modest, and often interrupted by my tears, in substance as follows: that I never had a single thought of wronging him (which was true), till I had seen him taking the last liberties with my servant-wench (here he colour'd prodigiously), and that my resentment at that, which I was over-awed from giving vent to by complaints, or explanations with him, had driven me to a course that I did not pretend to justify; but that as to the young man, he was entirely faultless; for that, in the view of making him the instrument of my revenge, I had downright seduced him to what he had done; and therefore hop'd, whatever he determined about me, he would distinguish between the guilty and the innocent; and that, for the rest, I was entirely at his mercy.

Mr. H . . ., on hearing what I said, hung his head a little: but instantly recovering himself, he said to me, as near as I can retain, to the following purpose:

"Madam, I am somewhat taken aback, and confess you have fairly turn'd the tables upon me. It is not with one of your cast of breeding and sentiments that I should enter into a discussion of the very great difference of the provocations: be it sufficient that I allow you so much reason on your side, as to have changed my resolutions, in consideration of what you reproach me with; and I own, too, that your clearing that rascal there, is fair and honest in you. Renew with you I cannot: the affront is too gross. I give you a week's warning to go out of these lodgings; whatever I have given you remains to you; and as I never intend to see you more, the landlord will pay you fifty pieces on my account, with which, and every debt paid, I hope you will own I do not leave you in a worse condition than what I took you up in, or than you deserve of me. Blame yourself only that it is no better."

Then, without giving me time to reply, he address'd himself to the young fellow:

"For you, spark, I shall, for your father's sake, take care of you: the town is no place for such a silly fool as you are; and tomorrow you shall set out, under the charge of one of my men, well recommended, in my name, to your father, not to let you return and be spoil'd here."

At these words he went out, after my vainly attempting to stop him by throwing myself at his feet. He shook me off, though he seemed greatly mov'd too, and took Will away with him, who, I dare swear, thought himself very cheaply off.

I was now once more adrift, left to my own resources by a gentleman whom I certainly did not deserve. And all the letters, arts, friends' entreaties that I employed within the week of grace in my lodging could never win on him so much as to see me again. He had irrevocably pronounc'd my doom, and submission to it was my only choice. Soon after he married a lady of birth and fortune, to whom, I have heard, he prov'd an irreproachable husband.

As for poor Will, he was immediately sent down to the country to his father, a well-to-do farmer. He had not been there four months before an innkeeper's buxom young widow, with a very good stock, both in money and trade, fancy'd, and perhaps pre-acquainted with his secret excellencies, marry'd him: and I am sure there was, at least, one good foundation for their living happily together.

Though I should have been charm'd to see him before he went, such measures were taken, by Mr. H...'s orders, that it was impossible; otherwise I should certainly have endeavour'd to detain him in town, and would have spared neither offers nor expense to have procured myself the satisfaction of keeping him with me. He had such a powerful hold upon my inclinations as were not easily to be shaken off, or replaced; as to my heart, it was quite out of the question: glad, however, I was from my soul, that nothing worse, and as things turn'd out, probably nothing better could have happened to him.

As to Mr. H..., though views of conveniency made me, at first, exert myself to regain his affection, I was giddy and thoughtless enough to be much easier reconcil'd to my failure than I ought to have been; but as I never had lov'd him, and his leaving me gave me a sort of liberty that I had often long'd for, I was soon comforted; and flattering myself that the stock of youth and beauty I was going into trade with could hardly fail of procuring me a maintenance, I saw myself under a necessity of trying my fortune with them, rather with pleasure and gaiety, than with the least idea of despondency.

In the meantime, several of my acquaintances among the sisterhood, who had soon got wind of my misfortune, flocked to insult me with their malicious consolations. Most of them had long envied me the affluence and splendour I had been maintain'd in; and though there was scarce one of them that did not at least deserve to be in my case, and would probably, sooner or later, come to it, it was equally easy to notice, even in their affected pity, their secret pleasure at seeing me thus disgrac'd and discarded, and their secret grief that it was no worse with me. Unaccountable malice of the human heart! and which is not confin'd to the class of life they were of.

But as the time approached for me to come to some resolution how to dispose of myself, and I was considering round where to shift my quarters to, *Mrs. Cole*, a middle-aged discreet sort of woman who had been brought into my acquaintance by one of the misses that visited me, upon learning my situation, came to offer her cordial advice and service to me; and as I had always taken to her more than to any of my female acquaintances, I listened the easier to her proposals. And, as it happened, I could not have put myself into worse, or into better hands in all London: into worse, because in keeping a house of ill-repute, there were no lengths in lewdness she would not advise me to go, in compliance with her customers, no schemes of pleasure, or even unbounded debauchery she did not take an evil delight in promoting; into better, because nobody having had more experience of the wicked part of the town than she had, was fitter to advise and guard one against the worst dangers of our profession; and what was rare to be met with in those of hers, she contented herself with a moderate living profit upon her industry and good offices, and had nothing of their greedy rapacious turn. She was really too a gentlewoman born and bred, but through a train of accidents reduc'd to this course, which she pursued, partly through necessity, partly through choice, as never woman delighted more in encouraging a brisk circulation of trade, for the sake of the trade itself, or better understood all the mysteries and refinements of it than she did; so that she was consummately at the top of her profession, and dealt only with customers of distinction: to answer the demands of whom she kept a competent number of her daughters in constant recruit (so she call'd those whom their youth and personal charms recommended to her adoption and management: several of whom by her means, and through her tuition and instructions, succeeded very well in the world).

This useful gentlewoman upon whose protection I now threw myself, having her reasons of state, respecting Mr. H . . . for not appearing too much in the thing herself, sent a friend of hers on the day appointed for my removal to conduct me to my new lodgings at a brushmaker's in *R*** street*, *Covent Garden*, the very next door to her own house, where she had no conveniences to lodge me herself: lodgings that, by having been for several successions tenanted by ladies of pleasure, the landlord of them was familiarized to their ways; and provided the rent was duly paid, everything else was as easy and commodious as one could desire.

The fifty guineas promis'd me by Mr. H . . . at his parting with me having been duly paid me, all my clothes and moveables chested up, which were at least of two hundred pounds value, I had them convey'd into a coach, where I soon followed them, after taking a civil leave of the landlord and his family, with whom I had never liv'd in a degree of familiarity enough to regret the removal; but still, the very circumstance of its being a removal drew tears from me. I left, too, a letter of thanks for Mr. H . . ., from whom I concluded myself, as I really was, irretrievably separated.

My maid I had discharged the day before, not only because I had her of Mr. H . . ., but that I suspected her of having somehow or other been the occasion of his discovering me, in revenge, perhaps, for my not having trusted her with him.

We soon got to my lodging, which, though not so handsomely furnish'd nor so showy as those I left, were in every way as convenient, and at half price, though on the first floor. My trunks were safely landed, and stow'd in my apartments, where my neighbour, and now *gouvernante*, Mrs. Cole, was ready with my landlord to receive me, to whom she took care to set me out in the most favourable light, that of one from whom there was the clearest reason to expect the regular payment of his rent: all the cardinal virtues attributed to me would not have had half the weight of that recommendation alone.

I was now settled in lodgings of my own, abandon'd to

my own conduct, and turned loose upon the town, to sink or swim, as I could manage with the current of it; and what were the consequences, together with the number of adventures which befell me in the exercise of my new profession, will compose the matter of another letter: for surely it is high time to put a period to this.

I am,

MADAM,

Yours, etc., etc., etc.

THE END OF THE FIRST LETTER

LETTER THE SECOND

Madam,

IF I have delay'd the sequel of my history, it has been purely to allow myself a little breathing time not without some hopes that, instead of pressing me to a continuation, you would have acquitted me of the task of pursuing a confession, in the course of which my self-esteem has so many wounds to sustain.

I imagined, indeed, that you would have been cloy'd and tired with uniformity of adventures and expressions, inseparable from a subject of this sort, whose bottom, or groundwork being, in the nature of things, eternally one and the same, whatever variety of forms and modes the situations are susceptible of, there is no escaping a repetition of the same images, the same figures, the same expressions, with this further inconvenience added to the disgust it creates, that the words JOYS, ARDOURS, TRANSPORTS, ECSTASIES, and the rest of those pathetic terms so congenial to, so received in the PRACTICE OF PLEASURE, flatten and lose much of their due spirit and energy by the frequency they indispensably recur with, in a narrative of which that PRACTICE professedly composes the whole basis. I must therefore trust to the candour of your judgement, for you allowing for the disadvantage I am necessarily under in that respect, and to your imagination and sensibility, the pleasing task of repairing it, by their supplements, where my descriptions flag or fail: the one will readily place the pictures I present before your eyes; the other give life to the colours where they are dull, or worn with too frequent handling.

What you say besides, by way of encouragement, concerning the extreme difficulty of continuing so long in one strain, in a mean temper'd with taste, between the revolting-ness of gross, rank, and vulgar expressions and the ridicule of mincing metaphors and affected circumlocutions, is so sensible, as well as good-natur'd, that you greatly justify me to myself for my compliance with a curiosity that is to be satisfied so extremely at my expense.

Resuming now where I broke off in my last, I am in my way to remark to you, that it was late in the evening before I arriv'd at my new lodgings, and Mrs. Cole, after helping me to arrange and secure my things, spent the whole evening with me in my apartment, where we supped together, in giving me the best advice and instruction with regard to this new stage of my profession I was now to enter upon; passing thus from a private devotee to pleasure into a public one, to become a more general good, with all the advantages requisite to put my person out to use, either for interest or pleasure, or both. But then, she observ'd, as I was a kind of new face upon the town, that it was an established rule and part of trade, for me to pass for a maid, and dispose of myself as such on the first good occasion, without prejudice, however, to such diversions as I might have a mind to in the interim; for that nobody could be a greater enemy than she was to the losing of time. That she would, in the meantime, do her best to find out a proper person, and would undertake to manage this nice point for me, if I would accept of her aid and advice to such good purpose, that in the loss of a fictitious maidenhead, I should reap all the advantages of a native one.

Though such a delicacy of sentiments did not really belong to my character at that time, I confess, against myself, that I perhaps too readily closed with a proposal which my candour and ingenuity gave me some repugnance to, but not enough to contradict the intent of one to whom I had now thoroughly abandoned the direction of all my steps. For Mrs. Cole had, I do not know how unless by one of those unaccountable invincible sympathies that, nevertheless, form the strongest links, especially of female friendship, won and got entire possession of me. On her side, she pretended that a strict resemblance, she fancied she saw in me, to an only daughter whom she had lost at my age, was the first motive of her taking to me so affectionately. It might be so: there exist as slender motives of attachment, that, gathering force from habit and liking, have proved often more solid and durable than those founded on much stronger reasons; but this I know, that tho' I had no other acquaintance with her, than seeing her at my lodgings, when I lived with Mr. H..., where she had made errands to sell me some millinery ware, she had by degrees insinuated herself so far into my confidence, that I threw myself blindly into her hands, and came, at length, to regard, love, and obey her implicitly; and, to do her justice, I never experienc'd at her hands other than a sincerity of tenderness, and care for my interest, hardly heard of in those of her profession. We parted that night, after having settled a perfect unreserv'd agreement; and the next morning Mrs. Cole came, and took me with her to her house for the first time. Here, at the first sight of things, I found everything breath'd an air of decency, modesty, and order.

In the outer parlour, or rather shop, sat three young women, very demurely employ'd on millinery work, which was the cover of a traffic in more precious commodities; but three beautifuller creatures could hardly be seen. Two of them were extremely fair, the eldest not above nineteen; and the third, much about that age, was a piquant brunette, whose black sparking eyes and perfect harmony of features and shape left her nothing to envy in her fairer companions. Their dress too had the more design in it, the less it appeared to have, being in a taste of uniform correct neatness, and elegant simplicity. These were the girls that composed the small domestic flock, which my governess train'd up with surprising order and management, considering the giddy wildness of young girls once got upon the loose. But then she never continued any in her house, whom, after a due noviciate, she found untractable, or unwilling to comply with the rules of it. Thus had she insensibly formed a little family of love, in which the members found so sensibly their account, in a rare alliance of pleasure with interest, and of a necessary outward decency, with unbounded secret liberty, that Mrs. Cole, who had pick'd them as much for their temper as their beauty, govern'd them with ease to herself and them too.

To these pupils then of hers, whom she had prepar'd, she presented me as a new boarder, and one that was to be immediately admitted to all the intimacies of the house; upon which these charming girls gave me all the marks of a welcome reception, and indeed of being perfectly pleased with my figure, that I could possibly expect from any of my own sex: but they had been effectually brought to sacrifice all jealousy, or competition of charms, to a common interest, and consider'd me a partner that was bringing no despicable stock of goods into the trade of the house. They gathered round me, view'd me on all sides; and as my admission into this joyous troop made a little holiday, the show of work was laid aside; and Mrs. Cole, giving me up, with special recommendation, to their caresses and entertainment, went about her ordinary business of the house.

The sameness of our sex, age, profession, and views soon created as unreserv'd a freedom and intimacy as if we had been for years acquainted. They took and shew'd me the house, their respective apartments, which were furnished with every article of conveniency and luxury; and above all, a spacious drawing-room, where a select revelling band usually met, in general parties of pleasure; the girls supping with their sparks, and acting their wanton pranks with unbounded licentiousness; whilst a defiance of awe, modesty, or jealousy were their standing rules, by which, according to the principles of their society, whatever pleasure was lost on the side of sentiment, was abundantly made up to the senses in the variety and the charms of ease and luxury. The authors and supporters of this secret institution would, in the height of their humour, style themselves the restorers of the golden age and its simplicity of pleasures, before their innocence became so injustly branded with the names of guilt and shame.

As soon then as the evening began, and the show of a shop was shut, the academy open'd; the mask of mock-modesty was completely taken off, the girls deliver'd over to their respective calls of pleasure or interest with their men: and none of that sex was promiscuously admitted, but only such as Mrs. Cole was previously satisfied with their character and discretion. In short, this was the safest, politest, and, at the same time, the most thorough house of accommodation in town: everything being conducted so, that decency made no entrenchment upon the most libertine pleasures, in the practice of which too, the choice familiars of the house had found the secret so rare and difficult of reconciling even all the refinements of taste and delicacy with the most gross and determinate gratifications of sensuality.

After having consum'd the morning in the endearments and instructions of my new acquaintance, we went to dinner, when Mrs. Cole, presiding at the head of her clique, gave me the first idea of her management and address, in inspiring these girls with so sensible a love and respect for her. There was no stiffness, no reserve, no airs of pique, or little jealousies, but all was unaffectedly gay, cheerful, and easy.

After dinner, Mrs. Cole, seconded by the young ladies, acquainted me that there was a chapter to be held that night in form, for the ceremony of my reception into the sisterhood; and in which, with all due reserve to my maidenhead, that was to be occasionally cook'd up for the first proper chapman, I was to undergo a ceremonial of initiation they were sure I should not be displeased with.

Embark'd as I was, and moreover captivated with the charms of my new companions, I was too much prejudic'd in favour of any proposal they could make, to so much as hesitate an assent; which, therefore, readily giving in the style of a *carte blanche*, I receiv'd fresh kisses of compliment from them all, in approval of my docility and good nature. Now I was "a sweet girl . . ." I came into things with a "good grace . . ." I was not "affectedly coy . . ." I should be "the pride of the house . . ." and the like.

This point thus adjusted, the young women left Mrs. Cole to talk and arrange matters with me: she explained to me that I should be introduc'd, that very evening, to four of her best friends, one of whom, she had, according to the custom of the house, favoured with the preference of engaging me in the first party of pleasure; assuring me, at the same time, that they were all young gentlemen agreeable in their persons, and unexceptionable in every respect; that united, and holding together by the hand of common pleasures, they composed the chief support of her house, and made very liberal presents to the girls that pleas'd and humour'd them, so that they were, properly speaking, the founders and patrons of this little seraglio. Not but that she had, at proper seasons, other customers to deal with, whom she stood less upon punctilio with, than with these; for instance, it was not on one of them she could attempt to pass me for a maid; they were not only too knowing, too much town-bred to bite at such a bait, but they were such generous benefactors to her that it would be unpardonable to think of it.

Amidst all the flutter and emotion which this promise of pleasure, for such I conceiv'd it, stirr'd up in me, I preserved so much of the woman as to feign just reluctance enough to make some merit of sacrificing it to the influence of my patroness, to whom I likewise, still in character, reminded that perhaps it would be better for me to go home and dress, in favour of my first impressions.

But Mrs. Cole, in opposition to this, assured me that the gentlemen I should be presented to were, by their rank and taste of things, infinitely superior to the being touched with any glare or dress or ornaments, such as silly women rather confound and overlay than set off their beauty with; that these veteran voluptuaries knew better than not to hold them in the highest contempt: they with whom the pure native charms alone could pass current, and who would at any time leave a sallow, washy, painted duchess on her own hands for a ruddy, healthy, firm-flesh'd country maid; and as for my part, that nature had done enough for me, to set me above owing the last favour to art; concluding withal, that for the instant occasion, there was no dress like an undress.

I thought my governess too good a judge of these matters not to be easily over-ruled by her: after which she went on preaching very pathetically the doctrine of passive obedience and non-resistance to all those arbitrary tastes of pleasure, which are by some styl'd the refinements, and by others the depravations of it; between whom it was not the business of a simple girl, who was to profit by pleasing, to decide, but to conform to. Whilst I was edifying by these wholesome lessons, tea was brought in, and the young ladies, returning, joined company with us.

After a great deal of mix'd chat, frolic, and humour, one of them, observing that there would be a good deal of time on hand before the assembly-hour, proposed that each girl should entertain the company with that critical period of her personal history in which she first exchanged the maiden state for womanhood. The proposal was approv'd, with only one restriction of Mrs. Cole, that she, on account of her age, and I, on account of my titular maidenhead, should be excused, at least till I had undergone the formalities of the house. This obtain'd me a dispensation, and the promotress of this amusement was desired to begin.

Her name was *Emily*; a girl fair to excess, and whose limbs were, if possible, too well made, since their plump fulness was rather to the prejudice of that delicate slimness requir'd by the nicer judges of beauty; her eyes were blue, and streamed inexpressible sweetness, and nothing could be prettier than her mouth and lips, which clos'd over a range of the evenest and whitest teeth. Thus she began:

"Neither my extraction, nor the most critical adventure of my life, is sublime enough to impeach me of any vanity in the advancement of the proposal you have approv'd of. My father and mother were, and for aught I knew, are still, farmers in the country, not above forty miles from town: their barbarity to me, in favour of a son, on whom only they vouchsafed to bestow their tenderness, had a thousand times determined me to fly their house, and throw myself on the wide world; but, at length, an accident forc'd me on this desperate attempt at the age of fifteen. I had broken a china-bowl, the pride and idol of both their hearts; and as an unmerciful beating was the least I had to depend on at their hands, in the silliness of those tender years, I left the house, and, at all adventures, took the road to London. How my loss was resented I do not know, for till this instant I have not heard a syllable about them. My whole stock was two broad pieces of my godmother's, a few shillings, silver shoe-buckles, and a silver thimble. Thus equipp'd, with no more clothes than the ordinary ones I had on my back, and frighten'd at every foot or noise heard behind me, I hurried on; and, I dare swear, walked a dozen miles before I stopped, through mere weariness and fatigue. At length I sat down on a stile, wept bitterly, and yet was still rather under increased impressions of fear on the account of my escape; which made me dread, worse than death, the going back to face my unnatural parents. Refresh'd by this little repose, and relieved by my tears, I was proceeding onward, when I was overtaken by a sturdy country lad, who was going to London to see what he could do for himself there, and, like me, had given his friends the slip. He could not be above seventeen, was ruddy, well featur'd enough, with uncomb'd flaxen hair, a little flapp'd hat, yarn stockings, in short, a perfect plough-boy. I saw him come whistling behind me, with a bundle tied to the end of a stick, his travelling equipage. We walk'd by one another for some time without speaking; at length we join'd company, and agreed to keep together till we got to our journey's end. What his designs or ideas were, I knew not: the innocence of mine I can solemnly protest.

"As night drew on, it became us to look out for some inn or shelter; to which perplexity another was added, and that was, what we should say for ourselves, if we were question'd. After some delay, the young fellow offered a proposal, which I thought the finest that could be; and what was that? why, that we should pass for husband and wife: I never once dream'd of the consequences. We came presently, after having agreed on this notable expedient, to one of those hedge-accommodations for foot passengers, at the door of which stood an old crazy beldam, who seeing us trudge by, invited us to lodge there. Glad of any cover, we went in, and my fellow traveller, taking all upon him, call'd for what the house afforded, and we supped together as man and wife; which, considering our figures and ages, could not have past on anyone but such as anything could passion. But when bedtime came on, we had neither of us the courage to contradict our first account of ourselves; and what was extremely pleasant, the young lad seem'd as perplex'd as I was, how to evade lying together, which was so natural for the state we had pretended to. Whilst we were in this quandary, the landlady takes the candle, and lights us to our apartment, through a long yard, at the end of which it stood, separate from the body of the house. Thus we suffer'd ourselves to be conducted, without saying a word in opposition to it; and there, in a wretched room, with a bed answerable, we were left to pass the night together, as a thing quite of course. For my part, I was so incredibly innocent, as not even then to think much more harm of going into bed with the young man, than with one of our dairy-wenches; nor had he, perhaps, any other notions than those of innocence, till such a fair occasion put them into his head.

"Before either of us undressed, however, he put out the candle; and the bitterness of the weather made it a kind of necessity for me to go into bed: slipping then my clothes off, I crept under the bedclothes, where I found the young stripling already nestled, and the touch of his warm flesh rather pleas'd than alarm'd me. I was indeed too much disturbed with the novelty of my condition to be able to sleep; but then I had not the least thought of harm. But, oh! how powerful are the instincts of nature! how little is there wanting to set them in action! The young man, sliding his arm under my body, drew me gently towards him, as if to keep himself and me warmer; and the heat I felt from joining our breasts kindled another that I had hitherto never felt and was, even then, a stranger to the nature of. Emboldened, I suppose, by my passiveness, he ventur'd to kiss me, and I insensibly returned it, without knowing the consequence of returning it: for, on this encouragement, he slipped his hand all down from my breast to that part of me where the sense of feeling is so exquisitely critical, as I then experienc'd by its instantly taking fire upon the touch and glowing with a strange tickling heat: there he pleas'd himself and me, by feeling, till, growing a little too bold, he hurt me, and made me complain. Then he took my hand, which he guided, not unwillingly on my part, between the twist of his closed thighs, which were extremely warm; there he lodged and pressed it, till raising it by degrees, he made me feel the proud distinction of his sex from mine. I was frighten'd at the novelty, and drew back my hand; yet, pressed and spurred on by sensations of a strange pleasure, I could not help asking him what that was for? He told me he would show me if I would let him; and, without waiting for my answer, which he prevented by stopping my mouth with kisses I was far from disrelishing, he got upon me, and inserting one of his thighs between mine, opened them so as to make way for himself, and fixed me to his purpose; whilst I was so much out of my usual sense, so subdu'd by the present power of a new one, that, between fear and desire, I lay utterly passive, till the piercing pain rous'd and made me cry out. But it was too late: he was too firm fix'd in the saddle for me to compass flinging him, with all the struggles I could use, some of which only served to further his point, and at length an irresistible thrust murdered at once my maidenhead, and almost me. I now lay a bleeding witness of the necessity impos'd on our sex, to gather the first honey off the thorns.

"But the pleasure rising as the pain subsided, I was soon reconciled to fresh trials, and before morning, nothing on earth could be dearer to me than this rifler of my virgin sweets: he was everything to me now. How we agreed to join fortunes; how we came up to town together, where we lived some time, till necessity parted us, and drove me into this course of life, in which I had been long ago battered and torn to pieces before I came to this age, as much through my easiness as through my inclination, had it not been for my finding refuge in this house: these are all circumstances which pass the mark I proposed, so that here my narrative ends."

In the order of our sitting, it was *Harriet's* turn to go on. Amongst all the beauties of our sex that I had before or have since seen, few indeed were the forms that could dispute excellence with hers; it was not delicate, but delicacy itself incarnate, such was the symmetry of her small but exactly fashion'd limbs. Her complexion, fair as it was, appeared yet more fair from the effect of two black eyes, the brilliancy of which gave her face more vivacity than belonged to the colour of it, which was only defended from paleness by a sweetly pleasing blush in her cheeks that grew fainter and fainter, till at length it died away insensibly into the overbearing white. Then her minature features join'd to finish the extreme sweetness of it, which was not belied by that of a temper turned to indolence, languor, and the pleasures of love. Press'd to subscribe her contingent, she smiled, blushed a little, and thus complied with our desires:

"My father was neither better nor worse than a miller near the city of *York*; and both he and my mother dying whilst I was an infant, I fell under the care of a widow and childless aunt, housekeeper to my lord N. . ., at his seat in the county of . . ., where she brought me up with all imaginable tenderness. I was not seventeen, as I am not now eighteen, before I had, on account of my person purely (for fortune I had notoriously none), several advantageous proposals; but whether nature was slow in making me sensible in her favourite passion, or that I had not seen any of the other sex who had stirr'd up the least emotion or curiosity to be better acquainted with it, I had, till that age, preserv'd a perfect innocence, even of thought: whilst my fears of I did not well know what, made me no more desirous of marrying than of dying. My aunt, good woman, favoured my timorousness, which she look'd on as childish affection, that her own experience might probably assure her would wear off in time, and gave my suitors proper answers for me.

"The family had not been down at that seat for years, so that it was neglected, and committed entirely to my aunt, and two old domestics to take care of it. Thus I had the full range of a spacious lonely house and gardens, situate at about half a mile distance from any other habitation, except, perhaps, a straggling cottage or so.

"Here, in tranquility and innocence, I grew up without any memorable accident, till one fatal day I had, as I had often done before, left my aunt fast asleep, and secure for some hours, after dinner; and resorting to a kind of ancient summer-house, at some distance from the house, I carried my work with me, and sat over a rivulet, which its door and window fac'd upon. Here I fell into a gentle breathing slumber, which stole upon my senses, as they fainted under the excessive heat of the season at that hour; a cane couch, with my work-basket for a pillow, were all the conveniencies of my short repose; for I was soon awake and alarmed by flounce and noise of splashing in the water. I got up to see what was the matter; and what indeed should it be but the son of a neighbouring gentleman, as I afterwards found (for I had never seen him before), who had strayed that way with his gun, and heated by his sport, and the sultriness of the day, had been tempted by the freshness of the clear stream; so that presently stripping, he jump'd into it on the other side, which bordered on a wood, some trees whereof, inclining down to the water, form'd a pleasing shady recess, commodious to undress and leave his clothes under.

"My first emotions at the sight of this youth, naked in the water, were, with all imaginable respect to truth, those of surprise and fear; and, I should immediately have run out, had not my modesty, fatally for itself, interposed the objection of the door and window being so situated that it was scarce possible to get out, and make my way along the bank to the house, without his seeing me: which I could not bear the thought of, so much ashamed and confounded was I at having seen him. Condemn'd then to stay till his departure should release me, I was greatly embarrassed how to dispose of myself: I kept some time between terror and modesty, even from looking through the window, which, being an old-fashion'd casement, without any light behind me, could hardly betray anyone's being there to him from within; then the door was so secure, that without violence, or my own consent, there was no opening it from without.

"But now, by my own experience, I found it too true, that objects which affright us, when we cannot get from them, draw our eyes as forcibly as those that please us. I could not long withstand that nameless impulse, which, without any desire of this novel sight, compelled me towards it; embolden'd too by my certainty of being at once unseen and safe, I ventur'd by degrees to cast my eyes on an object so terrible and alarming to my virgin modesty as a naked man. But as I snatched a look, the first gleam that struck me was in general the dewy lustre of the whitest skin imaginable, which the sun playing upon made the reflection of it perfectly beamy. His face, in the confusion I was in, I could not well distinguish the lineaments of, any further than that there was a great deal of youth and freshness in it. The frolic and various play of all his fine polish'd limbs, as they appeared above the surface, in the course of his swimming or wantoning with the water, amus'd and insensibly delighted me: sometimes he lay motionless, on his back, waterborne, and dragging after him a fine head of hair, that, floating, swept the stream in a bush of black curls. Then the overflowing water would make a separation between his breast and glossy white belly; at the bottom of which I could not escape observing so remarkable a distinction, as a black mossy tuft, out of which appeared to emerge a round, softish, limber, white something, that played every way, with ever the least motion or whirling eddy. I cannot say but that part chiefly, by a kind of natural instinct, attracted, detain'd, captived my attention: it was out of the power of all my modesty to command my eye away from it; and seeing nothing so very dreadful in its appearance, I insensibly lock'd away all my fears: but as fast as they gave way, new desires and strange wishes took place, and I melted as I gazed. The fire of nature, that had so long lain dormant or conceal'd, began to break out, and make me feel my sex the first time. He had changed his posture, and swam prone on his belly, striking out with his legs and arms, finer modell'd than which could not have been cast, whilst his floating locks played over a neck and shoulders whose whiteness they delightfully set off. Then the luxuriant swell of flesh that rose from the small of his back, and terminates its double globe at where the thighs are set off, perfectly dazzled one with its watery glistening gloss.

"By this time I was so affected by this inward involution of sentiments, so soften'd by this sight, that now, betrayed into a sudden transition from extreme fears to extreme desires, I found these last so strong upon me, the heat of the weather too perhaps conspiring to exalt their rage, that nature almost fainted under them. Not that I so much as knew precisely what was wanting to me: my only thought was that so sweet a creature, as this youth seemed to me, could only make me happy; but then, the little likelihood there was of compassing an acquaintance with him, or perhaps of ever seeing him again, dash'd my desires, and turn'd them into torments. I was still gazing, with all the powers of my sight, on this bewitching object, when, in an instant, down he went. I had heard of such things as a cramp seizing on even the best swimmers, and occasioning their being drowned; and imagining this so sudden eclipse to be owing to it, the inconceivable fondness this lad had given birth to, distracted me with the most killing terrors; insomuch, that my concern giving me wings, I flew to the door, open'd it, ran down to the canal, guided thither by the madness of my fears for him, and the intense desire of being an instrument to save him, though I was ignorant how, or by what means to effect it, but was it for fears, and a passion so sudden as mine, to reason! All this took up scarce the space of a few moments. I had then just life enough to reach the green borders of the waterpiece, where wildly looking round for the young man, and missing him still, my fright and concern sunk me down in a deep swoon, which must have lasted me some time; for I did not come to myself, till I was rous'd out of it by a sense of pain that pierced me to the vitals, and awaked me to the most surprising circumstance of finding myself not only in the arms of the very same young gentleman I had been so solicitous to save, but taken at such an advantage in my unresisting condition, that he had actually completed his entrance into me so far, that weakened as I was by preceding conflicts of mind I had suffer'd, and struck dumb by the violence of my surprise, I had neither the power to cry out, nor the strength to disengage myself from his strenuous embraces before, urging his point, he had forced his way and completely triumphed over my virginity, as he might now as well see by the streams of blood that follow'd his drawing out, as he had felt by the difficulties he had met with consummating his penetration. But the sight of the blood, and the sense of my condition, had (as he told me afterwards), since the ungovernable rage of his passion was somewhat appeas'd, now wrought so far on him, that at all risks, even of the worst consequences, he could not find in his heart to leave me, and make off, which he might easily have done. I still lay all discompos'd in bleeding ruin, palpitating, speechless, unable to get off, frightened, and fluttering like a poor wounded partridge, and ready to faint away again at the sense of what had befallen me. The young gentleman was by me, kneeling, kissing my hand, and with tears in his eyes, beseeching me to forgive him, and offering all the reparation in his power. It is certain that could I, at the instant of regaining my senses, have called out, or taken the bloodiest revenge, I would not have struck at it: the violation was attended too with such aggravating circumstances, though he was ignorant of them, since it was to my concern for the preservation of his life that I owed my ruin.

"But how quick is the shift of passions from one extreme to another! and how little are they acquainted with the human heart who dispute it! I could not see this amiable criminal, so suddenly the first object of my love, and as suddenly of my just hate, on his knees, bedewing my hand with his tears, without relenting. He was still stark naked, but my modesty had been already too much wounded, in essentials, to be so much shocked as I should have otherwise been with appearances only; in short, my anger ebbed so fast, and the tide of love return'd so strong upon me, that I felt it a point of my own happiness to forgive him. The reproaches I made him were murmur'd in so soft a tone, my eyes met his with such glances, expressing more languor than resentment, that he could not but presume his forgiveness was at no desperate distance; but still he would not quit his posture of submission till I had pronounced his pardon in form; which, after the most fervent entreaties, protestations, and promises, I had not the power to with-hold. On which, with the utmost marks of a fear of again offending, he ventured to kiss my lips, which I neither declined or resented: but on my mild expostulations with him upon the barbarity of his treatment, he explain'd the mystery of my ruin, if not entirely to the clearance, at least much to the alleviation of his guilt, in the eyes of a judge so partial in his favour as I was grown.

"It seems that the circumstance of his going down, or sinking, which in my extreme ignorance I had mistaken for something very fatal, was no other than a trick of diving, which I had not ever heard, or at least attended to, the mention of: and he was so long-breath'd at it, that in the few moments in which I ran out to save him, he had not yet emerged, before I fell into the swoon, in which, as he rose, seeing me extended on the bank, his first idea was that some young woman was upon some design of frolic or diversion with him, for he knew I could not have fallen asleep there without his having seen me before: agreeably to which notion he had ventured to approach, and finding me with-out sign of life, and still perplex'd as he was what to think of the adventure, he took me in his arms at all hazards, and carried me into the summer-house, of which he observed the door open; there he laid me down on the couch, and tried, as he protested in good faith, by several means to bring me to myself again, till fired, as he said, beyond all bearing by the sight and touch of several parts of me, which were unguardedly exposed to him, he could no longer govern his passion; and the less, as he was not quite sure that his first idea of this swoon being a feint, was not the very truth of the case: seduced then by this flattering notion, and over-come by the present, as he styled them, superhuman temptations, combined with the solitude and seeming security of the attempt, he was not enough his own master not to make it. Leaving me then just only whilst he fastened the door, he returned with redoubled eagerness to his prey: when, finding me still entranced, he ventured to place me as he pleased, whilst I felt, no more than the dead, what he was about, till the pain he put me to roused me just in time enough to be witness of a triumph I was not able to defeat, and now scarce regretted: for as he talked, the tone of his voice sounded, methought, so sweetly in my ears, the sensible nearness of so new and interesting an object to me wrought so powerfully upon me, that, in the rising perception of things in a new and pleasing light, I lost all sense of the past injury. The young gentleman soon discern'd the symptoms of a reconciliation in my softened looks, and hastening to receive the seal of it from my lips, press'd them tenderly to pass his pardon in the return of a kiss so melting fiery, that the impression of it being carried to my heart, and thence to my new-discover'd sphere of Venus, I was melted into a softness that could refuse him nothing. When now he managed his caresses and endearments so artfully, as to insinuate the most soothing consolations for the past pain and the most pleasing expectations of future pleasure, but whilst mere modesty kept my eyes from seeing his and rather declined them, I had a glimpse of that instrument of the mischief which was now, obviously even to me, who had scarce had snatches of a comparative observation of it, resuming its capacity to renew it, and grew greatly alarming with its increase of size, as he bore it no doubt designedly, hard and stiff against one of my hands carelessly dropt; but then he employ'd such tender prefacing, such winning progressions, that my returning passion of desire being now so strongly prompted by the engaging circumstances of the sight and incendiary touch of his naked glowing beauties, I yielded at length at the force of the present impressions, and he obtained of my tacit blushing consent all the gratifications of pleasure left in the power of my poor person to bestow, after he had cropt its richest flower, during my suspension of life, and abilities to guard it.

"Here, according to the rule laid down, I should stop; but I am so much in mention, that I could not if I would. I shall only add, however, that I got home without the least discovery, or suspicion of what had happened. I met my young ravisher several times after, whom I now passionately lov'd and who, tho' not of age to claim a small but independent fortune, would have married me; but as the accidents that prevented it, and their consequences, which threw me on the public, contain matters too moving and serious to introduce at present, I cut short here."

Louisa, the brunette whom I mentioned at first, now took her turn to treat the company with her history. I have already hinted to you the graces of her person, than which nothing could be more exquisitely touching; I repeat touching, as a just distinction from striking, which is ever a lasting effect, and more generally belongs to the fair complexions; but leaving that decision to everyone's taste, I proceed to give you Louisa's narrative as follows:

"According to practical maxims of life, I ought to boast of my birth, since I owe it to pure love, without marriage; but this I know, it was scarce possible to inherit a stronger propensity to that cause of my being than I did. I was the rare production of the first essay of a journeyman cabinet-maker on his master's maid: the consequence of which was a big belly, and the loss of a place. He was not in circumstances to do much for her; and yet, after all this blemish, she found means, after she had dropt her burthen, and disposed of me to a poor relation's in the country, to repair it by marrying a pastry-cook here in London, in thriving business; on whom she soon, under favour of the complete ascendant he had given her over him, passed me for a child she had by her first husband. I had, on that footing, been taken home, and was not six years old when this father-in-law died, and left my mother in tolerable circumstances, and without any children by him. As to my natural father, he had betaken himself to the sea; where, when the truth of things came out, I was told that he died, not immensely rich you may think, since he was no more than a common sailor. As I grew up, under the eyes of my mother, who kept on the business, I could not but see, in her severe watchfulness, the marks of a slip, which she did not care should be hereditary; but we no more choose our passions than our features or complexion, and the bent of mine was so strong to the forbidden pleasure that it got the better, at length, of all her care and precaution. I was scarce twelve years old before that part which she wanted so much to keep out of

harm's way made me feel its impatience to be taken notice
of and come into play: already had it put forth the signs of
forwardness in the sprout of a soft down over it, which had
often flatter'd, and I might also say, grown under my constant touch and visitation, so pleas'd was I with what
I took to be a kind of title to womanhood, that state I
pin'd to be entr'd of, for the pleasures I conceiv'd were
annexed to it; and now the growing importance of that
part to me, and the new sensations in it, demolish'd at
once all my girlish play-things and amusements. Nature
now pointed me strongly to more solid diversions, while all
the stings of desire settled so fiercely in that little centre of
them, that I could not mistake the spot I wanted a play-
fellow in.

"I now shunn'd all company in which there was no
hopes of coming at the object of my longings, and used to
shut myself up, to indulge in solitude some tender meditation on the pleasures I strongly perceiv'd the overture of, in
feeling and examining what nature assur'd me must be the
chosen avenue, the gates for unknown bliss to enter at, that
I panted after.

"But these meditations only increas'd my disorder, and
blew the fire that consumed me. I was yet worse when,
yielding at length to the insupportable irritations of the
little fairy charm that tormented me, I seiz'd it with my
fingers, teasing it to no end. Sometimes, in the furious
excitations of desire, I threw myself on the bed, spread my
thights apart, and lay as it were expecting the longed-for
relief, till finding my illusion, I shut and squeez'd them together again, burning and fretting. In short, this devilish
thing, with its impetuous girds and itching fires, led me such
a life, that I could neither, night or day, be at peace with it
or myself. In time, however, I thought I had gained a
prodigious prize, when figuring to myself that my fingers
were something of the shape of what I pined for, I worked
my way in for one of them with great agitation and delight;
yet not without pain too did I deflower myself as far as
it could reach; proceeding with such a fury of passion, in
this solitary and last shift of pleasure, as extended me at

length breathless on the bed in an amorous melting trance.

"But frequency of use dulling the sensation, I soon began to perceive that this work was but a paltry shallow expedient that went but a little way to relieve me, and rather rais'd more flame than its dry and insignificant titillation could rightly appease.

"Man alone, I almost instinctively knew, as well as by what I had industriously picked up at weddings and christenings, was possess'd of the only remedy that could reduce this rebellious disorder; but watch'd and overlook'd as I was, how to come at it was the point, and that, to all appearance, an invincible one; not that I did not rack my brains and invention how at once to elude my mother's vigilance, and procure myself the satisfaction of my impetuous curiosity and longings for this mighty and untasted pleasure. At length, however, a singular chance did at once the work of a long course of alertness. One day that we had dined at an acquaintance's over the way, together with a gentlewoman-lodger that occupied the first floor of the house, there started an indispensable necessity for my mother's going down to *Greenwich* to accompany her: the party was settled, when I do not know what genius whispered me to plead a headache, which I certainly had not, against my being included in a jaunt that I had not the least relish for. The pretext however passed, and my mother, with much reluctance, prevailed with herself to go without me; but took particular care to see me safe home, where she consign'd me into the hands of an old trusty maidservant, who served in the shop, for we had not a male creature in the house.

"As soon as she was gone, I told the maid I would go up and lie down on our lodger's bed, mine not being made, with a charge to her at the same time not to disturb me, as it was only rest I wanted. This injunction probably prov'd of eminent service to me. As soon as I was got into the bedchamber, I unlaced my stays, and threw myself on the outside of the bedclothes, in all the loosest undress. Here I gave myself up to the old insipid privy shifts of my self-viewing, self-touching, self-enjoying, *in fine*, to all the means of *self-knowledge* I could devise, in search of the pleasure that fled before me, and tantalized with that unknown something that was out of my reach; this all only serv'd to enflame myself, and to provoke violently my desires, whilst the one thing needful to their satisfaction was not at hand, and I could have but my fingers, for representing it so ill. After then wearying and fatiguing myself with grasping shadows, whilst that most sensible part of me disdain'd to content itself with less than realities, the strong yearnings, the urgent struggles of nature towards the melting relief, and the extreme self-agitations I had used to come at it, had wearied and thrown me into a kind of unquiet sleep: for, if I tossed and threw about my limbs in proportion to the distraction of my dreams, as I had reason to believe I did, a bystander could not have help'd seeing all for love. And one there was it seems; for waking out of my very short slumber, I found my hand lock'd in that of a young man, who was kneeling at my bedside, and begging my pardon for his boldness: but that being a son to the lady to whom this bed-chamber, he knew, belonged, he had slipp'd by the servant of the shop, as he supposed, unperceiv'd, when finding me asleep, his first ideas were to withdraw; but that he had been fix'd and detain'd there by a power he could better account for than resist.

"What shall I say? my emotions of fear and surprise were instantly subdued by those of the pleasure I bespoke in great presence of mind from the turn this adventure might take; he seem'd to me no other than a pitying angel, dropt out of the clouds: for he was young and perfectly handsome, which was more than even I had asked for; *man*, in general, being all that my utmost desires had pointed at. I thought then I could not put too much encouragement into my eyes and voice; I regretted no leading advances; no matter for his after opinion of my forwardness, so it might bring him to the point of answering my pressing demands of present case; it was not now with his thoughts, but his actions, that my business immediately lay. I rais'd then my head, and told him, in a soft tone, that tended to prescribe the same key to him, that his mamma was gone out and would not return till late at night: which I thought no bad hint; but as it prov'd, I had nothing of a novice to deal with. The impressions I had made on him from the discoveries I had betrayed of my person in the disordered motions of it, during his view of me asleep, had, as he afterwards told me, so fix'd and charmingly prepar'd him that, had I known his dispositions, I had more to hope from his violence than to fear from his respect; and even less than the extreme tenderness which I threw into my voice and eyes would have served to encourage him to make the most of the opportunity. Finding then that his kisses, imprinted on my hand, were taken as tamely as he could wish, he rose to my lips; and glewing his to them, made me so faint with overcoming joy and pleasure, that I fell back, and he with me, in course, on the bed, upon which I had, by insensibly shifting from the side to near the middle, invitingly made room for him. He is now lain down by me, and the minutes being too precious to consume in untimely ceremony, or dalliance, my youth proceeds immediately to those extremities, which all my looks, flushing, and palpitations, had assured him he might attempt without the fear of repulse: those rogues the men read us admirably on these occasions. I lay then at length panting for the imminent attack, with wishes far beyond my fears, and for which it was scarce possible for a girl, barely thirteen, but all and well grown, to have better dispositions. He threw up my petticoat and shift, whilst my thighs were, by an instinct of nature, unfolded to their best; and my desires had so thoroughly destroy'd all modesty in me that even their being now naked and all laid open to him was part of the prelude that pleasure deepn'd my blushes at, more than shame. But when his hand, and touches, naturally attracted to their centre, made me feel all their wantonness and warmth in and round it, oh! how immensely different a sense of things did I perceive there, than when under my own insipid handling! And now his waistcoat was unbuttoned, and the confinement of the breeches burst through, when out started to view the amazing, pleasing object of all my wishes, all my dreams, all my love, the king member indeed! I gaz'd at, I devoured it, at length and breadth, with my eyes intently directed to it, till his getting upon me, and placing it between my thighs, took from me the enjoyment of its sight, to give me a far more grateful one, in its touch, in that part where its touch is so exquisitely affecting. Applying it then to the minute opening, for such at that age it certainly was, I met with too much good will, I felt with too great a rapture of pleasure the first insertion of it, to heed much the pain that followed: I thought nothing too dear to pay for this the richest treat of the senses; so that, split up, torn, bleeding, mangled, I was still superiorly pleas'd, and hugg'd the dear author of all this delicious ruin. But when, soon after, he made his second attack, sore as everything was, the smart was soon put away by the sovereign cordial; all my soft complainings were silenc'd, and the pain melting fast away into pleasure. I abandon'd myself over to all its transports, and gave it the full possession of my whole body and soul; for now all thought was at an end with me; I lived but in what I felt only. And who could describe those feelings, those agitations, yet exalted by the charm of their novelty and surprise? when that part of me which had so long hunger'd for the dear morsel that now so delightfully crammed it forc'd all my vital sensations to fix their home there, during the stay of my beloved guest; who too soon paid me for his hearty welcome, in a dissolvent, richer far than that I have heard of some queen treating her paramour with, in liquify'd pearl, and ravishingly pour'd into me, where, now myself too much melted to give it a dry reception, I hail'd it with the warmest confluence on my side, amidst all those ecstatic raptures, not unfamiliar I presume to this good company! Thus, however, I arrived at the very top of all my wishes, by an accident unexpected indeed, but not so wonderful; for this young gentleman was just arriv'd in town from college, and came familiarly to his mother at her apartment, where he had once before been, though, by mere chance. I had not seen him: so that we knew one another by hearsay only; and finding me stretched on his mother's bed, he readily concluded, from her description, who it was. The rest you know.

"This affair had however no ruinous consequences, the

young gentleman escaping then, and many more times indiscover'd. But the warmth of my constitution, that made the pleasures of love a kind of necessary of life to me, having betray'd me into indiscretions fatal to my private fortune, I fell at length to the public; from which, it is probable, I might have met with the worst of ruin, if my better fate had not thrown me into this safe and agreeable refuge."

Here Louisa ended; and these little histories having brought the time for the girls to retire, and to prepare for the revels of the evening, I stay'd with Mrs. Cole, till Emily came, and told us the company was met, and waited for us.

Mrs. Cole on this, taking me by the hand, with a smile of encouragement, led me upstairs, preceded by Louisa, who was come to hasten us, and lighted us with two candles, one in each hand.

On the landing-place of the first pair of stairs, we were met by a young gentleman, extremely well dress'd, and a very pretty figure, to whom I was to be indebted for the first essay of the pleasures of the house. He saluted me with great gallantry, and handed me into the drawing-room, the floor of which was overspread with a Turkish carpet, and all its furniture voluptuously adapted to every demand of the most study'd luxury; now too it was, by means of a profuse illumination, enliven'd by a light scarce inferior, and perhaps more favourable to joy, more tenderly pleasing, than that of broad sunshine.

On my entrance into the room, I had the satisfaction to hear a buzz of approbation run through the whole company, which now consisted of four gentlemen, including my particular (this was the cant-term of the house for one's gallant for the time), the three young women, in a neat flowing deshabillé, the mistress of the academy and myself. I was welcomed and saluted by a kiss all round, in which, however, it was easy to discover, in the superior warmth of that of the men, the distinction of the sexes.

Aw'd and confounded as I was at seeing myself surrounded, caress'd, and made court to by so many strangers, I could not immediately familiarize myself to all that air of gaiety and joy which dictated their compliments, and animated their caresses.

They assur'd me that I was so perfectly to their taste, as to have but one fault against me, which I might easily be cur'd of, and that was my modesty: this, they observ'd, might pass for a beauty the more with those who wanted it for a heightener; but their maxim was that it was an impertinent mixture, and dash'd the cup so as to spoil the sincere draught of pleasure; they consider'd it accordingly as their mortal enemy, and gave it no quarter wherever they met with it. This was a prologue not unworthy of the revels that ensu'd.

In the midst of all the frolic and wantonnesses, which this joyous band had presently, and all naturally, run into, an elegant supper was serv'd in, and we sat down to it, my spark elect placing himself next to me, and the other couples without order or ceremony. The delicate cheer and good wine soon banish'd all reserve; the conversation grew as lively as could be wished, without taking too loose a turn: these professors of pleasure knew too well, to stale impressions of it, or evaporate the imagination in words, before the time of action. Kisses however were snatch'd at times, or where a handkerchief round the neck interpos'd its feeble barrier, it was not extremely respected: the hands of the men went to work with their usual petulance, till the provocations on both sides rose to such a pitch, that my particular's proposal for beginning the country-dances was received with instant assent: for, as he laughingly added, he fancied the instruments were in tune. This was a signal for preparation that the complaisant Mrs. Cole, who understood life, took for her cue of disappearing; no longer so fit for personal service herself, and content with having settled the order of battle, she left us the field, to fight it out at discretion.

As soon as she was gone, the table was remov'd from the middle, and became a side-board; a couch was brought into its place, of which when I whisperingly inquired the reason of my particular, he told me that as it was chiefly on my account that this convention was met, the parties inten-

137

ded at once to humour their taste of variety in pleasures, and by an open public enjoyment, to see me broke of any taint of reserve or modesty, which they look'd on as the poison of joy; that though they occasionally preached pleasure, and lived up to the text, they did not enthusiastically set up for missionaries, and only indulg'd themselves in the delights of a practical instruction of all the pretty women they lik'd well enough to bestow it upon, and who fell properly in the way of it; but that as such a proposal might be too violent, too shocking for a young beginner, the old standers were to set an example, which he hoped I would not be averse to follow, since it was to him I was devolv'd in favour of the first experiment; but that still I was perfectly at my liberty to refuse the party, which being in its nature one of pleasure, suppos'd an exclusion of all force or constraint.

My countenance expressed, no doubt, my surprise as my silence did my acquiescence. I was now embarked, and thoroughly determined on any voyage the company would take me on.

The first that stood up, to open the ball, were a cornet of horse, and that sweetest of olive-beauties, the soft and amorous Louisa. He led her to the couch "nothing loath", on which he gave her the fall, and extended her at her length with an air of roughness and vigour, relishing high of amorous eagerness and impatience. The girl, spreading herself to the best advantage, with her head upon the pillow, was so concentered in what she was about, that our presence seemed the least of her care and concern. Her petticoats, thrown up with her shift, discovered to the company the finest turn'd legs and thighs that could be imagined, and in broad display, that gave us a full view of that delicious cleft of flesh, into which the pleasing hairgrown mount over it, parted and presented a most inviting entrance, between two closehedges, delicately soft and pouting. Her gallant was now ready, having disencumber'd himself from his clothes, overloaded with lace, and presently, his shirt removed, shew'd us his forces in high plight, bandied and ready for action. But giving us no time to consider the dimensions, he threw himself instantly over his charming antagonist who receiv'd him as he pushed at once dead at mark, like a heroine, without flinching; for surely never was girl constitutionally truer to the taste of joy, or sincerer in the expressions of its sensations, than she was: we could observe pleasure lighten in her eyes, as he introduc'd his plenipotentiary instrument into her; till, at length, having indulg'd her to its utmost reach, its irritations grew so violent, and gave her the spurs so furiously, that collected within herself, and lost to everything but the enjoyment of her favourite feelings, she returned his thrusts with a just concert of springy heaves, keeping time so exactly with the most pathetic sighs, that one might have number'd the strokes in agitation by their distinct murmurs, whilst her active limbs kept wreathing and intertwisting with his, in convulsive folds: then the turtlebilling kisses, and the poignant painless love-bites, which they both exchang'd, in a rage of delight, all conspiring towards the melting period. It soon came on, when Louisa, in the ravings of her pleasure-frenzy, impotent of all restraint, cried out: "Oh, Sir! . . . Good Sir! . . . pray do not spare me! ah! ah! . . ." All her accents now faltering into heartfetched sighs, she clos'd her eyes in the sweet death, in the instant of which she was embalm'd by an injection, of which we could easily see the signs in the quiet, dying, languid posture of her late so furious driver, who was stopp'd of a sudden, breathing short, panting, and, for that time, giving up the spirit of pleasure. As soon as he was dismounted, Louisa sprung up, shook her petticoats, and running up to me, gave me a kiss, and drew me to the side-board, to which she was herself handed by her gallant, where they made me pledge them in a glass of wine, and toast a droll health of Louisa's proposal in high frolic.

By this time the second couple was ready to enter the lists: which were a young baronet, and that delicatest of charmers, the winning, tender Harriet. My gentle esquire came to acquaint me with it, and brought me back to the scene of action.

And, surely, never did one of her profession accompany

her dispositions for the bare-faced part she was engaged to play with such a peculiar grace of sweetness, modesty, and yielding coyness, as she did. All her air and motions breath'd only unreserv'd, unlimited complaisance without the least mixture of impudence or prostitution. But what was yet more surprising, her spark-elect, in the midst of the dissolution of a public open enjoyment, doted on her to distraction, and had, by dint of love and sentiments, touched her heart, tho' for a while the restraint of their engagement to the house laid him under a kind of necessity of complying with an institution which himself had had the greatest share in establishing.

Harriet was then led to the vacant couch by her gallant, blushing as she look'd at me, and with eyes made to justify anything, tenderly bespeaking of me the most favourable construction of the step she was thus irresistibly drawn into.

Her lover, for such he was, sat her down at the foot of the couch, and passing his arm round her neck, preluded with a kiss fervently applied to her lips, that visibly gave her life and spirit to go thro' with the scene; and as he kiss'd, he gently inclined her head, till it fell back on a pillow disposed to receive it, and leaning himself down all the way with her, at once countenanc'd and endear'd her fall to her. There, as if he had guess'd our wishes, or meant to gratify at once his pleasure and his pride, in being the master, by the title of present possession, of beauties delicate beyond imagination, he discovered her breasts to his own touch, and our common view; but oh! what delicious manuals of love devotion! how inimitably fine moulded! small, round, firm, and excellently white: the grain of their skin, so soothing, so flattering to the touch! and their nipples, that crown'd them, the sweetest buds of beauty. When he had feasted his eyes with the touch and perusal, feasted his lips with kisses of the highest relish, imprinted on those all-delicious twin orbs, he proceeded downwards.

Her legs still kept the ground; and now, with the tenderest attention not to shock or alarm her too suddenly, he, by degrees, rather stole than rolled up her petticoats; at which, as if a signal had been given, Louisa and Emily took hold of her legs, in pure wantonness, and, in ease to her, kept them stretched wide abroad. Then lay exposed, or, to speak more properly, display'd the greatest parade in nature of female charms. The whole company, who, except myself, had often seen them, seemed as much dazzled, surpriz'd, and delighted, as anyone could be who had now beheld them for the first time. Beauties so excessive could not but enjoy the privileges of eternal novelty. Her thighs were so exquisitely fashioned, that either more in, or more out of flesh than they were, they would have declined from that point of perfection they presented. But what infinitely enrich'd and adorn'd them was the sweet intersection formed, where they met, at the bottom of the smoothest, roundest, whitest belly, by that central furrow which nature had sunk there, between the soft relieve of two pouting ridges, and which, in this girl, was in perfect symmetry of delicacy and miniature with the rest of her frame. No! nothing in nature could be of a beautifuller cut; then, the dark umbrage of the downy spring-moss that overarched it, bestowed, on the luxury of the landscape, a touching warmth, a tender finishing, beyond the expression of words, or even the pain of thought.

The truly enamour'd gallant, who had stood absorbed and engrossed by the pleasure of the sight long enough to afford us time to feast ours (no fear of glutting!) addressed himself at length to the materials of enjoyment, and lifting the linen veil that hung between us and his master member of the revels, exhibited one whose eminent size proclaimed the owner a true woman's hero. He was, besides, in every other respect an accomplish'd gentleman, and in the bloom and vigour of youth. Standing then between Harriet's legs, which were supported by her two companions at their widest extension, with one hand he gently disclosed the lips of that luscious mouth of nature, whilst with the other, he stooped his mighty machine to its lure, from the height of his stiff stand-up towards his belly; the lips, kept open by his fingers, received its broad shelving head of coral hue: and when he had nestled it in, he hovered there a little, and the girls then deliver'd over to his hips the agreeable office of supporting her thighs; and now, as if meant to spin out his pleasure, and give it the more play for its life, he passed up his instrument so slow that we lost sight of it inch by inch, till at length it was wholly taken into the soft laboratory of love, and the mossy mounts of each fairly met together. In the mean time, we could plainly mark the prodigious effect the progressions of this delightful energy wrought in this delicious girl, gradually heightening her beauty as they heightened her pleasure. Her countenance and whole frame grew more animated; the faint blush of her cheeks, gaining ground on the white, deepened into a florid vivid vermillion glow, her naturally brilliant eyes now sparkled with ten-fold lustre; her languor was vanish'd, and she appeared quick spirited and alive all over. He had now fixed, nailed, this tender creature, with his home-driven wedge, so that she lay passive by force, and unable to stir, till beginning to play a strain of arms against this vein of delicacy, as he urged the to-and-fro friction, he awaken'd, rous'd, and touch'd her so to the heart, that, unable to contain herself, she could not but reply to his motions, as briskly as her nicety of frame would admit of, till the raging stings of the pleasure rising towards the point made her wild with the intolerable sensations of it, and she now threw her legs and arms about at random, as she lay lost in the sweet transport; which on his side declared itself by quicker, eager thrusts, convulsive grasps, burning sighs, swift laborious breathings, eyes darting humid fires: all faithful tokens of the imminent approaches of the last gasp of joy. It came on at length: the baronet led the ecstasy, she sympathically joined in, as she felt the melting symptoms from him, in the nick of which glewing more ardently than ever his lips to hers, he shewed all the signs of that agony of bliss being strong upon him, in which he gave her the finishing titillation; inly thrill'd with which, we saw plainly that she answered it down with all effusion of spirit and matter she was mistress of, whilst a general soft shudder ran through all her limbs, which she gave a stretchout of, and lay motionless, breathless, dying with dear delight; and in the height of its expression, showing, through the nearly closed lids of her eyes, just the edges of their black, the rest being rolled strongly upwards in their ecstasy; then her sweet mouth appear'd languishingly open, with the tip of her tongue leaning negligently towards the lower range of her white teeth, whilst the natural ruby colour of her lips glowed with heightened life. Was not this a subject to dwell upon? And accordingly her lover still kept on her, with an abiding delectation, till compressed, squeezed, and distilled to the last drop, he took leave with one fervent kiss, expressing satisfy'd desires, but unextinguish'd love.

As soon as he was off, I ran to her, and sitting down on the couch by her, rais'd her head, which she declin'd gently, and hung on my bosom, to hide her blushes and confusion at what had pass'd, till by degrees she recomposed herself, and accepted of a restorative glass of wine from my spark, who had left me to fetch it her, whilst her own was re-adjusting his affairs and buttoning up; after which he led her, leaning languishingly upon him, to our stand of view round the couch.

And now Emily's partner had taken her out for her share in the dance, when this transcendently fair and sweet tempered creature readily stood up; and if a complexion to put the rose and lily out of countenance, extreme pretty features, and that florid health and bloom for which the country-girls are so lovely might pass her for a beauty, this she certainly was, and one of the most striking of the fair ones.

Her gallant began first, as she stood, to disengage her breasts, and restore them to the liberty of nature, from the easy confinement of no more than a pair of jumps; but on their coming out to view, we thought a new light was added to the room, so superiorly shining was their whiteness; then they rose in so happy a swell as to compose her a well-formed fullness of bosom that had such an effect on the eye as to seem flesh hardening into marble, of which it emulated the polished gloss, and far surpassed even the whitest, in the life and lustre of its colours, white veined with blue. Refrain who could from such provoking enticements to it in reach? He touched her breasts, first lightly, when the glossy smoothness of the skin eluded his hand, and made it slip along the surface; he press'd them, and the springy flesh that filled them, thus pitted by force, rose again reboundingly with his hand, and on the instant effac'd the pressure: and alike indeed was the consistence of all those parts of her body throughout, where the fulness of flesh compacts and constitutes all that fine firmness which the touch is so highly attach'd to. When he had thus largely pleased himself with this branch of dalliance and delight, he truss'd up her petticoat and shift, in a wisp to her waist, where being tuck'd in, she stood fairly naked on every side; a blush at this overspread her lovely face, and her eyes downcast to the ground, seemed to be for quarter, when she had so great a right to triumph in all the treasures of youth and beauty that she now so victoriously display'd. Her legs were perfectly well shaped and her thighs, which she kept pretty close, shewed so white, so round, so substantial and abounding in firm flesh, that nothing could offer a stronger recommendation to the luxury of the touch, which he accordingly did not fail to indulge himself in. Then gently removing her hand, which in the first emotion of natural modesty, she had carried thither, he gave us rather a glimpse than a view of that soft narrow chink running its little length downwards and hiding the remains of it between her thighs; but plain was to be seen the fringe of light-brown curls, in beauteous growth over it, that with their silky gloss created a pleasing variety from the surrounding white skin, whose lustre too, their gentle embrowning shade, considerably raised. Her spark then endeavoured, as she stood, by disclosing her thighs, to gain us a completer sight of that central charm of attraction, but not obtaining it so conveniently in that attitude, he led her to the foot of the couch, and bringing to it one of the pillows, gently inclin'd her head down, so that as she leaned with it over her crossed hands, straddling with her thighs wide spread, and jutting her body out, she presented a full back view of her person, naked to her waist. Her posteriors, plump, smooth, and prominent, form'd luxuriant tracts of animated snow, that splendidly filled the eye, till it was commanded down the parting or separation of those exquisitely white cliffs, by their narrow vale, and was there stopt, and attracted by the embowered bottom-cavity that terminated this delightful vista and stood moderately gaping from the influence of her bended posture, so that the agreeable interior red of the sides of the orifice came into view, and with respect to the white that dazzled round it, gave somewhat the idea of a pink slash in the glossiest white satin. Her gallant, who was a gentleman about thirty, somewhat inclin'd to a fatness that was in no sort displeasing, improving the hint thus tendered him of this mode of enjoyment, after settling her well in this posture, and encouraging her with kisses and caresses to stand him through, drew out his affair ready erected, and whose extreme length, rather disproportion'd to its breadth, was the more surprising, as that excess is not often the case with those of his corpulent habit; making then the right and direct application, he drove it up to the guard, whilst the round bulge of those Turkish beauties of hers tallying with the hollow made with the bent of his belly and thighs, as they curved inwards, brought all those parts, surely not undelightfully, into warm touch, and close conjunction; his hands he kept passing round her body, and employed in toying with her enchanting breasts. As soon too as she felt him at home as he could reach, she lifted her head a little from the pillow, and turning her neck, without much straining, but her cheeks glowing with the deepest scarlet, and a smile of the tenderest satisfaction, met the kiss he press'd forward to give her as they were thus close joined together: when leaving him to pursue his delights, she hid again her face and blushes with her hands and pillow, and thus stood passively and as favourably too as she could, whilst he kept laying at her with repeated thrusts and making the meeting flesh on both sides resound again with the violence of them; then ever as he backen'd from her, we could see between them part of his long white staff foamingly in motion, till, as he went on again and closed with her, the interposing hillocks took it out of sight. Sometimes he took his hands from the semi-globes of her bosom, and transferred the pressure of them to those larger ones, the present subjects of his soft blockade, which he squeez'd, grasp'd, and play'd with, till at length a pursuit of driving, so hotly urged, brought on the height of the fit with such overpowering pleasure that his fair partner became now necessary to support him, panting, fainting, and dying as he discharged; which she no sooner felt the killing sweetness of than, unable to keep her legs, and yielding to the mighty intoxication, she reeled, and falling forward on the couch, made it a necessity for him, if he would preserve the warm pleasure-hold, to fall upon her, where they perfected, in a continued conjunction of body and ecstatic flow, their scheme of joys for that time.

As soon as he had disengag'd, the charming Emily got up, and we crowded round her with congratulations and other officious little services; for it is to be noted, that though all modesty and reserve were banished from the transaction of these pleasures, good manners and politeness were inviolably observ'd: here was no gross ribaldry, no offensive or rude behaviour, or ungenerous reproaches to the girls for their compliance with the humours and desires of the men; on the contrary, nothing was wanting to soothe, encourage, and soften the sense of their condition to them. Men know not in general how much they destroy of their own pleasure, when they break through the respect and tenderness due to our sex, and even to those of it who live only by pleasing them. And this was a maxim perfectly well understood by these polite voluptuaries, these profound adepts in the great art and science of pleasure, who never shew'd these votaries of theirs a more tender respect than at the time of those exercises of their complaisance, when they unlock'd their treasures of concealed beauty, and showed out in the pride of their native charms, evermore touching surely than when they parade it in the artificial ones of dress and ornament.

The frolick was now come round to me, and it being my turn of subscription to the will and pleasure of my particular elect, as well as to that of the company, he came to me, and saluting me very tenderly, with a flattering eagerness, put me in mind of the compliances my presence there authoriz'd the hopes of, and at the same time repeated to me that if all this force of example had not surmounted any repugnance I might have to concur with the humours and desires of the company, that though the play was bespoke for my benefit, and great as his own private disappointment might be, he would suffer anything, sooner than be the instrument of imposing a disagreeable task on me.

To this I answered, without the least hesitation, or mincing grimace, that had I not even contracted a kind of engagement to be at his disposal without the least reserve, the example of such agreeable companions would alone determine me and that I was in no pain about any thing but my appearing to so great a disadvantage after such superior beauties. And take notice, that I thought as I spoke. The frankness of the answer pleas'd them all; my particular was complimented on his acquisition, and, by way of indirect flattery to me, openly envied.

Mrs. Cole, by the way, could not have given me a greater mark of her regard than in managing for me the choice of this young gentleman for my master of the ceremonies: for, independent of his noble birth and the great fortune he was heir to, his person was even uncommonly pleasing, well shaped and tall; his face mark'd with the small-pox, but no more than what added a grace of more manliness to features rather turned to softness and delicacy, was marvellously enliven'd by eyes which were of the clearest sparkling black; in short, he was one whom any woman would, in the familiar style, readily call a very pretty fellow.

I was now handed by him to the cockpit of our match, where, as I was dressed in nothing but a white morning gown, he vouchsafed to play the male-Abigail on this occasion, and spared me the confusion that would have attended the forwardness of undressing myself: my gown then was loosen'd in a trice, and I divested of it; my stay next offered an obstacle which readily gave way, Louisa very readily furnishing a pair of scissors to cut the lace; off went that shell and dropping my uppercoat, I was reduced to my under one and my shift, the open bosom of which gave the hands and eyes all the liberty they could wish. Here I imagin'd the stripping was to stop, but I reckoned short:

my spark, at the desire of the rest, tenderly begged that I would not suffer the small remains of a covering to rob them of a full view of my whole person; and for me, who was too flexibly obsequious to dispute any point with them, and who considered the little more that remain'd as very immaterial, I readily assented to whateve he pleased. In an instant, then, my under petticoat was untied and at my feet, and my shift drawn over my head, so that my cap, slightly fasten'd, came off with it, and brought all my hair down (of which, be it again remembered without vanity, that I had a very fine head) in loose disorderly ringlets, over my neck and shoulders, to the not unfavourable set-off of my skin.

I now stood before my judges in all the truth of nature, to whom I could not appear a very disagreeable figure, if you please to recollect what I have before said of my person, which time, that at certain periods of life robs us every instant of our charms, had, at that of mine, then greatly improved into full and open bloom, for I wanted some months of eighteen. My breasts, which in the state of nudity are ever capital points, now in no more than in graceful plenitude, maintained a firmness and steady independence of any stay of support, that dared and invited the test of the touch. Then I was as tall, as slim-shaped as could be consistent with all that juicy plumpness of flesh, ever the most grateful to the senses of sight and touch, which I owed to the health and youth of my constitution. I had not, however, so thoroughly renounc'd all innate shame, as not to suffer great confusion at the state I saw myself in; but the whole troop round me, men and women, relieved me with every mark of applause and satisfaction, every flattering attention to raise and inspire me with even sentiments of pride on the figure I made, which my friend gallantly protested, infinitely out-shone all other *birthday* finery whatever; so that had I leave to set down, for sincere, all the compliments these connoisseurs overwhelmed me with upon this occasion, I might flatter myself with having pass'd my examination with the approbation of the learned.

My friend however, who for this time had alone the disposal of me, humoured their curiosity, and perhaps his own, so far, that he placed me in all the variety of postures and lights imaginable, pointing out every beauty under every aspect of it, not without such parentheses of kisses, such inflammatory liberties of his roving hands, as made all shame fly before them, and a blushing glow give place to a warmer one of desire, which led me even to find some relish in the present scene.

But in this general survey, you may be sure, the most material spot of me was not excus'd the strictest visitation! nor was it but agreed, that I had not the least reason to be diffident of passing even for a maid, on occasion: so inconsiderable a flaw had my preceding adventures created there, and so soon had the blemish of an over-stretch been repaired and worn out at my age, and in my naturally small make in that part.

Now, whether my partner had exhausted all the modes of regaling the touch or sight, or whether he was now ungovernably wound up to strike, I know not; but briskly throwing off his clothes, the prodigious heat bred by a close room, a great fire, numerous candles, and even the inflammatory warmth of these scenes, induced him to lay aside his shirt too, when his breeches, before loosen'd, now gave up their contents to view, and shew'd in front the enemy I had to engage with, stifly bearing up the port of its head unhooded, and glowing red. Then I plainly saw what I had to trust to: it was one of those just true-siz'd instruments, of which the masters have a better command than the more unwieldy, inordinate siz'd ones are generally under. Straining me then close to his bosom, as he stood up fore-right against me and applying to the obvious niche its peculiar idol, he aimed at inserting it, which, as I forwardly favoured, he effected at once, by canting up my thighs over his naked hips, and made me receive every inch, and close home; so that stuck upon the plesaure-pivot, and clinging round his neck, in which and in his hair I hid my face, burningly flushing with my present feelings as much as with shame, my bosom glew'd to his; he carried me once round the couch, on which he then, without quitting the middle-fastness, or dischannelling, laid me down, and began the pleasure-grist. But so provokingly predisposed and primed as we were, by all the moving sights of the night, our imagination was too much heated not to melt us of the soonest: and accordingly, I no sooner felt the warm spray darted up my inwards from him, but I was punctually on flow, to share the momentary ecstasy; but I had yet greater reason to boast of our harmony: for finding that all the flames of desire were not yet quench'd within me, but that rather, like wetted coals, I glowed the fiercer for this sprinkling, my hot-mettled spark, sympathizing with me, and loaded for a double fire, recontinu'd the sweet battery with undying vigour; greatly pleas'd at which, I gratefully endeavoured to accommodate all my motions to his best advantage and delight; kisses, squeezes, tender murmurs, all came into play, till our joys growing more turbulent and riotous, threw us into a fond disorder, and as they raged to a point, bore us far from ourselves into an ocean of boundless pleasures, into which we both plunged together in a transport of lust. Now all the impressions of burning desire, from the lively scenes I had been spectatress of, ripened by the heat of this exercise, and collecting to a head, throbb'd and agitated me with insupportable irritations: I perfectly fevered and madden'd with their excess. I did not now enjoy a calm of reason enough to perceive, but I ecstatically, indeed, *felt* the power of such rare and exquisite provocatives, as the examples of the night had proved towards thus exalting our pleasures: which, with great joy, I sensibly found my gallant shared in, by his nervous and home expressions of it: his eyes flashing eloquent flames, his action infuriated with the stings of it, all conspiring to rise my delight, by assuring me of his. Lifted then to the utmost pitch of joy that human life can bear, undestroyed by excess, I touch'd that sweetly critical point, whence scarce prevented by the injection from my partner, I dissolved, and breaking out into a deep drawn sigh, sent my whole sensitive soul down to that passage where escape was denied it, by its being so deliciously plugged and chok'd up. Thus we lay a few blissful instants, overpowered, still, and languid; till, as the sense of pleasure stagnated, we recover'd from our trance, and he slipt out of me, not however before he had protested his extreme satisfaction by the tenderest kiss and embrace, as well as by the most cordial expressions.

The company, who had stood round us in a profound silence, when all was over, help'd me to hurry on my clothes in an instant, and complimented me on the sincere homage they could not escape observing had been done (as they termed it) to the sovereignty of my charms, in my receiving a double payment of tribute at one juncture. But my partner, now dress'd again, signaliz'd, above all, a fondness unbated by the circumstance of recent enjoyment; the girls too kiss'd and embraced me, assuring me that for that time, or indeed any other, unless I pleased, I was to go thro' no farther public trials, and that I was now consummatedly initiated, and one of them.

As it was an inviolable law for every gallant to keep to his partner, for the night especially, and even till he relinquish'd possession over to the community, in order to preserve a pleasing property, and to avoid the disgusts and indelicacy of another arrangement, the company, after a short refection of biscuits and wine, tea and chocolate, served in at now about one in the morning, broke up, and went off in pairs. Mrs. Cole had prepared my spark and me an occasional field-bed, to which we retir'd, and there ended the night in one continued strain of pleasure, sprightly and uncloy'd enough for us not to have formed one wish for its ever knowing an end. In the morning, after a restorative breakfast in bed, he got up, and with very tender assurances of a particular regard for me, left me to the composure and refreshment of a sweet slumber; waking out of which, and getting up to dress before Mrs. Cole should come in, I found in one of my pockets a purse of guineas, which he had slipt there; and just as I was musing on a liberality I had certainly not expected, Mrs. Cole came in, to whom I immediately communicated the present, and naturally offered her whatever share she pleas'd: but assuring me that the gentleman had very nobly rewarded her, she would on no terms, no entreaties, no shape I could put it in, receive any part of it. Her denial, she observed, was not affectation of grimace, and proceeded to read me such admirable lessons on the economy of my person and my purse, as I became amply paid for my *general* attention and conformity to, in the course of my acquaintance with the town. After which, changing the discourse, she fell on the pleasures of the preceding night, where I learn'd, without much surprise, as I began to enter on her character, that she had seen everything that had passed, from a convenient place managed solely for that purpose, and of which she readily made me the confidence.

She had scarce finish'd this, when the little troop of love, the girls my companions, broke in, and renewed their compliments and caresses. I observed with pleasure that the fatigues and exercises of the night had not usurped in the least on the life of their complexion, or the freshness of their bloom: this I found, by their confession, was owing to the management and advice of our rare directress. They went down then to figure it, as usual, in the shop; whilst I repair'd to my lodgings, where I employed myself till I returned to dinner at Mrs. Cole's.

Here I staid in constant amusement, with one or other of these charming girls, till about five in the evening; when seiz'd with a sudden drowsy fit, I was prevailed on to go up and doze it off on Harriet's bed, who left me on it to my repose. There then I lay down in my clothes, and fell fast asleep, and had now enjoyed, by guess, about an hour's rest, when I was pleasingly disturbed by my new and favourite gallant, who, enquiring for me, was readily directed where to find me. Coming then into my chamber, and seeing me lie alone, with my face turn'd from the light towards the inside of the bed, he, without more ado, just slipped off his breeches, for the greater ease and enjoyment of the naked touch; and softly turning up my petticoat and shift behind, opened the prospect of the back avenue to the genial seat of pleasure; where, as I lay at my side length, inclining rather face downward, I appeared full fair, and liable to be entered. Laying himself then gently down by me, he invested me behind, and giving me to feel the warmth of his body, as he applied his thighs and belly close to me, and the endeavours of that machine, whose touch has something so exquisitely singular in it, to make its way good into me. I wak'd pretty much startled at first, but seeing who it was, disposed myself to turn to him, when he gave me a kiss, and desiring me to keep my posture, just lifted up my upper thigh, and ascertaining the right opening, soon drove it up to the farthest: satisfied with which, and solacing himself with lying so close in those parts, he suspended motion, and thus steeped in pleasure, kept me lying on my side, into him, spoon-fashion, as he term'd it, from the snug indent of the back part of my thighs, and all upwards, into the space of the bending between his thighs and belly; till, after some time, that restless and turbulent inmate, impatient by nature of longer quiet, urg'd him to action, which now prosecuting with all the usual train of toying, kissing, and the like, ended at length in the liquid proof on both sides that we had not exhausted, or at least were quickly recruited of last night's draughts of pleasure in us.

With this noble and agreeable youth liv'd I in perfect joy and constancy. He was full bent on keeping me to himself, for the honey-month at least; but his stay in *London* was not even so long, his father, who had a post in *Ireland*, taking him abruptly with him, on his repairing thither; yet even then I was near keeping hold of his affection and person, as he had propos'd, and I had consented to follow him in order to go to Ireland after him, as soon as he could be settled there; but meeting with an agreeable and advantageous match in that kingdom, he chose the wiser part, and forebore sending for me, but at the same time took care that I should receive a very magnificent present, which did not however compensate for all my deep regret on my loss of him.

This event also created a chasm in our little society, which Mrs. Cole, on the foot of her usual caution, was in no haste to fill up; but then it redoubled her attention to procure me, in the advantages of a traffic for a counterfeit maidenhead, some consolation for the sort of widowhood I had been left in; and this was a scheme she had never lost prospect of, and only waited for a proper person to bring it to bear with.

But I was, it seems, fated to be my own caterer in this, as I had been in my first trial of the market.

I had now pass'd near a month in the enjoyment of all the pleasures of familiarity and society with my companions, whose particular favourites (the baronet excepted, who soon after took Harriet home) had all, on the terms of community establish'd in the house, solicited the gratification of their taste for variety in my embraces; but I had with the utmost art and address, on various pretexts, eluded their pursuit, without giving them cause to complain; and this reserve I used neither out of dislike of them, or disgust of the thing, but my true reason was my attachment to my own, and my tenderness of invading the choice of my companions, who outwardly exempt, as they seem'd, from jealousy, could not but in secret like me the better for the regard I had for, without making a merit of it to them. Thus easy, and beloved, by the whole family, did I go on; when one day, that, about five in the afternoon, I stepped over to a fruiterer's shop in *Covent Garden*, to pick some table fruit for myself and the young woman, I met with the following adventure.

Whilst I was chaffering for the fruit I wanted, I observ'd myself follow'd by a young gentleman, whose rich dress first attracted my notice; for the rest, he had nothing remarkable in his person, except that he was pale, thinmade, and ventur'd himself upon legs rather of the slenderest. Easy was it to perceive, without seeming to perceive it, that it was me he wanted to be at; and keeping his eyes fixed on me, till he came to the same basket that I stood at, and cheapening, or rather giving the first price ask'd for the fruit, began his approaches. Now most certainly I was not at all out of figure to pass for a modest girl. I had neither the feathers, nor *fumet* of a tawdry town-miss: a straw hat, a white gown, clean linen, and above all, a certain natural and easy air of modesty (which the appearances of never forsook me, even on those occasions that I most broke in upon it, in practice) were all signs that gave him no opening to conjecture my condition. He spoke to me; and this address from a stranger

154

throwing a blush into my cheeks that still set him wider off the truth, I answered him, with an awkwardness and confusion the more apt to impose, as there was really a mixture of the genuine in them. But when proceeding, on the foot of having broken the ice, to join discourse, he went into other leading questions, I put so much innocence, simplicity and even childishness into my answers that on no better foundation, liking my person as he did, I will answer for it, he would have been sworn for my modesty. There is, in short, in the men, when once they are caught, by the eye especially, a fund of gullibility that their lordly wisdom little dreams of, and in virtue of which the most sagacious of them are seen so often our dupes. Amongst other queries he put to me, one was whether I was married. I replied that I was too young to think of that this many a year. To that of my age, I answered, and sunk a year upon him, passing myself for not seventeen. As to my way of life, I told him I had serv'd an apprenticeship to a milliner in *Preston*, and was come to town after a relation, that I had found, on my arrival, was dead, and now liv'd journey-woman to a milliner in town. That last article, indeed, was not much of the side of what I pretended to pass for; but it did pass, under favour of the growing passion I had inspir'd him with. After he had next got out of me, very dextrously as he thought, what I had no sort of design to make reserve of, my own, my mistress's name, and place of abode, he loaded me with fruit, all the rarest and dearest he could pick out and sent me home, pondering on what might be the consequence of this adventure.

As soon then as I came to Mrs. Cole's I related to her all that past, on which she very judiciously concluded, that if he did not come after me there was no harm done, and that, if he did, as her presage suggested to her he would, his character and his views should be well sifted, so as to know whether the game was worth the candle; that in the meantime nothing was easier than my part in it, since no more rested on me than to follow her cue and promptership throughout, to the last act.

The next morning, after an evening spent on his side, as

we afterwards learnt, in perquisitions into Mrs. Cole's character in the neighbourhood (than which nothing could be more favourable to her design upon him), my gentleman came in his chariot to the shop, where Mrs. Cole alone had an inkling of his errand. Asking then for her, he easily made a beginning of acquaintance by bespeaking some millinery ware: when, as I sat without lifting up my eyes, and pursuing the hem of a ruffle with the utmost composure and simplicity of industry, Mrs. Cole took notice that the first impressions I made on him ran no risk of being destroyed by those of Louisa and Emily, who were then sitting at work by me. After vainly endeavouring to catch my eyes in encounter with his (as I held my head down, affecting a kind of consciousness of guilt for having, by speaking to him given him encouragement and means of following me), and after giving Mrs. Cole direction when to bring the things home herself, and the time he should expect them, he went out, taking with him some goods, that he paid for liberally, for the better grace of his introduction.

The girls all this time did not in the least cloak the mystery of this new customer; but Mrs. Cole, as soon as we were conveniently alone, insur'd me, in virtue of her long experience in these matters, that for this bout my charms had not miss'd fire; for that by his eagerness, his manner and looks, she was sure he had it: the only point now in doubt was his character and circumstances, which her knowledge of the town would soon gain her sufficient acquaintance with, to take her measures upon.

And effectively, in a few hours, her intelligence serv'd her so well, that she learn'd that this conquest of mine was no other than Mr. *Norbert*, a gentleman orginally of great fortune, which, with a constitution naturally not the best, he had vastly impaired by his over-violent pursuit of the vices of the town; in the course of which, having worn out and stal'd all the more common modes of debauchery, he had fallen into a taste of maiden-hunting; in which chase he had ruin'd a number of girls, sparing no expense to compass his ends, and generally using them well till tired, or cool'd by enjoyment, or springing a new face, he could with more ease disembarrass himself of the old ones, and resign them to their fate, as his sphere of achievements of that sort lay only amongst such as he could proceed with by way of bargain and sale.

Concluding from these premises, Mrs. Cole observ'd that a character of this sort was ever a lawful prize; that the sin would be, not to make the best of our market of him; and that she thought such a girl as I only too good for him at any rate, and on any terms.

She went then, at the hour appointed, to his lodgings in one of our inns of court, which were furnished in a taste of grandeur that had a special eye to all the conveniences of luxury and pleasure. Here she found him in ready waiting; and after finishing her pretence of business, and a long circuit of discussions concerning her trade, which she said was very bad, the qualities of her servants, 'prentices, journey-women, the discourse naturally landed at length on me, when Mrs. Cole, acting admirably the good old prating gossip, who lets everything escape her when her tongue is set in motion, cooked him up a story so plausible of me, throwing in every now and then such strokes of art, with all the simplest air of nature, in praise of my person and temper, as finished him finely for her purpose, whilst nothing could be better counterfeited than her innocence of his. But when now fir'd and on edge, he proceeded to drop hints of his design or views upon me, after he had with much confusion and pains brought her to the point (she kept as long aloof from as she thought proper) of understanding him, without now affecting to pass for a dragoness of virtue, by flying out into those violent and ever suspicious passions, she stuck with the better grace and effect to the character of a plain, good sort of a woman, that knew no harm, and that getting her bread in an honest way, was made of stuff easy and flexible enough to be wrought upon to his ends, by his superior skill and address; but, however, she managed so artfully that three or four meetings took place before he could obtain the least favourable hope of her assistance; without which, he had, by a number of fruitless messages, letters, and other direct trials of my disposition, convinced himself there was no coming at me, all which too rais'd at once my character and price with him.

Regardful, however, of not carrying these difficulties to such a length as might afford time for starting discoveries, or incidents, unfavourable to her plan, she at last, pretended to be won over by mere dint of entreaties, promises, and, above all, by the dazzling sum she took care to wind him up to the specification of, when it was now even a piece of art to feign, at once, a yielding to the allurements of a great interest, as a pretext for her yielding at all, and the manner of it such as might persuade him she had never dipp'd her virtuous fingers in an affair of that sort.

Thus she led him through all the gradations of difficulty, and obstacles, necessary to enhance the value of the prize he aim'd at; and in conclusion, he was so struck with the little beauty I was mistress of, and so eagerly bent on gaining his ends of me, that he left her even no room to boast of her management in bringing him up to her mark, he drove so plum of himself into everything tending to make him swallow the bait. Not but, in other respects, Mr. Norbert was not clear-sighted enough, or that he did not perfectly know the town, and even by experience, the very branch of imposition now in practice upon him: but we had his passion our friend so much, he was so blinded and hurried on by it, that he would have thought any undeception a very ill office done to his pleasure thus concurring even precipitately, to the point she wanted him at, Mrs. Cole brought him at last to hug himself on the cheap bargain he consider'd the purchase of my imaginary jewel was to him, at no more than three hundred guineas to myself, and a hundred to the brokeress: being a slender recompense for all her pains, and all the scruples of conscience she had now sacrificed to him for this the first time of her life; which sums were to be paid down on the nail, upon livery of my person, exclusive of some not inconsiderable presents that had been made in the course of the negociation: during which I had occasionally, but sparingly been introduc'd into his company, at proper times and hours; in which it is incredible how little it seem'd necessary to strain my natural disposition to modesty higher, in order to pass it upon him for that of a very maid: all my looks and gestures ever breathing nothing but that innocence which the men so ardently require in us, for no other end than to feast themselves with the pleasures of destroying it, and which they are so grievously, with all their skill, subject to mistakes in.

When the articles of the treaty had been fully agreed on, the stipulated payments duly secur'd, and nothing now remained but the execution of the main point, which center'd in the surrender of my person up to his free disposal and use, Mrs. Cole managed her objections, especially to his lodgings, and insinuations so nicely, that it became his own mere notion and urgent request that this copy of a wedding should be finish'd at her house: At first, indeed, she did not care, said she, to have such doings in it . . . she would not for a thousand pounds have any of the servants or 'prentices know it . . . her precious good name would be gone for ever . . . with the like excuses. However, on superior objections to all other expedients, whilst she took care to start none but those which were most liable to them, it came round at last to the necessity of her obliging him in that conveniency, and of doing a little more where she had already done so much.

The night then was fix'd, with all possible respect to the eagerness of his impatience, and in the meantime Mrs. Cole had omitted no instructions, nor even neglected any preparation, that might enable me to come off with honour, in regard to the appearance of my virginity, except that, favour'd as I was by nature with all the narrowness of stricture in that part requisite to conduct my designs, I had no occasion to borrow those auxiliaries of art that create a momentary one, easily discover'd by the test of a warm bath. And as to the usual sanguinary symptoms of deflorations, which, if not always, are generally attendants on it, Mrs. Cole had made me the mistress of an invention of her own, which could hardly miss its effect, and of which more in its place.

Everything then being disposed and fix'd for Mr. Norbert's reception, he was, at the hour of eleven at night with all the mysteries of silence and secrecy, let in by Mrs. Cole herself, and introduced into her bedchamber, where, in an old fashioned bed of hers, I lay, fully undressed, and panting, if not with the fears of a real maid, at least with those perhaps greater of a dissembled one which gave me an air of confusion and bashfulness that maiden-modesty had all the honour of, and was indeed scarce distinguishable from it, even by less partial eyes than those of my lover: so let me call him, for I ever thought the term "*cully*" too cruel a reproach to the men, for their abused weakness for us.

As soon as Mrs. Cole, after the old gossipery, on these occasions, us'd to young women abandoned for the first time to the will of man, had left us alone in her room, which, by-the-bye, was well lighted up, at his previous desire, that seemed to bode a stricter examination than he afterwards made, Mr. Norbert, still dressed, sprung towards the bed, where I got my head under the clothes, and defended them a good while before he could even get at my lips, to kiss them: so true it is, that a false virtue, on this occasion, even makes a greater rout and resistance than a true one. From thence he descended to my breasts, the feel I disputed tooth and nail with him till, tired with my resistance, and thinking probably to give a better account of me, when got into bed to me, he hurry'd his clothes off in an instant, and came into bed.

Meanwhile, by the glimpse I stole of him, I could easily discover a person far from promising any such doughty performances as the storming of maidenheads generally requires, and whose flimsy consumptive texture gave him more the air of an invalid that was pressed, than of a volunteer, on such hot service.

At scarce thirty, he had already reduced his strength of appetite down to a wretched dependence on forc'd provocatives, very little seconded by the natural power of a body jaded, and racked off to the lees by constant repeated overdraughts of pleasure, which had done the work of sixty winters on his springs of life: leaving him at the same time all the fire and heat of youth in his imagination, which served at once to torment and spur him down the precipice.

As soon as he was in bed, he threw off the bedclothes, which I suffered him to force from my hold, and I now lay as expos'd as he could wish, not only to his attacks, but his visitation of the sheets; where in the various agitations of the body, through my endeavours to defend myself, he could easily assure himself there was no preparation: though, to do him justice, he seem'd a less strict examiner than I had apprehended from so experienc'd a practitioner. My shift then he fairly tore open, finding I made too much use of it to barricade my breasts, as well as the more important avenue: yet in everything else he proceeded with all the marks of tenderness and regard to me, whilst the art of my play was to show none for him. I acted then all the niceties, apprehensions, and terrors, supposable for a girl perfectly innocent to feel at so great a novelty as a naked man in bed with her for the first time. He scarce even obtained a kiss but what he ravished; I put my hand away twenty times from my breasts, where he had satisfied himself of their hardness and consistence, with passing for hitherto un-handled goods. But when grown impatient for the main point, he now threw himself upon me, and first trying to examine me with his finger, sought to make himself further way, I complained of his usage bitterly: I thought he would not have serv'd a body so ... I was ruin'd ... I did not know what I had done ... I would get up, so I would ...; and at the same time kept my thighs so fast locked, that it was not for strength like his to force them open, or do any good. Finding thus my advantages, and that I had both my own and his motions at command, the deceiving him came so easy, that it was perfectly playing upon velvet. In the mean-time, his machine, which was one of those sizes that slip in and out without being minded, kept pretty stiffly bearing against that part, which the shutting my thighs barr'd access to; but finding, at length, he could do no good by mere dint of bodily strength, he resorted to entreaties and arguments: to which I only answer'd, with a tone of shame and timidity, that I was afraid he would kill me ... Lord! ... I would not be served so ... I was never so used in all my born days . . . I wondered he was not ashamed of himself, so I didi . . ., with such silly childish moods of repulse and complaint as I judged best adapted to express the character of innocence and affright. Pretending, however, to yield at length to the vehemence of his insistence, in action and words, I sparingly disclosed my thighs, so that he could just touch the cloven inlet with the tip of his instrument, but as he fatigued and toil'd to get it in, a twist of my body, so as to receive it obliquely, not only thwarted his admission, but giving a scream, as if he had pierced me to the heart, I shook him off me with such violence that he could not with all his might to it, keep the saddle. Vex'd indeed at this he seemed, but not in the style of any displeasure with me for my skittishness; on the contrary, I dare swear he held me the dearer, and hugged himself for the difficulties that even hurt his instant pleasure. Fired, however, now beyond all bearance of delay, he remounts, and begg'd of me to have patience, stroking and soothing me to it by all the tenderest endearments and protestations of what he would moreover do for me; at which, feigning to be something softened, and abating of the anger that I had shewn at his hurting me so prodigiously, I suffered him to lay my thighs aside, and make way for a new trial; but I watched the directions and management of his point so well, that no sooner was the orifice in the least open to it, but I gave such a timely jerk as seemed to proceed not from the evasion of his entry, but pain his efforts at it put me to: a circumstance too that I did not fail to accompany with proper gestures, sighs and cries of complaint, of which, that he had hurt me . . . he kill'd me . . . I should die . . . were the most frequent interjections. But now, after repeated attempts, in which he had not made the least impression towards gaining his point, at least for that time, the pleasure rose so fast upon him, that he could not check or delay it, and in the vigour and fury which the approaches of the height of it inspir'd him, he made one fierce thrust, that had almost put me by my guard, and lodged it so far that I could feel the warm inspersion just within the exterior orifice, which I had the cruelty not to let him finish there, but threw him out again, not without a most piercing loud exclamation, as if the pain had put me beyond all regard of being overheard. It was easy then to observe that he was more satisfy'd, more highly pleased with the supposed motives of his baulk of consummation than he would have been at the full attainment of it. It was on this foot that I solved to myself all the falsity I employed to procure him that blissful pleasure in it, which most certainly he would not have tasted in the truth of things. Eas'd however, and relieved by one discharge, he now apply'd himself to soothe, encourage and put me into humour and patience to bear his next attempt, which he began to prepare and gather force for, from all the incentives of the touch and sight which he could think of, by examining every individual part of my whole body, which he declared his satisfaction with, in raptures of applauses, kisses universally imprinted, and sparing no part of me, in all the eagerest wantonness of feeling, seeing, and toying; his vigour however did not return so soon, and I felt him more than once pushing at the door, but so little in a condition to break in, that I question whether he had the power to enter, had I held it ever so open; but this he then thought me too little acquainted with the nature of things to have any regret or confusion about, and he kept fatiguing himself and me for a long time, before he was in any state to resume his attacks with any prospect of success; and then I breath'd him so warmly, and kept him so at bay, that before he had made any sensible progress in point of penetration, he was deliciously sweated, and weary'd out indeed: so that it was deep in the morning before he achieved his second let-go, about half way of entrance, I all the while crying and complaining of his prodigious vigour, and the immensity of what I appear'd to suffer splitting up with. Tired, however, at length, with such athletic drudgery, my champion began now to give out, and to gladly embrace the refreshment of some rest. Kissing me then with much affection, and recommending me to my repose he presently fell fast asleep: which, as soon as I had well satisfy'd myself of, I with much composure of body, so as not to wake him by any motion, with much ease and safety too, played of Mrs. Cole's device for perfecting the signs of my virginity.

In each of the head bed-posts, just above where the bed-steads are inserted into them, there was a small drawer, so artfully adapted to the mouldings of the timber-work that it might have escap'd even the most curious search: which drawers were easily open'd or shut by the touch of a spring, and were fitted each with a shallow glass tumbler, full of a prepared fluid blood, in which lay soak'd, for ready use, a sponge, that required no more than gently reaching the hand to it, taking it out and properly squeezing between the thighs, when it yielded a great deal more of the red liquid than would save a girl's honour; after which, replacing it, and touching the spring, all possibility of discovery, or even of suspicion, was taken away; and all this was not the work of the fourth part of a minute, and of which ever side one lay, the thing was equally easy and practicable, by the double care taken to have each bed-post provided alike. True it is, that had he waked and caught me in the fact, it would at least have covered me with shame and confusion; but then, that he did not, was, with the precautions I took, a risk of a thousand to one in my favour.

At ease now, and out of all fear of any doubt or suspicion on his side, I address'd myself in good earnest to my repose, but could obtain none; and in about half an hour's time my gentleman waked again, and turning towards me, I feigned a sound sleep, which he did not long respect; but girding himself again to renew the onset, he began to kiss and caress me, when now making as if I just wak'd, I complained of the disturbance, and of the cruel pain that this little rest had stole my senses from. Eager, however, for the pleasure, as well of consummating an entire triumph over my virginity, he said everything that could overcome my resistance, and bribe my patience to the end, which now I was ready to listen to, from being secure of the bloody proofs I had prepared of his victorious violence, though I still thought of good policy not to let him in yet a while. I answered then only to his importunities in sighs and moans that I was so hurt, I could not bear it . . . I was sure he had done me a mischief; that he had . . . he was such a sad man! At this, turning down the clothes, and viewing the field of battle by the glimmer of a dying taper, he saw plainly my thighs, shift, and sheets, all stained with what he readily took for a virgin effusion, proceeding from his last half-penetration: convinc'd, and transported at which, nothing could equal his joy and exultation. The illusion was complete, no other conception entered his head but that of his having been at work upon an unopen'd mine; which idea, upon so strong an evidence, redoubled at once his tenderness for me, and his ardour for breaking it wholly up. Kissing me then with the utmost rapture, he comforted me, and begg'd my pardon for the pain he had put me to: observing withal that it was only a thing in course, but the worst was certainly past, and that with a little courage and constancy, I should get it once well over, and never after experience anything but the greatest pleasure. By little and little I suffer'd myself to be prevailed on, and giving, as it were, up the point to him, I made my thighs, insensibly spreading them, yield him liberty of access, which improving, he got a little within me, when by a well managed reception I work'd the female screw so nicely, that I kept him from the easy mid-channel direction, and by dextrous wreathing and con-tortions, creating an artificial difficulty of entrance, made him win it inch by inch, with the most laborious struggles, I all the while sorely complaining: till at length, with might and main, winging his way in, he got it completely home, and giving my virginity, as he thought, the *coup de grâce*, furnished me with the cue of setting up a terrible outcry, whilst he, triumphant and like a cock clapping his wings over his down-trod mistress, pursu'd his pleasure; which presently rose, in virtue of this idea of a complete victory, to a pitch that made me soon sensible of his melting period; whilst I now lay acting the deep wounded, breathless, frighten'd, undone, no longer maid.

You would ask me, perhaps, whether all this time I enjoy'd any perception of pleasure? I assure you, little or none, till just towards the latter end, a faintish sense of it came on mechanically, from so long a struggle and constant friction in that ever sensible part; but, in the first place, I had no taste for the person I was suffering the embraces of, on a pure mercenary account; and then, I was not entirely delighted with myself for the jade's part I was playing, whatever excuses I might have to plead for my being brought into it; but then this insensibility kept me so much the mistress of my mind and motions, that I could the better manage so close a counterfeit, through the whole scene of deception.

Recover'd at length to a mere show of life by his tender condolences, kisses, and embraces, I upbraided him and reproach'd him with my ruin, in such natural terms as added to his satisfaction with himself, for having accomplish'd it; and guessing, by certain observations of mine, that it would be rather favourable to him, to spare him, when he some time after, feebly enough, came on again to the assault, I resolutely withstood any further endeavours, on a pretext that flattered his prowess, of my being so violently hurt and sore, that I could not possibly endure a fresh trial; he then graciously granted me a respite, and the next morning soon after advancing, I got rid of further importunity, till Mrs. Cole, being rang for by him, came in and was made acquainted, in terms of the utmost joy and rapture, with his triumphant certainty of my virtue, and the finishing stroke he had given it, in the course of the night: of which, he added, she would see proof enough, in bloody characters, on the sheets.

You may guess how a woman of her turn of address and experience humour'd the jest, and played him off with mixed exclamations of shame, anger, compassion for me, and of her being pleased that all was so well over, in which last, I believe, she was certainly sincere. And now, as the objection which she had represented as an invincible one, to my lying the first night at his lodgings (which were studiously calculated for freedom of intrigues) on the account of my maiden fears and terrors, at the thoughts of going to a gentleman's chambers, and being alone with him in bed, was surmounted, she pretended to persuade me, in favour to him, that I should go there to him, whenever he pleas'd, and still keep up all the necessary appearances of working with her, that I might not lose, with my character, the prospect of getting a good husband, and at the same time her house would be kept the safer from scandal. All this seem'd so reasonable, so considerate to Mr. Norbert, that he never once perceived that she did not want him to resort to her house, lest he might in time discover certain inconsistencies with the character she had set out with to him: besides that, his plan greatly flattered his own ease, and views of liberty.

Leaving me then to my much wanted rest, he got up, and Mrs. Cole, after settling with him all points relating to me, got him undiscovered out of the house. After which, as I was awake, she came in, and gave me due praises for my success. Behaving too with her usual moderation and disinterestedness, she refus'd any share of the sum I had thus earned, and put me into such a secure and easy way of disposing of my affairs, which now amounted to a kind of little fortune, that a child of ten years old might have kept the account and property of them safe in its hands.

I was now restor'd again to my former state of a kept mistress, and used punctually to wait on Mr. Norbert at his chambers whenever he sent a messenger for me, which I constantly took care to be in the way of, and manag'd with so much caution, that he never once penetrated the nature of my connections with Mrs. Cole; but indolently given up to ease and the town dissipations, the perpetual hurry of them hinder'd him from looking into his own affairs, much less to mine.

In the meantime, if I may judge from my own experience, none are better paid, or better treated, during their reign, than the mistresses of those who, enervate by nature, debaucheries, or age, have the least employment for the sex: sensible that a woman must be satisfy'd some way, they ply her with a thousand little tender attentions, presents, caresses, confidences, and exhaust their inventions in means and devices to make up for the capital deficiency; and even towards lessening that, what arts, what modes, what refinements of pleasure have they not recourse to, to raise their languid powers, and press nature into the service of their sensuality? But here is their misfortune, that when by a course of teasing, worrying, handling, wanton postures, lascivious motions, they have at length accomplish'd a flashy enervate enjoyment, they at the same time lighted up a flame in the object of their passion, that, not having the means themselves to quench, drives her for relief into the next person's arms, who can finish their work; and thus they become bawds to some favourite, tried and approv'd of, for a more vigorous and satisfactory execution; for with women, of our turn especially, however well our hearts may be dispos'd, there is a controlling part, or queen-seat in us, that governs itself by its own maxims of state, amongst which not one is stronger in practice with it, than, in the matter of its dues, never to accept the will for the deed.

Mr. Norbert, who was much in this ungracious case, though he profess'd to like me extremely, could but seldom consummate the main joy itself with me without such a length and variety of preparations as were at once wearisome and inflammatory.

Sometimes he would strip me stark naked on a carpet, by a good fire, when he would contemplate me almost by the hour, disposing me in all the figures and attitudes of body that it was susceptible of being viewed in; kissing me in every part, the most secret and critical one so far from excepted, that it received most of that branch of homage. Then his touches were so exquisitely wanton, so luxuriously diffus'd and penetrative at times, that he had me perfectly rage with titillating fires, when, after all, and with much ado, he had gained a short-lived erection, he would perhaps melt it away in a washy sweat, or a premature abortive effusion, that provokingly mock'd my eager desires: or, if carried home, how falter'd and unnervous the execution! how insufficient the sprinkle of a few heat-drops to extinguish all the flames he had kindled!

One evening, I cannot help remembering that, returning home from him, with a spirit he had raised in a circle his wand had prov'd too weak to lay, as I turn'd the corner of a street, I was overtaken by a young sailor. I was then in that spruce, neat, plain dress, which I ever affected, and perhaps might have, in my trip, a certain air of restlessness unknown to the composure of cooler thoughts. However, he seiz'd me as prize, and without further ceremony threw his arms round my neck, and kiss'd me boisterously and sweetly. I looked at him with a beginning of anger and indignation at his rudeness, that softened away into other sentiments as I viewed him: for he was tall, manly carriaged, handsome of body and face, so that I ended my stare, with asking him, in a tone turn'd to tenderness, what he meant; at which, with the same frankness and vivacity as he had begun with me, he proposed treating me with a glass of wine. Now, certain it is, that had I been in a calmer state of blood than I was, had I not been under the dominion of unappeas'd irritations and desires, I should have refused him without hesitation; I do not know how it was, my pressing calls, his figure, the occasion, and if you will, the powerful combination of all these, with a start of curiosity to see the end of an adventure, so novel too as being treated like a common street-player, made me give a silent consent; in short, it was not my head that I now obeyed, I suffered myself to be towed along as it were by this man-of-war, who took me under his arm as familiarly as if he had known me all his life-time and led me into the next convenient tavern, where we were shown into a little room on one side of the passage. Here, scarce allowing himself patience till the drawer brought in the wine call'd for, he fell directly on board me: when, untucking my handkerchief, and giving me a snatching kiss, he laid my breasts bare at once, which he handled with that keenness that abridges a ceremonial ever more tiresome than pleasing on such pressing occasions; and now, hurrying towards the main-point, we found no conveniency to our purpose, two or three disabled chairs, and a rickety table composing the whole furniture of the room. Without more ado, he plants me with my back standing against the wall, and my petticoats up; and coming out with a splitter indeed, made it shine, as he brandished it, in my eyes; and going to work with an impetuosity and eagerness, bred very likely by a long fast at sea, went to give me a taste of it. I straddled, I humoured my posture, and did my best in short to buckle to it; I took part of it in too, but still things did not go to his thorough liking: changing then in a trice his system of battery, he leads me to the table and with a master hand lays my head down on the edge of it, and, with the other canting up my petticoats and shift, bares my naked posteriors to his blind and furious guide; it forces its way between them, and I feeling pretty sensibly that it was not going by the right door, and knocking desperately at the wrong one, I told him of it: – "Pooh!" says he, "my dear, any port in a storm." Altering, however, directly his course, and lowering his point, he fixed it right, and driving it up with a delicious stiffness, made all foam again, and gave me the *tout* with such fire and spirit, that in the fine disposition I was in when I submitted to him, and stirr'd up so fiercely as I was, I got the start of him, and went away into the melting swoon, and squeezing him, whilst in the convulsive grasp of it, drew from him such a plenteous bedewal, as, join'd to my own effusion, perfectly floated those parts, and drown'd in a deluge all my raging conflagration of desire.

When this was over, how to make my retreat was my concern; for, though I had been so extremely pleas'd with the difference between this warm broadside, pour'd so briskly into me, and the tiresome pawing and toying to which I had owed the unappeas'd flames that had driven me into this step, now I was grown cooler, I began to apprehend the danger of contracting an acquaintance with this, however agreeable, stranger; who, on his side, spoke of passing the evening with me and continuing our intimacy, with an air of determination that made me afraid of it's being not so easy to get away from him as I could wish. In the meantime I carefully conceal'd my uneasiness, and readily pretended to consent to stay with him, telling him I should only step to my lodgings to leave a necessary direction, and then instantly return. This he very glibly swallowed, on the notion of my being one of those unhappy street-errants, who devote themselves to the pleasure of the first ruffian that will stoop to pick them up, and of course, that I would scarce bilk myself of my hire, by my not returning to make the most of the job. Thus he parted with me, not before, however, he had order'd in my hearing a supper, which I had the barbarity to refuse.

But when I got home, and told Mrs. Cole my adventure, she represented so strongly to me the nature and dangerous consequences of my folly, particularly the risks to my health, in being so open-legg'd and free, that I not only took resolutions never to venture so rashly again, which I inviolably preserv'd, but pass'd a good many days in continual uneasiness, lest I should have me with other reasons, besides the pleasure of that re-encounter, to remember it; but these fears wronged my pretty sailor, for which I gladly make him this reparation.

I had now liv'd with Mr. Norbert near a quarter of a year, in which space I circulated my time very pleasantly between my amusements at Mrs. Cole's and a proper attendance on that gentleman, who paid me profusely for the unlimited complaisance with which I passively humoured every caprice of pleasure, and which had won upon him so greatly, that finding, as he said, all that variety in me alone, which he had sought for in a number of women, I had made him lose his taste for inconstancy and new faces. But what was yet at least agreeable, as well as more flattering to me as his fondness and attachment, as well as much more flattering the love I had inspir'd him with, bred a deference to me, that was of great service to his health: for having by degrees, and with most pathetic representations brought him to some husbandry of it, and to insure the duration of his pleasures by moderating their use, and correcting those excesses in them he was so addicted to, and which had shatter'd his constitution and destroyed his powers of life in the very point for which he seemed chiefly desirous to live, he was grown more delicate, more temperate, and in course more healthy; his gratitude was taking a turn very favourable for my fortune, when once more the caprice of it dash'd the cup from my lips.

His sister, Lady L . . ., for whom he had a great affection, desiring him to accompany her down to *Bath* for her health, he could not refuse her such a favour; and accordingly, though he counted on staying away from me no more than a week at the most, he took his leave of me with an ominous heaviness of heart, and left me a sum far above the state of his fortune, and very inconsistent with the intended shortness of his journey; but it ended in the longest that can be, and is never but once taken: for, arriv'd at Bath, he was not there two days before he fell into a debauch of drinking with some gentlemen that threw him into a high fever and carry'd him off in four days' time, never once out of a delirium. Had he been in his senses to make a will, perhaps he might have made favourable mention of me in it. Thus, however, I lost him; and as no condition of life is more subject to revolutions than that of a woman of pleasure, I soon regain'd my cheerfulness, and now beholding myself one more struck off the list of kept mistresses, returned into the bosom of the community from which I had been in some manner taken.

Mrs. Cole, still continuing her friendship, offered me her assistance and advice towards another choice; but I was now in ease and affluence enough to look about me at leisure; and as to any constitutional calls of pleasure, their pressure, or sensibility, was greatly lessen'd by a consciousness of the ease with which they were to be satisfy'd at Mrs. Cole's house, where Louisa and Emily still continu'd in the old way; and my great favourite Harriet used often to come and see me, and entertain me, with her head and heart full of the happiness she enjoy'd with her dear baronet, whom she loved with tenderness and constancy, even though he was her keeper, and what is yet more, had made her independent, by a handsome provision for her and hers. I was then in this vacancy from any regular employ of my person, in my way of business, when one day, Mrs. Cole, in the course of the constant confidence we lived in, acquainted me that there was one Mr. Barville, who used her house, just come to town, whom she was not a little perplex'd about providing a suitable companion for; which was indeed a point of difficulty, as he was under the tyranny of a cruel taste: that of an ardent desire, not only of being unmercifully whipp'd himself, but of whipping others, in such sort, that tho' he paid extravagantly those who had the courage and complaisance to submit to his humour, there were few, delicate as he was in the choice of his subjects, who would exchange turns with him so terrible at the expense of their skin. But what yet increased the oddity of this strange fancy was the gentleman being young; whereas it generally attacks, it seems, such as are, through age, obliged to have recourse to this experiment, for quickening the circulation of their sluggish juices, and determining a conflux of the spirits of pleasure towards those flagging, shrively parts, that rise to life only by virtue of those titillating ardours created by the discipline of their opposites, with which they have so surprising a consent.

This Mrs. Cole could not well acquaint me with, in any expectation of my offering my service: for, sufficiently easy as I was in my circumstances, it must have been the temptation of an immense interest indeed that could have induced me to embrace such a job; neither had I ever express'd, nor indeed felt, the least impulse or curiosity to know more of a taste, that promis'd so much more pain than pleasure to those that stood in no need of such violent goads: what then should move me to subscribe myself voluntarily to a party of pain, fore-knowing it such? Why, to tell the plain truth, it was a sudden caprice, a gust of fancy for trying a new experiment, mix'd with the vanity of approving my personal courage to Mrs. Cole, that determined me, at all risks, to propose myself to her and relieve her from any further lookout. Accordingly, I at once pleas'd and surpris'd her, with a frank and unreserved render of my person to her and her friend's absolute disposal on this occasion.

My good temporal mother was, however, so kind as to use all the arguments she could imagine to dissuade me: but, as I found they only turn'd on a motive of tenderness to me, I persisted in my resolution, and thereby acquitted my offer of any suspicion of its not having been sincerely made, or out of compliment only. Acquiescing then thankfully in it, Mrs. Cole assur'd me that, hating the pain I should be put to, she had no scruples to engage me to this party, which she assur'd me I should be liberally paid for, and which the secrecy of the transaction preserved safe from the ridicule that otherwise vulgarly attended it; that for her part, she considered pleasure, of one sort or other, as the universal port of destination, and every wing that blew thither a good one, provided it blew nobody any harm; that she rather compassionated, than blam'd those unhappy persons, who are under a subjection they cannot shake off, to those arbitrary tastes that rule their appetites of pleasures with an unaccountable control: tastes too, as infinitely diversify'd, as superior to, and independent of all reasoning as the different relishes or palates of mankind in their viands, some delicate stomachs nauseating plain meats, and finding no savour but in high-seasoned, luxurious dishes, whilst others again pique themselves upon detesting them.

I stood now in no need of this preambule of encouragement, or justification: my word was given, and I was determin'd to fulfil my engagements. Accordingly the night was set, and I had all the necessary previous instructions how to act and conduct myself. The dining-room was duly prepared and lighted up, and the young gentleman posted there in waiting, for my introduction to him.

I was then, by Mrs. Cole, brought in, and presented to him, in a loose *déshabillé* fitted, by her direction, to the exercise I was to go through, all in the finest linen and a thorough white uniform: gown, petticoat, stockings, and satin slippers, like a victim led to sacrifice; whilst my dark auburn hair, falling in drop-curls over my neck, created a pleasing distinction of colour from the rest of my dress.

As soon as Mr. Barville saw me, he got up, with a visible air of pleasure and surprise, and saluting me, asked Mrs. Cole if it was possible that so fine and delicate a creature would voluntarily submit to such sufferings and rigours, as were the subject of his assignation. She answer'd him properly, and now, reading in his eyes that she could not too soon leave us together, she went out, after recommending to him to use moderation with so tender a novice.

But whilst she was employing his attention, mine had been taken up with examining the figure and person of this unhappy young gentleman, who was thus unaccountably condemn'd to have his pleasure lashed into him, as boys have their learning.

He was exceedingly fair and smooth complexion'd, and appeared to me no more than twenty at most, tho' he was three years older than what my conjectures gave him; but then he ow'd this favourable mistake to a habit of fatness, which spread through a short, squat stature, and a round, plump, fresh coloured face gave him greatly the look of a *Bacchus*, had not an air of austerity, not to say sternness, very unsuitable even to his shape of face, dash'd that character of joy, necessary to complete the resemblance. His dress was extremely neat, but plain, and far inferior to the ample fortune he was in full possession of; this too was a taste in him, and not avarice.

As soon as Mrs. Cole was gone, he seated me near him, when now his face turned upon me, into an expression of the most pleasing sweetness and good humour, the more remarkable for its sudden shift from the other extreme, which, I found afterwards, when I knew more of his character, was owing to a habitual state of conflict with and dislike of himself for being enslaved to so peculiar a taste, by the fatality of a constitutional ascendant, that render'd him incapable of receiving any pleasure till he submitted to these extraordinary means of procuring it at the hands of pain, whilst the constancy of this repining consciousness stamp'd at length that cast of sourness and severity on his features: which was, in fact, very foreign to the natural sweetness of his temper.

After a competent preparation by apologies, and encouragement to go through my part with spirit and constancy, he stood up near the fire, whilst I went to fetch the instruments of discipline out of a closet hard by: these were several rods, made each of two or three strong twigs of birch tied together, which he took, handled, and view'd with as much pleasure as I did with a kind of shuddering presage.

Next we took from the side of the room a long broad bench, made easy to lie at length on by a soft cushion in a calico-cover: and everything being now ready, he took his coat and waistcoat off; and at his motion and desire, I unbutton'd his breeches, and rolling up his shirt rather above his waist, tuck'd it in securely there: when, directing naturally my eyes to that humoursome master-movement, in whose favour all these dispositions were making, it seemed almost shrunk into his body, scarce shewing its tip above the sprout of hairy curls that clothed those parts, as you may have seen a wren peep its head out of the grass.

Stooping then to untie his garters, he gave them me for the use of tying him down to the legs of the bench: a circumstance no further necessary than, as I suppose, it made part of the humour of the thing, since he prescribed it to himself, amongst the rest of the ceremonial.

I led him then to the bench, and according to my cue, play'd at forcing him to lie down: which, after some little show of reluctance, for form's sake, he submitted to; he was straightway extended flat upon his belly, on the bench, with a pillow under his face; and as he thus tamely lay, I tied him tightly, hand and foot, to the legs of it; which done, his shirt remaining truss'd up over the small of his back, I drew his breeches quite down to his knees; and now he lay, in all the fairest, broadest display of that part of the back-view; in which a pair of chubby, smooth-cheek'd and passing white posteriors rose cushioning upwards from two stout, fleshful thighs, and, ending their cleft, or separation, by a union at the small of the back, presented a bold mark, that swell'd, as it were, to meet the scourge.

Seizing now one of the rods, I stood over him, and according to his direction, gave him, in one breath, ten lashes with much good-will and the utmost nerve and vigour of arm that I could put to them, so as to make those fleshy orbs quiver again under them; whilst he himself seem'd no more concern'd, or to mind them, than a lobster would a flea-bite. In the meantime, I viewed intently the effects of them, which to me at least appear'd surprisingly cruel: every lash had skimmed the surface of those white cliffs, which they deeply reddened, and lapping round the side of the furthermost from me, cut specially, into the dimple of it, such livid weals, as the blood either spurt'd out from, or stood in large drops on; and, from some of the cuts, I picked out the splinters of the rod that had stuck in the skin. Nor was this raw work to be wonder'd at, considering the greenness of the twigs and the severity of the infliction, whilst the whole surface of his skin was so smooth-stretched over the hard and firm pulp of flesh that fill'd it, as to yield no play, or elusive swagging under the stroke: which thereby took place the more plum, and cut into the quick.

I was however already so mov'd at the piteous sight, that I from my heart repented the undertaking, and would willingly have given over, thinking he had full enough; but, he encouraging and beseeching me earnestly to proceed, I gave him ten more lashes; and then, resting, survey'd the increase of bloody appearances. And at length, steel'd to the sight, by his stoutness in suffering, I continued the discipline, by intervals, till I observ'd him writhing and twisting his body in a way that I could plainly perceive was not the effect of pain, but of some new and powerful sensation: curious to delve into the meaning, in one of my pauses of intermission I approached, as he still kept working and grinding his belly against the cushion under him; and, first stroking the untouched and unhurt side of the fleshmount next me, then softly insinuating my hand under this thigh, felt the posture things were in forwards, which was indeed surprising: for that machine of his, which I had, by its appearance, taken for an impalpable, or at best a very diminutive subject, was now, in virtue of all that smart and havoc of his skin behind, grown not only to a prodigious stiffness of erection, but to a size that frighted even me: a non-pareil thickness indeed! the head of it alone fill'd the utmost capacity of my grasp. And when, as he heav'd and wriggled to and fro, in the agitation of his strange pleasure, it came into view, it had something of the air of a round fillet of the whitest veal, and like its owner, squat, and short in proportion to its breadth; but when he felt my hand there, he begg'd I would go on briskly with my jerking, or he should never arrive at the last stage of pleasure.

Resuming then the rod and the exercise of it, I had fairly worn out three bundles, when, after an increase of struggles and motion, and a deep sigh or two, I saw him lie still and motionless; and now he desir'd me to desist, which I instantly did; and proceeding to untie him, I could not but be amazed at his passive fortitude, on viewing the skin of his butcher'd, mangled posteriors late so white, smooth and polish'd, now all one side of them a confused network of weals, livid flesh, gashes and gore, so much so that when he stood up he could scarce walk; in short, he was in sweet-briars.

Then I plainly perceived, on the cushion, the marks of a plenteous effusion, and already had his sluggard member run up to its old nestling-place, and enforced itself again, as if ashamed to show its head; which nothing, it seems, could raise but stripes inflicted on its opposite neighbours who were thus constantly obliged to suffer for his caprice.

My gentleman had now put on his clothes and recomposed himself, when, giving me a kiss, and placing me by him, he sat himself down as gingerly as possible, with one side off the cushion, which was too sore for him to bear resting any part of his weight on.

Here he thanked me for the extreme pleasure I had procured him, and seeing, perhaps, some marks in my countenance of terror and apprehension of retaliation on my own skin, for what I had been the instrument of his suffering in his, he assured me he was ready to give up to me any engagement I might deem myself under to stand him, as he had done me, but if that proceeded in my consent to it, he would consider the difference of my sex, its greater delicacy and incapacity to undergo pain. Rehearten'd at which, and piqu'd in honour, as I thought, not to flinch so near the trial, especially as I well knew Mrs. Cole was an eyewitness to the whole of our transactions, I was now less afraid of my skin than of his not furnishing me with an opportunity of signalizing my resolution.

Consonant to this disposition was my answer, but my courage was still more in my head than in my heart; and, as cowards rush into the danger they fear, in order to be the sooner rid of the pain of that sensation, I was entirely pleas'd with his hastening matters into execution.

He had then little to do but to unloose the strings of my petticoats, and lift them, together with my shift, navel-high, where he just tuck'd them up loosely girt, and might be slipt up higher at pleasure. Then viewing me round with great seeming delight, he laid me at length on my face upon the bench, and when I expected he would tie me, as I had done him, and held out my hands, not without fear and a little trembling, he told me he would by no means terrify me unnecessarily with such a confinement; for that though he meant to put my constancy to some trial, the standing it was to be completely voluntary on my side, and therefore I might be at full liberty to get up whenever I found the pain too much for me. You cannot imagine how much I thought myself bound, by being thus allow'd to remain loose, and how much spirit this confidence in me gave me, so that I was even from my heart careless how much my flesh might suffer in honour of it.

All my back parts, naked half-way up, were now fully at his mercy: and first, he stood at a convenient distance, delighting himself with a gloating survey of the attitude I lay in, and of all the secret stores I thus expos'd to him in fair display. Then, springing eagerly towards me, he cover'd all those naked parts with a fond profusion of kisses; and now, taking hold of the rod, rather wanton'd with me, in gentle inflictions on those tender trembling masses of my flesh behind, than in any way hurt them, till by degrees, he began to tingle them with smarter lashes, so as to provoke a red colour into them, which I knew, as well by the flagrant glow I felt there, as by his telling me, they now emulated the native roses of my other cheeks. When he had thus amus'd himself with admiring, and toying with them, he went on to strike harder, and more hard; so that I needed all my patience not to cry out, or complain at least. At last, he twigg'd me so smartly as to fetch blood in more than one lash: at sight of which he flung down the rod, flew to me, kissed away the starting drops, and, sucking the wounds, eased a good deal of my pain. But now raising me on my knees, and making me kneel with them straddling wide, that tender part of me, naturally the province of pleasure, not of pain, came in for its share of suffering: for now, eyeing it wistfully, he directed the rod so that the sharp ends of the twigs lighted there, so sensibly, that I could not help wincing, and writhing my limbs with pain; so that my contortions of body must necessarily throw it into infinite variety of postures and points of view, fit to feast the luxury of the eye. But still I bore everything without crying out: when presently, giving me another pause, he rush'd, as it were, on that part whose lips, and round-about, had felt this cruelty, and by way of reparation, glues his own to them; then he opened, shut, squeez'd them, pluck'd softly the overgrowing moss, and all this in a style of wild passionate rapture and enthusiasm, that express'd excess of pleasure; till, betaking himself to the rod again, encourag'd by my passiveness and infuriated with this strange taste of delight, he made my poor posteriors pay for the ungovernableness of it; for now showing them no quarter, the traitor cut me so that I wanted but little of fainting away, when he gave over. And yet I did not utter one groan, or make any angry expostulation; but in heart I resolv'd never to expose myself again to the like severities.

You may guess what a curious pickle those soft flesh-cushions of mine were, all sore, raw, and terribly clawed off; but so far from feeling any pleasure in it, that the recent pain made me pout a little, and not with the greatest air of satisfaction receive the compliments and after-caresses of the author of my pain.

As soon as my clothes were huddled on in a little decency, a supper was brought in by the discreet Mrs. Cole herself, which might have piqued the sensuality of a cardinal, accompanied with a choice of the richest wines: all which she set before us, and went out again, without having, by a word or even by a smile, given us the least interruption or confusion, in those moments of secrecy, that we were not yet ripe to the admission of a third to.

I sat down then, still scarce in charity with my butcher, for such I could not help considering him, and was moreover not a little piqued at the gay satisfied air of his countenance, which I thought myself insulted by. But when the now necessary refreshment to me of a glass of wine, a little eating (all the time observing a profound silence) had somewhat cheer'd and restor'd me to spirits, and as the pain began to go away, my good humour return'd accordingly: which alteration not escaping him, he said and did everything that could confirm me in, and indeed exalt it.

But scarce was supper well over, before a change so incredible was wrought in me, such violent, yet pleasingly irksome sensations took possession of me that I scarce knew how to contain myself; the smart of the lashes was now converted into such a prickly heat, such fiery tinglings, as made me sigh, squeeze my thighs together, shift and wriggle about my seat with a furious restlessness; whilst these itching ardours, thus excited in those parts on which the storm of discipline had principally fallen, detach'd legions of burning, subtle, stimulating spirits to their opposite spot and centre of assemblage, where their titillation rag'd so furiously, that I was even stinging mad with them. No wonder then, that in such a taking, and devour'd by flames that licked up all modesty and reserve, my eyes, now charg'd brimful of the most intense desire, fired on my companion very intelligible signals of distress: my companion, I say, who grew in them every instant more amiable, and more necessary to my urgent wishes and hopes of immediate ease. Mr. Barville, no stranger, by experience, to these situations, soon knew the pass I was brought to from my extreme disorder; in favour of which, removing the table out of the way, he began a prelude that flatter'd me with instant relief, to which I was not, however, so near as I imagin'd: for as he was unbuttoned to me, and tried to provoke and rouse to action his unactive torpid machine, he blushingly own'd that no good was to be expected from it, unless I took it in hand to re-excite its languid loitering powers, by just refreshing the smart of the yet recent blood-drawn cuts, seeing it could, no more than a boy's top, keep up without lashing. Sensible then that I should work so much for my own profit as his, I hurried my compliance with his desire, and abridging the ceremonial, whilst he lean'd his head against the back of a chair, I had scarce gently made him feel the lash, before I saw the object of my wishes give signs of life, and presently, as it were with a magic touch, it started up into a noble size and distinction indeed! Hastening then to give me the benefit of it, he threw me down on the bench; but such was the refresh'd soreness of those parts behind, on my leaning so hard on them, as became me to compass the admission of that stupendous head of his machine, that I could not possibly bear it. I got up then, and tried, by leaning forwards, and turning the crupper on my assailant, to let him at the back avenue: but here it was likewise impossible to stand his bearing so fiercely against me, in his agitations and endeavours to enter that way, whilst his belly battered directly against the recent sore. What should we do now? both intolerably heated, both in a fury; but pleasure is ever inventive for its own ends: he strips me in a trice, stark naked, and placing a broad settee-cushion on the carpet before the fire, oversets me gently, topsy-turvy, on it; and handling me only at the waist, whilst you may be sure I favour'd all my dispositions, brought my legs round his neck: so that my head was kept from the floor only by my hands and the velvet cushion, which was now bespread with my flowing hair: thus I stood on my head and hands, supported by him in such manner, that whilst my thighs clung round him, so as to expose to his sight all my back figure, including the theatre of his bloody pleasure, the centre of my fore part fairly bearded the object of its rage, that now stood in fine condition to give me satisfaction for the injuries of its neighbours. But as this posture was certainly not the easiest, and our imaginations, wound up to the height, could suffer no delay, he first, with the utmost eagerness and effort, just liplodg'd that broad acorn-fashion'd head of his instrument; and still frenzied by the fury with which he had made that impression, he soon stuffed in the rest; when now, with a pursuit of thrusts, fiercely urg'd, he absolutely overpower'd and absorb'd all sense of pain and uneasiness, whether from my wounds behind, my most untoward posture, of the oversize of his stretcher, in an infinitely predominant delight; when now all my whole spirits of life and sensation, rushing impetuously to the cockpit, where the prize of pleasure was hotly in dispute and clustering to a point there, I soon receiv'd the dear relief of nature from these overviolent strains and provocations of it; harmonizing with which, my gallant spouted into me such a potent overflow of the balsamic injection, as soften'd and unedg'd all those irritating stings of a new species of titillation, which I had been so intolerably madden'd with, and restor'd the ferment of my senses to some degree of composure.

I had now achiev'd this rare adventure ultimately much more to my satisfaction than I had bespoken the nature of it to turn out; nor was it much lessn'd, you may think, by my spark's lavish praises of my constancy and complaisance, which he gave weight to by a present that greatly surpassed my utmost expectation, besides his gratification to Mrs. Cole.

I was not, however, at any time, re-enticed to renew with him, or resort again to the violent expedient of lashing nature into more haste than good speed: which, by the way, I conceive acts somewhat in the manner of a dose of Spanish flies; with more pain perhaps, but less danger; and might be necessary to him, but was nothing less to than to me, whose appetite wanted the bridle more than the spur.

Mrs. Cole, to whom this adventurous exploit had more and more endear'd me, looked on me now as a girl after her own heart, afraid of nothing, and, on a good account hardly enough to fight all the weapons of pleasure through. Attentive then, in consequence of these favourable conceptions, to promote either my profit or pleasure, she had special regard for the first, in a new gallant of a very singular turn, that she procur'd for and introduced to me.

This was a grave, staid, solemn, elderly gentleman, whose peculiar humour was a delight in combing fine tresses of hair; and as I was perfectly heated to his taste, he us'd to come constantly at my toilette hours, when I let down my hair as loose as nature, and abandon'd it to him to do what he pleased with it; and accordingly he would keep me an hour or more in play with it, drawing the comb through it, winding the curls round his fingers, even kissing it as he smooth'd it; and all this led to no other use of my person, or any other liberties whatever, any more than if a distinction of sexes had not existed.

Another peculiarity of taste he had, which was to present me with a dozen pairs of the whitest kid gloves at a time: these he would divert himself with drawing on me, and then biting off the finger ends; all which fooleries of a sickly appetite the old gentleman paid more liberally for, than most others did for more essential favours. This lasted till a violent cough, seizing and laying him up, deliver'd me from this most innocent and insipid trifler, for I never heard more of him after his first retreat.

You may be sure a by-jod of this sort interfer'd with no other pursuit, or plan of life; which I led, in truth, with a modesty and reserve that was less the work of virtue than of exhausted novelty, a glut of pleasure, and easy circumstances, that made me indifferent to any engagements in which pleasure and profit were not eminently united; and such I could, with the less impatience, wait for at the hands of time and fortune, as I was satisfy'd I could never mend my pennyworths, having evidently been serv'd at the top of market, and even been pamper'd with dainties: besides that, in the sacrifice of a few momentary impulses, I found a secret satisfaction in respecting myself, as well as preserving the life and freshness of my complexion. Louisa and Emily did not carry indeed their reserve so high as I did; but still they were far from cheap or abandon'd, tho' two of their adventures seem'd to contradict this general character, which, for their singularity, I shall give you in course, beginning first with Emily's:

Louisa and she went one night to a ball, the first in the habit of a shepherdess, Emily in that of a shepherd: I saw them in their dresses before they went, and nothing in nature could represent a prettier boy than this last did, being so fair and well limbed. They had kept together for some time, when Louisa, meeting an old acquaintance of hers, very cordially gives her companion the drop, and leaves her under the protection of her boy's habit, which was not much, and of her discretion, which was, it seems, still less. Emily, finding herself deserted, sauntered thoughtless about a while, and, as much for coolness and air as anything else, at length pull'd off her mask and went to the sideboard; where, eyed and mark'd out by a gentleman in a very handsome domino, she was accosted by, and fell into chat with him. The domino, after a little discourse, in which Emily doubtless distinguish'd her good nature and easiness more than her wit, began to make violent love to her, and drawing her insensibly to some benches at the lower end of the masquerade room, got her to sit by him, where he squeez'd her hands, pinch'd her cheeks, prais'd and played with her fine hair, admired her complexion, and all in a style of courtship dash'd with a certain oddity that, not comprehending the mystery of, poor Emily attributed to his falling in with the humour of her disguise; and being naturally not the cruellest of her profession, began to incline to a parley on those essentials. But here was the joke: he took her really for what she appear'd to be, a smock-fac'd boy; and she, forgetting her dress, and of course ranging quite wide of ideas, took all those addresses to be paid to herself as a woman, which she precisely owed to his not thinking her one. However, this double error was push'd to such a height on both sides, that Emily, who saw nothing in him but a gentleman of distinction by those points of dress to which his disguise did not extend, warmed too by the wine he had ply'd her with and the caresses he had lavished upon her, suffered herself to be persuaded to go to a bagnio with him; and thus, losing sight of Mrs. Cole's cautions, with a blind confidence, put herself into his hands, to be carried wherever he pleased. For his part, equally blinded by his wishes, whilst her gregious simplicity favoured his deception more than the most exquisite art could have done, he supposed, no doubt, that he had lighted on some soft simpleton, fit for his purpose, or some kept minion broken to his hand, who understood him perfectly well, and enter'd into his designs. But, be that as it may, he led her to a coach, went into it with her, and brought her to a very handsome apartment, with a bed in it, but whether it was a bagnio or not, she could not tell, having spoken to nobody but himself. But when they were alone together, and her *enamorato* began to proceed to those extremities which instantly discover the sex, she remark'd that no description could paint up to the life, the mixture of pique, confusion and disappointment that appeared in his countenance, joined to the mournful exclamation: "By heavens, a woman!" This at once opened her eyes, which had hitherto been shut in downright stupidity. However, as if he had meant to retrieve that escape, he still continu'd to toy with and fondle her, but with so staring an alteration from extreme warmth into a chill and forced civility that even Emily herself could not but take notice of it, and now began to wish she had paid more regard to Mrs. Cole's premonitions against ever engaging with a stranger. And now an excess of timidity succeeded to an excess of confidence, and she thought herself so much at his mercy and discretion that she stood passive throughout the whole progress of his prelude: for now, whether the impressions of so great a beauty had even made him forgive her her sex, or whether her appearance of figure in that dress still humour'd his first illusion, he recover'd by degrees a good part of his first warmth, and keeping Emily with her breeches still unbuttoned, stript them down to her knees, and gently impelling her to lean down, with her face against the bedside, placed her so, that the double way, between the double rising behind, presented the choice fair to him, and he was so fairly set on a misdirection as to give the girl no small alarm for fear of losing a maidenhead she had not dreamt of. However, her complaints, and a resistance, gentle but firm, check'd and brought him to himself again; so that turning his steed's head, he drove him at length in the right road, in which his imagination having probably made the most of those resemblances that flatter'd his taste, he got, with much ado, to his journey's end: after which, he led her out himself, and walking with her two or three streets length, got her a chair, when, making her a present not anything inferior to what she could have expected, he left her, well recommended to the chairmen, who, on her directions, brought her home.

This she related to Mrs. Cole and me the same morning, not without the visible remains of the fear and confusion she had been in still stamp'd on her countenance. Mrs. Cole's remark was, that her indiscretion proceeding from a constitutional facility, there were little hopes of anything curing her of it but repeated severe experience. Mine was, that I could not conceive how it was possible for mankind to run into a taste, not only universally odious, but absurd, and impossible to gratify; since, according to the notions and experience I had of things, it was not in nature to force such immense disproportions. Mrs. Cole only smil'd at my ignorance, and said nothing towards my undeception, which was not affected but by ocular demonstration, some months after, which a most singular accident furnish'd me, and which I will here set down, that I may not return again to so disagreeable a subject.

I had, on a visit intended to Harriet, who had taken lodgings at *Hampton-court*, hired a chariot to go out thither, Mrs. Cole having promis'd to accompany me; but some indispensable business intervening to detain her, I was obliged to set out alone; and scarce had I got a third of my way, before the axle-tree broke down, and I was well off to get out, safe and unhurt, into a public-house of a tolerable handsome appearance, on the road. Here the people told me that the stage would come by in a couple of hours at farthest; upon which, determining to wait for it, sooner than lose the jaunt I had got so far forward on, I was carried into a very clean decent room, up one pair of stairs, which I took possession of for the time I had to stay, in right of calling for sufficient to do the house justice.

Here, whilst I was amusing myself with looking out of the window, a single horse-chaise stopt at the door, out of which lightly leap'd two young gentlemen, for so they seem'd, who came in only as it were to refresh themselves a little, for they gave their horse to be held in readiness until they came out. And presently I heard the door of the next room, where they were let in, and call'd about them briskly; and as soon as they were serv'd, I could just hear that they shut and fastened the door on the inside.

A spirit of curiosity, far from sudden, since I do not know when I was without it, prompted me, without any particular suspicion, or other drift or view, to see what they were, and examine their persons and behaviour. The partition of our rooms was one of those moveable ones that, when taken down, serv'd occasionally to lay them into one, for the conveniency of a large company; and now, my nicest search could not show me the shadow of a peep-hole, a circumstance which probably had not escap'd the review of the parties on the other side, whom much it stood upon not to be deceived in it; but at length I observed a paper patch of the same colour as the wainscot, which I took to conceal some flaw: but then it was so high, that I was obliged to stand upon a chair to reach it, which I did as softly as possibly, and, with a point of a bodkin, soon pierc'd it. And now, applying my eye close, I commanded the room perfectly, and could see my two young sparks romping and pulling one another about, entirely, to my imagination, in frolic and innocent play.

The eldest might have been, on my nearest guess, towards nineteen, a tall comely young man, in a white fustian frock, with a green velvet cape, and a cut bob-wig.

The youngest could not have been above seventeen; fair, ruddy, completely well made, and to say the truth, a sweet pretty stripling: he was I fancy too, a country lad, by his dress, which was a green plush frock, and breeches of the same, white waistcoat and stockings, a jockey cap, with his yellowish hair, long and loose, in natural curls.

But after a look of circumspection, which I saw the eldest cast every way round the room, probably in too much hurry and heat not to overlook the very small opening I was posted at, especially at the height it was, whilst my eye close to it kept the light from shining through and betraying it, he said something to his companion that presently chang'd the face of things.

For now the elder began to embrace, to press and kiss the younger, to put his hands into his bosom, and give him such manifest signs of an amorous intention, as made me conclude the other to be a girl in disguise: a mistake that nature kept me in countenance for, for she had certainly made one, when she gave him the male stamp.

In the rashness then of their age, and bent as they were to accomplish their project of preposterous pleasure, at the risk of the very worst of consequences, where a discovery was nothing less than improbable, they now proceeded to such lengths as soon satisfied me what they were.

The criminal scene, I had the patience to see to an end, purely that I might gather more facts and certainly against them in my design to do their deserts instant justice; accordingly, when they had re-adjusted themselves, and were preparing to go out, burning as I was with rage and indignation, I jump'd down from the chair, in order to raise the house upon them, but with such an unlucky impetuosity, that some nail or ruggedness in the floor caught my foot, and flung me on my face with such violence, that I fell senseless on the ground, and must have lain there some time e'er anyone came to my relief: so that they, alarmed, I suppose, by the noise of my fall, had more than the necessary time to make a safe retreat. This they effected, as I learnt, with a precipitation nobody could account for, till, when come to myself, and compos'd enough to speak, I acquainted those of the house with the whole transaction I had been evidence to.

When I came home again, and told Mrs. Cole this adventure, she very sensibly observ'd to me, that there was no doubt of due vengeance one time or other overtaking these miscreants, however they might escape for the present; and that, had I been the temporal instrument of it, I should have been at least put to a great deal more trouble and confusion than I imagined; that, as to the thing itself, the less said of it the better; but that though she might be suspected of partiality, from its being the common cause of womankind, out of whose mouths this practise tended to make something more than bread, yet she protested against any mixture of passion, with a declaration extorted from her by pure regard to truth; which was, that whatever effect this infamous passion had in other ages and other countries, it seem'd a peculiar blessing on our air and climate, that there was a plague-spot visibly imprinted on all that are tainted with it, in this nation at least; for that among numbers of that stamp whom she had known, or at least universally under the scandalous suspicion of it, she would not name an exception hardly of one of them, whose character was not, in all other respects, the most worthless and despicable that could be, stript of all the manly virtues of their own sex, and fill'd up with only the worst vices and follies of ours: that, *in fine*, they were scarce less execrable than ridiculous in their monstrous inconsistence, of loathing and condemning women, and all at the same time apeing their manners, airs, lips, skuttle, and, in general, all their little modes of affectation, which become them at least better, than they do these unsex'd, male-misses.

But here, washing my hands of them, I re-plunge into the stream of my history, into which I may very properly add a terrible sally of Louisa's, since I had some share in it myself, and have besides engag'd myself to relate it, in point of countenance to poor Emily. It will add, too, one more example to thousands, in confirmation of the maxim that once women get out of compass, there are no lengths of licentiousness that they are not capable of running.

One morning then, that both Mrs. Cole and Emily were gone out for the day, and only Louisa and I (not to mention the house-maid) were left in charge of the house, whilst we were loitering away the time, in looking through the shop windows, the son of a poor woman, who earned very hard bread indeed by mending of stockings, in a stall in the neighbourhood, offer'd us some nosegays, rang'd round a small basket; by selling of which the poor boy eked out his mother's maintenance of them both: nor was he fit for any other way of livelihood, since he was not only a perfect changeling, or idiot, but stammer'd so that there was no understanding even those sounds his half-dozen at most, animal ideas, prompted him to utter.

The boys and servants in the neighbourhood had given him the nickname of *Good-natured Dick*, from the soft simpleton's doing everything he was bid at the first word, and from his naturally having no turn to mischief; then, by the way, he was perfectly well made, stout, clean-limb'd, tall for his age, as strong as a horse and, withal, pretty featur'd; so that he was not, absolutely, such a figure to be snuffled at neither, if your nicety could, in favour of such essentials, have dispens'd with a face un-washed, hair tangled for want of combing, and so ragged a plight, that he might have disputed points of show with e'er a heathen philosopher of them all.

This boy we had often seen, and bought his flowers, out of pure compassion, and nothing more; but just then, as he stood presenting us his basket, a sudden whim, a start of wayward fancy, seiz'd Louisa; and, without consulting me, she calls him in, and beginning to examine his nosegays, culls out two, one for herself, another for me, and pulling out half a crown, very currently gives it him to change, as if she had really expected he could have changed it: but the boy, scratching his head, made his signs explain his in-ability in place of words, which he could not, with all his struggling, articulate.

Louisa, at this, says: "Well, my lad, come upstairs with me, and I will give you your due," winking at the same time to me, and beckoning me to accompany her, which I did, securing first the street-door, that by this means, together with the shop, became wholly the care of the faithful house-maid.

As we went up, Louisa whispered to me that she had conceiv'd a strange longing to be satisfy'd, whether the general rule held good with regard to this changeling, and how far nature had made him amends, in her best bodily gifts, for her denial of the sublimer intellectual ones; begging, at the same time, my assistance in procuring her this satisfaction. A want of complaisance was never my vice, and I was so far from opposing this extravagant frolic that now, bit with the same maggot, and my curiosity conspiring with hers, I enter'd straightway into it on my own account.

Consequently, as soon as we came into Louisa's bed-chamber, whilst she was amusing him with picking out his nosegays, I undertook the lead, and began the attack. As it was not then very material to keep much measures with a mere natural, I made presently very free with him, though at my first motion of meddling, his surprise and confusion made him receive my advances but awkwardly; nay, so much so that he bashfully shy'd, and shy'd back a little; till encouraging him with my eyes, plucking him playfully by the hair, sleeking his cheeks, and forwarding my point by a number of little wantonnesses, I soon turn'd him familiar, and gave nature her sweetest alarm: so that arous'd, and beginning to feel himself, we could, amidst all the innocent laugh and grin I had provoked him into, perceive the fire lighting in his eyes, and, diffusing over his cheeks, blend its glow with that of his blushes. The emotion in short of animal pleasure glar'd distinctly in the simpleton's countenance; yet, struck with the novelty of the scene, he did not know which way to look or move; but tame, passive, simpering, with his mouth half open, in stupid rapture, stood and tractably suffer'd me to do what I pleased with him. His basket was dropt out of his hands, which Louisa took care of.

I had now, through more than one rent, discovered and felt his thighs, the sink of which seemed the smoother and fairer for the coarseness, and even dirt of his dress, as the teeth of Negroes seem the whiter for the surrounding black; and poor indeed of habit, poor of understanding, he was, however, abundantly rich in personal treasures, such as flesh, firm, plump, and replete with the juice of youth, and robust well-knit limbs. My fingers too had now got within reach of the true, the genuine sensitive plant, which, instead of shrinking from the touch, joys to meet it, and swells and vegetates under it: mine pleasingly informed me that matters were so ripe for the discovery we meditated, that they were too mighty for the confinement they were ready to break. A waistband that I unskewer'd, and a rag of a shirt that I removed, and which could not have cover'd a quarter of it, revealed the whole of the idiot's standard of distinction, erect, in full pride and display: but such a one! it was positively of so tremendous a size that, prepared as we were to see something extraordinary, it still, out of measure, surpass'd our expectation, and astonish'd even me, who had not been used to trade in trifles. *In fine,* it might have answered very well the making a show of; its enormous head seemed, in hue and size, not unlike a common sheep's heart; then you might have troll'd dice securely along the broad back of the body of it; the length of it too was prodigious; then the rich appendage of the treasure-bag beneath, large in proportion, gather'd and crisp'd up round in shallow furrows, helped to fill the eye, and complete the proof of his being a natural, not quite in vain; since it was full manifest that he inherited, and largely too, the prerogative of majesty which distinguishes that otherwise most unfortunate condition, and gives rise to the vulgar saying: "*A fool's bauble is a lady's play-fellow.*" Not wholly without reason: for, generally speaking, it is in love as it is in war, where longest weapon carries it. Nature, in short, had done so much for him in those parts, that she perhaps held herself acquitted in doing so little for his head.

For my part, who had sincerely no intention to push the joke further than simply satisfying my curiosity with the sight of it alone, I was content, in spite of the temptation that star'd me in the face, with having rais'd a May-pole for another to hand a garland on: for, by this time, easily reading Louisa's desires in her wishful eyes, I acted the commodious part and made her, who sought no better sport, significant terms of encouragement to go through with her adventure; intimating too that I would stay and see fair play: in which, indeed, I had in view to humour a new-born curiosity, to observe what appearances active nature would put on in such a simpleton, in the course of this her darling operation.

Louisa, whose appetite was up, and who, like the industrious bee, was, it seems, not above gathering the sweets of so rare a flower, tho' she found it planted on a dunghill, was but too readily disposed to take the benefit of my cession. Urg'd then strongly by her own desires, and embolden'd by me, she presently determined to risk a trial of parts with the idiot, who was by this time nobly inflam'd for her purpose by all the irritations we had used to put the principles of pleasure effectually into motion, and to wind up the springs of its organ to their supreme pitch; and it stood accordingly stiff and straining, ready to burst with the blood and spirits that swelled it . . . No! I shall never forget it!

Louisa then, taking and holding the fine handle that so invitingly offer'd itself, led the ductile youth, by that master tool of his, as she stepped backwards towards the bed; while he joyfully gave way under the incitations of instinct, and palpably deliver'd up to the goad of desire.

Stopped then by the bed, she took the fall she lov'd, and lean'd to the most, gently backward upon it, still holding fast what she held, and taking care to give her clothes a convenient toss up, so that her thighs, duly disclos'd, and elevated, laid open all the outward prospect of the treasury of love: the rose-lipt overture presenting the cockpit so fair, that it was not in nature even for an idiot to miss it. Nor did he: for Louisa, fully bent on grappling with it, and impatient of dalliance or delay, directed faithfully the point of the battering-piece, then bounded up with a rage of so voracious appetite, to meet and favour the thrust of insertion, that the fierce activity on both sides effected it with such pain of distention, that Louisa cry'd out violently that she was hurt beyond bearing, that she was killed. But it was too late: the storm was up, and force was on her to give way to it; for now the man-machine, strongly work'd upon by the sensual passion, felt so manfully his advantages and superiority, felt withal the sting of pleasure so intolerable, that maddening with it, his joys began to assume a character of furiousness, which made me tremble for the too tender Louisa. He seemed, at this juncture, greater than himself; his countenance, before so void of meaning, or expression, now grew big with the importance of the act he was upon. In short, it was not now that he was to be play'd the fool with. But, what is pleasant enough, I myself was aw'd into a sort of respect for him, by the comely terrors his motions dressed him in: his eyes shooting sparks of fire; his face glowing with ardours that gave another life to it; his teeth churning; his whole frame agitated with a raging ungovernable impetuosity: all sensibly betraying the formidable fierceness with which the genial instinct acted upon him. Butting then and goring all before him, and mad and wild like an over-driven steer, he ploughs up the tender furrow, all insensible to Louisa's complaints; nothing can stop, nothing can keep out a fury like his: with which, having once got its head in, its blind rage soon made way for the rest: piercing, rending, and breaking open all obstruction. The torn, split, wounded girl cries, struggles, invokes me to her rescue, and endeavours to get from under the young savage, or shake him off, but alas! in vain: her breath might as soon have still'd, or stemm'd a storm in winter, as all her strength have quell'd his rough assault, or put him out of his course. And indeed, all her efforts and struggles were manag'd with such disorder, that they serv'd rather to entangle, and fold her the faster in the twine of his boisterous arms; so that she was tied to the stake, and oblig'd to fight the match out, if she died for it. For his part, instinct-ridden as he was, the expressions of his animal passion, partaking something of ferocity, were rather worrying than kisses, intermix'd with eager ravenous love-bites on her cheeks and neck, the prints of which did not wear out for some days after.

Poor Louisa, however, bore up at length better than could have been expected; and though she suffer'd, and greatly too, yet, ever true to the good old cause, she suffer'd with pleasure and enjoyed her pain. And soon now, by dint of an enrag'd enforcement, the brute-machine, driven like a whirlwind, made all smoke again, and wedging its way up, to the utmost extremity, left her, in point of penetration, nothing to fear or to desire: and now, "*gorg'd with the dearest morsel of the earth,*" Louisa lay, pleas'd to the heart, pleas'd to her utmost capacity of being so, with every fibre in those parts stretched almost to breaking, on a rack of joy, whilst the instrument of all this overfulness searched her senses with its sweet excess, till the pleasure gained upon her so, its point stung her so home, that catching at length the rage from her furious driver and sharing the riot of his wild rapture, she went wholly out of her mind into that favourite part of her body, the whole intenseness of which was so mightily fill'd, and employ'd: there alone she existed, all lost in those delirious transports, those ecstasies of the senses, which her winking eyes, the brighten'd vermilion of her lips and cheeks, and sighs of pleasure deeply fetched, so pathetically express'd. In short, she was now as mere a machine as much wrought on, and had her motions as little at her own command as the idiot himself, who, thus broke in upon her, made her feel with a vengeance his tempestuous tenderness, and the force of the mettle he battered with; their active loins quivered again with the violence of their conflict, till the surge of pleasure, foaming and raging to a height, drew down the pearly shower that was to allay this hurricane. The purely sensitive idiot then first shed those tears of joy that attend its last moments, not without an agony of delight, and even almost a roar of rapture, as the gush escaped him; so rapturous too for Louisa that she kept him faithful company, going off, in consent, with the old symptoms: a delicious delirium, a tremulous convulsive shudder, and the critical dying: Oh! And now, on his getting off, she lay pleasure-drench'd, and regorging its essential sweets; but quite spent, and gasping for breath, without other sensation of life than in those exquisite vibrations that trembled yet on the strings of delight, which had been too intensively touched, and which nature had been so intensely stirred with, for the senses to be quickly at peace from.

As for the changeling, whose curious engine had been thus successfully played off, his shift of countenance and gesture had even something droll, or rather tragi-comic in it: there was now an air of sad repining foolishness, added to his natural air of stupidity, as he stood with his label of manhood now lank, unstiffen'd, becalm'd and flapping against his thighs, down which it reach'd half-way, terrible even in its fall, whilst under the dejection of spirit and flesh, which naturally followed, his eyes, by turns, cast down towards his struck standard, or piteously lifted to Louisa, seemed to require at her hands what he had so sensibly parted from to her, and now ruefully miss'd. But the vigour of nature, soon returning, dissipated the blast of faintness which the common law of enjoyment had subjected him to; and now his basket re-became his main concern, which I look'd for, and brought him, whilst Louisa restor'd his dress to its usual condition, and afterwards pleased him perhaps more by taking all his flowers off his hands, and paying him, at his rate for them, than if she had embarrass'd him by a present that he would have been puzzled to account for, and might have put others on tracing the motives of.

Whether she ever return'd to the attack I know not, and, to say the truth, I believe not. She had had her freak out, and had pretty plentifully drown'd her curiosity in a glut of pleasure, which, as it happened, had no other consequence than that the lad, who retain'd only a confused memory of the transaction, would, when he saw her, for some time after, express a grin of joy and familiarity, after his idiot manner, and soon forgot her in favour of the next woman, tempted, on the report of his parts, to take him in.

Louisa herself did not long outstay this adventure at Mrs. Cole's (to whom, by the bye, we took care not to boast of our exploit, till all fear of consequences were clearly over): for an occasion presenting itself of proving her passion for a young fellow, at the expense of her discretion, proceeding all in character, she pack'd up her toilet, at half a day's warning, and went with him abroad, since which I entirely lost sight of her, and it never fell in my way to hear what became of her.

But a few days after she had left us, two very pretty young gentlemen, who were Mrs. Cole's especial favourites, and free of her academy, easily obtain'd her consent for Emily's and my acceptance of a party of pleasure, at a little but agreeable house, belonging to one of them situated not far up the river Thames, on the Surry side.

Everything being settled, and it being a fine summer day, but rather of the warmest, we set out after dinner, and got to our rendezvous about four in the afternoon; where, landing at the foot of a neat, joyous pavilion, Emily and I were ushered by our squires, and there drank tea with a cheerfulness and gaiety that the beauty of the prospect, the serenity of the weather, and the tender politeness of our sprightly gallants naturally led us.

After tea, and taking a turn in the garden, my particular, who was the master of the house, and had in no sense schem'd this party of pleasure for a dry one, propos'd to us, with that frankness which his familiarity at Mrs. Cole's entitled him to, as the weather was excessively hot, to bathe together, under a commodious shelter that he had prepared expressly for that purpose, in a creek of the river, with which a side door of the pavilion immediately communicated, and where we might be sure of having our diversion out, safe from interruption, and with the utmost privacy.

Emily, who never refus'd anything, and I, who ever delighted in bathing, and had no exception to the person who propos'd it, or to those pleasures it was easy to guess it implied, took care, on this occasion, not to forget our training at Mrs. Cole's, and agreed to it with as good a grace as we could. Upon which, without loss of time, we return'd instantly to the pavilion, one door of which open'd into a tent, pitch'd before it, that with its marquise, formed a pleasing defence against the sun, or the weather, and was besides as private as we could wish. The lining of it, emboss'd cloth, represented a wild, forest-foliage, from the top, down to the sides, which, in the same stuff, were figur'd with fluted pilasters, with their spaces between fill'd with flower-vases, the whole having a gay effect upon the eye, wherever you turn'd it.

Then it reached sufficiently into the water, yet contain'd convenient benches round it, on the dry ground, either to keep our clothes, or . . . or . . . in short for more uses than resting upon. There was a side-table too, loaded with sweetmeats, jellies, and other eatables, and bottles of wine and cordials, by way of occasional relief from any rawness, or chill of the water, or from any faintness from whatever cause; and in fact, my gallant, who understood *chère entière* perfectly, and who, for taste (even if you would not approve this specimen of it) might have been comptroller of pleasures to a Roman emperor, had left no requisite towards convenience or luxury unprovided.

As soon as we had look'd round this inviting spot, and every preliminary of privacy was duly settled, strip was the word: when the young gentlemen soon dispatch'd the undressing each his partner and reduced us to the naked confession of all those secrets of person which dress generally hides, and which the discovery of was, naturally speaking, not to our disadvantage. Our hands, indeed, mechanically carried towards the most interesting part of us, screened, at first, all from the tufted cliff downwards, till we took them away at their desire, and employed them in doing them the same office, of helping off with their clothes; in the process of which, there pass'd all the little wantonnesses and frolicks that you may easily imagine.

As for my spark, he was presently undressed, all to his shirt, the fore-lappet of which, as he lean'd languishingly on me, he smilingly pointed to me to observe, as it bellied out, or rose and fell, according to the unruly starts of the motion behind it; but it was soon fix'd, for now, taking off his shirt, and naked as a Cupid, he shew'd it me at so upright a stand, as prepar'd me indeed for his application to me for instant ease; but, tho' the sight of its fine size was fit enough to fire me, the cooling air, as I stood in this state of nature, join'd to the desire I had of bathing first, enabled me to put him off, and tranquillize him, with the remark that a little suspense would only set a keener edge on the pleasure. Leading then the way, and shewing our friends an example of continency, which they were giving signs of losing respect to, we went hand in hand into the stream, till it took us up to our neck, where the no more than grateful coolness of the water gave my senses a delicious refreshment from the sultriness of the season, and made more alive, more happy in myself, and, in course, more alert, and open to voluptuous impressions.

Here I lav'd and wanton'd with the water, or sportively play'd with my companion, leaving Emily to deal with hers at discretion. Mine, at length, not content with making me take the plunge over head and ears, kept splashing me, and provoking me with all the little playful tricks he could devise, and which I strove not to remain in his debt for. We gave, in short, a loose to mirth; and now, nothing would serve him but giving his hands the regale of going over every part of me, neck, breast, belly, thighs, and all the rest, so dear to the imagination, under the pretext of washing and rubbing them; as we both stood in the water, no higher now than the pit of our stomachs, and which did not hinder him from feeling, and toying with that leak that distinguishes our sex, and it so wonderfully water-tight: for his fingers, in vain dilating and opening it, only let more flame than water into it, be it said without a figure. At the same time he made me feel his own engine, which was so well wound up, as to stand even the working in water, and he accordingly threw one arm round my neck, and was endeavouring to get the better of that harsher construction bred by the surrounding fluid; and had in effect won his way so far as to make me sensible of the pleasing stretch of those nether-lips from the in-driving machine; when, independent of my not liking that awkward mode of enjoyment, I could not help interrupting him, in order to become joint spectators of a plan of joy in hot operation between Emily and her partner; who, impatient of the fooleries and dalliance of the bath, had led his nymph to one of the benches on the green bank, where he was very cordially proceeding to teach her the difference between jest and earnest.

There, setting her on his knee, and gliding one hand over the surface of that smooth polish'd snow-white skin of hers, which now doubly shone with a dew-bright lustre, and presented to the touch something like what one would imagine of animated ivory, especially in those ruby-nippled globes, which the touch is so fond of and delights to make love to, with the other he was lusciously exploring the sweet secret of nature, in order to make room for a stately piece of machinery, that stood uprear'd, between her thighs, as she continued sitting on his lap, and pressed hard for instant admission, which the tender Emily, in a fit of humour, deliciously protracted, affecting to decline and elude the very pleasure she sigh'd for, but in a style of waywardness so prettily put on, and managed, as to render it ten times more poignant; then her eyes, all amidst the softest dying languishment, express'd at once a mock denial and extreme desire, whilst her sweetness was zested with a coyness so pleasingly provoking, her moods of keeping him of were so attractive, that they redoubled the impetuous rage with which he cover'd her with kisses.

Thus Emily, who knew no art but that which nature itself, in favour of her principal end, pleasure, had inspir'd her with, the art of yielding, coy'd it indeed, but coy'd it to the purpose; for with all her straining, her wrestling, and striving to break from the clasp of his arms, she was so far wiser yet than to mean it, that in her struggles, it was visible she aim'd at nothing more than multiplying points of touch with him, and drawing yet closer the folds that held them everywhere entwined, like two tendrils of a vine intercurling together; so that the same effect, as when Louisa strove in good earnest to disengage from the idiot, was now produced by different motives.

Meanwhile, their emersion out of the cold water had caused a general glow, a tender suffusion of heighten'd carnation over their bodies, both equally white and smooth-skinned, so that as their limbs were thus amorously inter-woven, in sweet confusion, it was scarce possible to dis-tinguish who they respectively belonged to, but for the brawnier, bolder muscles of the stronger sex.

In a little time, however, the champion was fairly in with her, and had tied at all points the true lover's knot; when now, adieu all the little refinements of a finessed reluctance; adieu the friendly feint! She was presently driven forcibly out of the power of using any art; and indeed, what art must not give way, when nature, corresponding with her assailant, invaded in the heart of her capital and carried by storm, lay at the mercy of the proud conqueror, who had made his entry triumphantly and completely? Soon, however, to become a tributary: for the engagement grow-ing hotter and hotter, at close quarters, she presently brought him to the pass of paying down the dear debt to nature; which she had no sooner collected in, but, like a duellist who has laid his antagonist at his feet, when he has himself received a mortal wound, Emily had scarce time to plume herself upon her victory, but, shot with the same discharge, she, in a loud expiring sigh, in the closure of her eyes, the stretch-out of her limbs, and a shudder of her whole frame, gave manifest signs that all was as it should be.

For my part, I had not with the calmest patience stood in the water all this time to view this warm action. I lean'd tenderly on my gallant, and at the close of it, seem'd to ask him with my eyes what he thought of it; but he, more eager to satisfy me by his actions than by words or looks, as we shoal'd the water towards the shore, shewed me the staff of love so intensely set up, that had not even charity beginning at home in this case, urged me to our mutual relief, it would have been cruel indeed to have suffered the youth to burst with straining, when the remedy was so obvious and so near at hand.

Accordingly we took to a bench, whilst Emily and her spark, who belonged it seems to the sea, stood at the sideboard, drinking to our good voyage: for, as the last observ'd, we were well under weigh, with a fair wind up channel, and full-freighted; nor indeed were we long before we finished our trip to Cythera, and unloaded in the old haven; but, as the circumstances did not admit of much variation, I shall spare you the description.

At the same time, allow me to place you here an excuse I am conscious of owing, you for having, perhaps, too much affected the figurative style; though surely, it can pass nowhere more allowably than in a subject which is so properly the province of poetry, nay, is poetry itself, pregnant with every flower of imagination and loving metaphors, even if the natural expressions, for respects of fashion and sound, necessarily forbid it.

Resuming now my history, you may please to know, that what with a competent number of repetitions, all in the same strain (and, by the bye, we have a certain natural sense that those repetitions are very much to the taste), what with a circle of pleasures delicately varied, there was not a moment lost to joy all the time we stay'd there, till late in the night we were re-escorted home by our squires, who delivered us safe to Mrs. Cole, with generous thanks for our company.

This too was Emily's last adventure in our way: for scarce a week after, she was, by an accident too trivial to detail to you the particulars, found out by her parents, who were in good circumstances, and who had been punish'd for their partiality to their son, in the loss of him, occasion'd by a circumstance of their over-indulgence to his appetite; upon which the so long engross'd stream of fondness, running violently in favour of this lost and inhumanly abandon'd child whom, if they had not neglected inquiry about they might long before have recovered, they were now so overjoyed at the retrieval of her, that, I presume, it made them much less strict in examining the bottom of things: for they seem'd very glad to take for granted, in the lump, everything that the grave and decent Mrs. Cole was pleased to pass upon them; and soon afterwards sent her, from the country, a handsome acknowledgement.

But it was not so easy to replace to our community the loss of so sweet a member of it: for, not to mention her beauty, she was one of those mild, pliant characters, that if one does not entirely esteem, one can scarce help loving, which is not such a bad compensation neither. Owing all her weakness to a good nature, and an indolent facility that kept her too much at the mercy of first impressions, she had just sense enough to know that she wanted leading strings, and thought herself so much obliged to any who would take the pains to think for her, and guide her, that with a very little management, she was capable of being made a most agreeable, nay, a most virtuous wife: for vice, it is probable, had never been her choice, or her fate, if it had not been for occasion, or example, or had she not depended less upon herself than upon her circumstances. This presumption her conduct afterwards verified: for presently meeting with a match that was ready cut and dry for her, with a neighbour's son of her own rank, and a young man of sense and order, who took her as the widow of one lost at sea (for so it seems one of her gallants, whose name she had made free with, really was), she naturally struck into all the duties of their domestic life, with as much simplicity of affection, with as much constancy and regularity, as if she had never swerv'd from a state of undebauch'd innocence and youth.

These desertions had, however, now so far thinned Mrs. Cole's brood, that she was left with only me, like a hen with one chicken; but tho' she was earnestly entreated and encourag'd to recruit her *corps*, her growing infirmities, and, above all, the tortures of a stubborn hip-gout, which she found would yield to no remedy, determin'd her to break up her business, and retire with a decent pittance into the country, where I promis'd myself nothing so sure, as my going down to live with her, as soon as I had seen a little more of life, and improv'd my small matters into a competency that would create in me an independence in the world: for I was, now, thanks to Mrs. Cole, wise enough to keep that essential in view.

Thus was I then to lose my faithful preceptress, as did the Philosophers of the town the White Crow of her profession. For besides that she never ransacked her customers, whose taste too she ever studiously consulted, besides that she never racked her pupils with unconscionable extortions, nor ever put their hard earnings, as she call'd them, under the contribution of poundage, she was a severe enemy to the seduction for innocence, and confin'd her acquisitions solely to those unfortunate young women, who, having lost it, were but the juster objects of compassion: among these, indeed, she pick'd but such as suited her views and, taking them under her protection, rescu'd them from the danger of the public sinks of ruin and misery, to place, or for them, well or ill, in the manner you have seen. Having then settled her affairs, she set out on her journey, after taking the most tender leave of me, and at the end of some excellent instructions, recommending me to myself, with an anxiety perfectly maternal. In short, she affected me so much, that I was not presently reconcil'd to myself for suffering her at any rate to go without me; but fate had, it seems, otherwise dispos'd of me.

I had, on my separation from Mrs. Cole, taken a pleasant convenient house at *Marlybone*, but easy to rent and manage from its smallness, which I furnishe'd neatly and modestly. There, with a reserve of eight hundred pounds, the fruit of my deference to Mrs. Cole's counsels, exclusive of clothes, some jewels, some plate, I saw myself in purse for a long time, to wait without impatience for what the chapter of accidents might produce in my favour.

Here, under the new character of a young gentlewoman whose husband was gone to sea, I had mark'd me out such lines of life and conduct, as leaving me at a competent liberty to pursue my views either out of pleasure of fortune, bounded me nevertheless strictly within the rules of decency and discretion: a disposition in which you cannot escape observing a true pupil of Mrs. Cole.

I was scarce, however, well warm in my new abode, when going out one morning pretty early to enjoy the freshness of it, in the pleasing outlet of the fields, accompanied only by a maid, whom I had newly hired, as we were carelessly walking among the trees we were alarmed with the noise of a violent coughing: turning our heads towards which, we distinguish'd a plain well-dressed elderly gentleman, who, attack'd with a sudden fit, was so much overcome, as to be forc'd to give way to it and sit down at the foot of a tree, where he seemed suffocating with the severity of it, being perfectly black in the face: not less mov'd than frighten'd with which, I flew on the instant to his relief, and using the rite of practice I had observ'd on the like occasion, I loosened his cravat and clapped him on the back; whether to any purpose, or whether the cough had had its course, I know not, but the fit immediately went off; and now recover'd to his speech and legs, he returned me thanks with as much emphasis as if I had sav'd his life. This naturally engaging a conversation, he acquainted me where he lived, which was at a considerable distance from where I met with him, and where he had stray'd insensibly on the same intention of a morning walk.

He was, as I afterwards learn'd in the course of the intimacy which this little accident gave birth to, an old bachelor, turn'd sixty, but of a fresh vigorous complexion, insomuch that he scarce looked five and forty, having never rack'd his constitution by permitting his desires to overtax his ability.

As to his birth and condition, his parents, honest and fail'd mechanics, had, by the best traces he could get of them, left him an infant orphan on the parish; so that it was from a charity-school, that, by honesty and industry, he made his way into a merchant's counting house; from whence, being sent to a house in Cadiz, he there, by his talents and activity, acquired a fortune, but an immense one, with which he returned to his native country; where he could not, however, so much as fish out one single relation out of the obscurity he was born in. Taking then a taste for retirement, and pleas'd to enjoy life, like a mistress in the dark, he passed his days in all the ease of opulence, without the least parade of it; and, rather studying the concealment than the show of a fortune, looked down on a world he perfectly knew; himself, to his wish, unknown and unmarked by.

But, as I propose to devote a letter entirely to the pleasure of retracing to you all the particulars of my acquaintance with this ever, to me, memorable friend, I shall, in this, transiently touch on no more than may serve as mortar to cement, to form the connection of my history, and to obviate your surprise that one of my high blood and relish of life should count a gallant of threescore such a catch.

Referring then to a more explicit narrative, to explain by what progressions our acquaintance, certainly innocent at first, insensibly changed nature, and ran into unplatonic lengths, as might well be expected from one of my condition of life, and above all, from that principle of electricity that scarce ever fails of producing fire when the sexes meet, I shall only here acquaint you, that as age had not subdued his tenderness for our sex, neither had it robbed him of the power of pleasing, since whatever he lacked in the bewitching charms of youth, he aton'd for, or supplemented with the advantages of experience, the sweetness of his manners, and above all, his flattering address in touching the heart, by an application to the understanding. From him it was I first learn'd, to any purpose, and not without infinite pleasure, that I had such a portion of me worth bestowing some regard on; from him I received my first essential encouragement, and instructions how to put it in that train of cultivation, which I have since pushed to the little degree of improvement you see it at; he it was who first taught me to be sensible that the pleasures of the mind were superior to those of the body; at the same time, that they were so far from obnoxious to, or incompatible with each other, that, besides the sweetness in the variety and transition, the one serv'd to exalt and perfect the taste of the other, to a degree that the senses alone can never arrive at.

Himself a rational pleasurist, as being much too wise to be asham'd of the pleasures of humanity, loved me indeed, but loved me with dignity; in a manner equally remov'd from the sourness, or forwardness, by which age is unpleasingly characteriz'd, and from that childish silly dotage that so often disgraces it, and which he himself used to turn into ridicule, and compare to an old goat affecting the frisk of a young kid.

In short, everything that is generally unamiable in his season of life was, in him, repair'd by so many advantages that he was a proof, manifest at least to me, that it is not out of the power of age to please, if it sets out to please, and if, making just allowances, those in that class do not forget, that it must cost them more pains and attention, than what youth, the natural spring-time of joy, stands in need of: as fruits out of season require proportionately more skill and cultivation to force them.

With the gentleman then, who took me home soon after our acquaintance commenc'd, I lived near eight months; in which time, my constant complaisance and docility, my attention to deserve his confidence and love, and a conduct, in general, devoid of the least art and founded on my sincere regard and esteem for him, won and attach'd him so firmly to me, that, after having generously trusted me with a genteel, independent settlement, proceeding to heap marks of affection on me, he appointed me, by an authentic will, his sole heiress and executrix: a disposition which he did not outlive two months, being taken from me by a violent cold that he contracted as he unadvisedly ran to the window, on an alarm of fire, at some streets distant, and stood there naked-breasted, and exposed to the fatal impressions of a damp night air.

After acquitting myself of my duty towards my deceas'd benefactor, and paying him a tribute of unfeign'd sorrow, which a little time chang'd into a most tender, grateful memory of him, that I shall ever retain, I grew somewhat comforted by the prospect that now open'd to me, if not of happiness, at least of affluence and independence.

I saw myself then in the full bloom and pride of youth (for I was not yet nineteen), actually at the head of so large a fortune that would have been even the height of imprudence in me to have raised my wishes, much more my hopes, to; and that this unexpected elevation did not turn my head I ow'd to the pains my benefactor had taken to form and prepare me for it, as I ow'd his opinion of my management of the vast possessions he left me to what he had observ'd of the prudential economy I had learned under Mrs. Cole, of which the reserve he saw I had made was a proof and encouragement to him.

But, alas, how easily is the enjoyment of the greatest sweets in life, in present possession, poisoned by the regret of an absent one! but my regret was a mighty and just one, since it had my only truly beloved *Charles* for its object.

Given him up I had, indeed, completely, having never once heard from him since our separation; which, as I found afterwards, had been my misfortune, and not his neglect, for he wrote me several letters which had all been lost; but forgotten him I never had. And amidst all my personal infidelities, not one had made a pin's point impression on a heart impenetrable to the true love-passion, but for him.

As soon, however, as I was mistress of his unexpected fortune, I felt more than ever how dear he was to me, from its insufficiency to make me happy, whilst he was not to share it with me. My earliest care, consequently, was to endeavour at getting some account of him; but all my researches produc'd me no more light, than that his father had been dead for some time, not so well as even with the world; and that Charles had reached his port of destination in the *South Seas,* where, finding the estate he was sent to recover, dwindled to a trifle, by the loss of two ships in which the bulk of his uncle's fortune lay, he was come away with the small remainder, and might, perhaps, according to the best advice, in a few months return to England, from whence he had, at the time of this my inquiry, been absent two years and seven months. A little eternity in love!

You cannot conceive with what joy I embraced the hopes thus given me of seeing the delight of my heart again. But, as the term of months was assigned it, in order to divert and amuse my impatience for his return, after settling my affairs with much ease and security, I set out on a journey for Lancashire, with an equipage suitable to my fortune, and with a design purely to revisit my place of nativity, for which I could not help retaining a great tenderness; and might naturally not be sorry to show myself there, to the advantage I was now in pass to do, after the report Esther Davis had spread of my being spirited away to the plantations; for on no other supposition could she account for the suppression of myself to her, since her leaving me so abruptly at the inn. Another intention I had was to look out for my relations, though I had none besides distant ones, and prove a benefactress to them. Then Mrs. Cole's place of retirement lying in my way, was not amongst the least of the pleasures I had proposed to myself in this expedition.

I had taken nobody with me but a discreet woman for my companion, besides my servants, and was scarce got into an inn, about twenty miles from London, where I was to sup and pass the night, when such a storm of wind and rain sprang up as made me congratulate myself on having got under shelter before it began.

This had continu'd a good half hour, when bethinking me of some directions to be given to the coachman, I sent for him, and not caring that his shoes should soil the very clean parlour, in which the cloth was laid, I stept into the hall-kitchen, where he was, and where, whilst I was talking to him, I slantingly observ'd two horsemen driven in by the weather, and both wringing wet; one of whom was asking if they could not be assisted with a change, while their clothes were dried. But, heavens! who can express what I felt at the sound of a voice, ever present to my heart, and that it now rebounded at! or when pointing my eyes towards the person it came from, they confirm'd its information, in spite of so long an absence, and of a dress one would have imagin'd studied for a disguise: a horseman's great coat, with a stand-up cape, and his hat flapp'd . . . but what could escape the piercing alertness of a sense surely guided by love? A transport then like mine was above all consideration, or schemes of surprise; and I, that instant, with the rapidity of the emotions that I felt the spur of, shot into his arms, crying out, as I threw mine round his neck: "My life! . . . my soul! . . . my *Charles*!" and without further power of speech swoon'd away, under the pressing agitations of joy and surprise.

Recover'd out of my entrancement, I found myself in my charmer's arms, but in the parlour, surrounded by a crowd which this event had gather'd round us, and which immediately, on a signal from the discreet landlady, who currently took him for my husband, clear'd the room, and desirably left us alone to the raptures of this reunion; my joy at which had like to have prov'd, at the expense of my life, power superior to that of grief at our fatal separation.

The first object then, that my eyes open'd on, was their supreme idol, and my supreme wish, Charles, on one knee, holding me fast by the hand and gazing on me with a transport of fondness. Observing my recovery, he attempted to speak, and give vent to his patience of hearing my voice again, to satisfy him once more that it was *me*; but the mightiness and suddenness of the surprise continuing to stun him, choked his utterance: he could only stammer out a few broken, half formed, faltering accents, which, my ears greedily drinking in, spelt, and put together, so as to make out their sense: "After so long! ... so cruel ... an absence! ... my dearest *Fanny*! ... can it? ... can it be you? ..." stifling me at the same time with kisses, that, stopping my mouth, at once prevented the answer that he panted for, and increas'd the delicious disorder in which all my senses were rapturously lost. Amidst however, this host of ideas, and all blissful ones, there intruded only one cruel doubt, that poison'd nearly all the transcendent happiness: and what was it, but my dread of its being too excessive to be real? I trembled now with the fear of its being no more than a dream, and of my waking out of it into the horrors of finding it one. Under this foolish apprehension, imagining I could not make too much of the present prodigious joy, before it should vanish and leave me in the desert again, nor verify its reality too strongly, I clung to him, I clasp'd him, as if to hinder him from escaping me again: "Where have you been? ... how could you ... could you leave me? ... Say you are still mine ... that you still love me ... and thus! thus!" (kissing him as if I would fuse my lips with his) "I forgive you ... forgive my hard fortune in favour of this restoration!"

All these interjections breaking from me, in that wildness of expression that justly passes for eloquence in love, drew from him all the returns my fond heart could wish or require. Our caresses, our questions, our answers, for some time observ'd no order; all crossing, or interrupting one another in sweet confusion, whilst we exchang'd hearts at our eyes, and renew'd the ratifications of a love unbated by time or absence: not a breath, not a motion, not a gesture on either side, but what was strongly impressed with it. Our hands, lock'd in each other, repeated the most passionate squeezes, so that their fiery thrill went to the heart again.

Thus absorb'd, and concenter'd in this unutterable delight, I had not attended to the sweet author of it, being thoroughly wet, and in danger of catching cold; when, in good time, the landlady, whom the appearance of my equipage (which, by the bye, Charles knew nothing of) had gain'd me an interest in, for me and mine, interrupted us by bringing in a decent shift of linen and clothes, which now, somewhat recover'd into a calmer composure by the coming in of a third person, I prest him to take the benefit of, with a tender concern and anxiety that made me tremble for his health.

The landlady leaving us again, he proceeded to shift; in the act of which, tho' he proceeded with all that modesty which became these first solemner instants of our re-meeting, after so long an absence, I could not contain certain snatches of my eyes, lur'd by the dazzling discoveries of his naked skin, that escaped him as he chang'd his linen, and which I could not observe the unfaded life and complexion of without emotions of tenderness and joy, that had himself too purely for their object, to partake of a loose or mistim'd desire.

He was soon drest in these temporary clothes, which neither fitted him, nor became the light my passion plac'd him in, to me at least; yet, as they were on him, they look'd extremely well, in virtue of that magic charm which love put into everything that he touch'd, or had relation to him: and where, indeed, was that dress that a figure like this would not give grace to? For now, as I ey'd him more in detail, I could not but observe the even favourable alteration which the time of his absence had producted in his person.

There were still the requisite lineaments, still the same vivid vermilion and bloom reigning in his face; but now the roses were more fully blown; the tan of his travels, and a beard somewhat more distinguishable, had, at the expense of no more delicacy than what he could well spare, given it an air of becoming manliness and maturity, that symmetriz'd nobly with that air of distinction and empire with which nature had stamp'd it, in a rare mixture with the sweetness of it; still nothing had he lost of that smooth plumpness of flesh, which, glowing with freshness, blooms florid to the eye, and delicious to the touch; then his shoulders were grown more square, his shape more form'd, more portly, but still free and airy. In short, his figure show'd riper, greater, and perfecter to the experienced eye, than in his tender youth; and now he was not much more than two and twenty.

In this interval, however, I pick'd out of the broken, often pleasingly interrupted account of himself that he was, at that instant, actually on his road to London, in not a very paramount plight or condition, having been wreck'd on the Irish coast for which he had prematurely embark'd, and lost the little he had brought with him from the South Seas; so that he had not till after great shifts and hardships, in the company of his fellow-traveller, the captain, got so far on his journey; that so it was (having heard of his father's death and circumstances) he had now the world to begin again, on a new account: a situation, which he assur'd me, in a vein of sincerity, that flowing from his heart, penetrated mine, gave him to further pain, than that he had it not in his power to make me as happy as he could wish. My fortune, you will please to observe, I had not enter'd upon any overture of, reserving to feast myself with the surprise of it to him, in calmer instants. And, as to my dress, it could give him no idea of the truth, not only as it was mourning, but likewise in a style of plainness and simplicity that I had ever kept to with studied art. He press'd me indeed tenderly to satisfy his ardent curiosity, both with regard to my past and present state of life, since his being torn away from me: but I had the address to elude his questions, by answers that, showing his satisfaction at no great distance, won upon him to wave his impatience, in favour of the thorough confidence he had in my not delaying it, but for respects I should in good time acquaint him with.

Charles, however, thus returned to my longing arms, tender, faithful, and in health, was already a blessing too mighty for my conception: but Charles in distress! ... Charles reduc'd, and broken down to his naked personal merit, was such a circumstance, in favour of the sentiments I had for him, as exceeded my utmost desires; and accordingly I seemed so visibly charm'd, so out of time and measure pleas'd at his mention of his ruin'd fortune, that he could account for it no way, but that the joy of seeing him again had swallow'd up every other sense, or concern.

In the meantime, my woman had taken all possible care of Charles's travelling companion; and as supper was coming in, he was introduc'd to me, and I receiv'd him as became my regard for all of Charles's acquaintance or friends.

We four then supp'd together, in the style of joy, congratulation and pleasing disorder that you may guess. For my part, though all these agitations had left me not the least stomach, but for that uncloying feast, the sight of my ador'd youth, I endeavour'd to force it, by way of example for him, who I conjectur'd must want such a recruit after riding; and, indeed, he ate like a traveller, but gaz'd at, and addressed me all the time like a lover.

After the cloth was taken away, and the hour of repose came on, Charles and I were, without further ceremony, in quality of man and wife, shown up together to a very handsome apartment and, all in course, the bed, which they said was the best in the inn.

And here, Decency, forgive me! if once more I violate thy laws and, keeping the curtains undrawn, sacrifice thee for the last time to that confidence, without reserve, with which I engaged to recount to you the most striking circumstances of my youthful disorders.

As soon, then, as we were in the room together, left to ourselves, the sight of the bed awaking the remembrance of our first joys, and the thought of my being instantly to share it with the dear possessor of my virgin heart mov'd me so strongly, that it was well I lean'd upon him, or I must have fainted again under the overpowering sweet alarm. Charles saw my confusion, and forgot his own, that was scarce less, to apply himself to the removal of mine.

But now the true refining passion had regain'd thorough possession of me, with all its train of symptoms: a sweet sensibility, a tender timidity, love-sick yearnings temper'd with diffidence and modesty, all held me in a subjection of soul, incomparably dearer to me than the liberty of heart which I had been long, too long! the mistress of, in the course of those grosser gallantries, the consciousness of which now made me sigh with a virtuous confusion and regret. No real virgin, in short, in view of the nuptial bed, could give more bashful blushes to unblemish'd innocence, than I did to a sense of guilt; and indeed I lov'd Charles too truly not to feel severely that I did not deserve him.

As I kept hesitating and disconcerted under this soft distraction, Charles, with a fond impatience, took the pains to undress me; and all I can remember amidst the flutter and discomposure of my senses was some flattering exclamations of joy and admiration, more specially at the feel of my breasts, now set at liberty from my stays, and which panting and rising in tumultuous throbs, swell'd upon his dear touch, and gave it the welcome pleasure of finding them well form'd, and unfail'd in firmness.

I was soon laid in bed, and scarce languish'd an instant for the darling partner of it, before he was undress'd and got between the sheets, with his arms clasp'd round me, giving and taking, with passion inexpressible, a kiss of welcome, that my heart rising to my lips stamp'd with its warmest impression, concurring to my bliss, with that delicate and voluptuous emotion which Charles alone had the secret to excite, and which constitutes the very life, the essence of pleasure.

Meanwhile, two candles lighted on a side-table near us and a joyous wood fire threw a light onto the bed, that took from one sense, of great importance to our joys, all pretext for complaining of its being shut out of its share of them; and indeed, the sight of my idolized youth was alone, from the ardour with which I had wished for it, without other circumstance, a pleasure to die of.

But as action was now a necessity to desires so much on edge as ours, Charles, after a very short preparatory dalliance, lifting up my linen and his own, laid the broad treasures of his manly chest close to my bosom, both beating with the tenderest alarms: when now, the sense of his glowing body, in naked touch with mine, took all power over my thoughts out of my own disposal, and deliver'd up every faculty of the soul to the sensiblest of joys, that, affecting me infinitely more with my distinction of the person than of the sex, now brought my conscious heart deliciously into play: my heart, eternally constant to Charles, had never taken any part in my occasional sacrifices to the calls of constitution, complaisance, or interest. But ah! what became of me, when as the powers of solid pleasure thickened upon me, I could not help feeling the stiff stake that had been adorn'd with the trophies of my despoil'd virginity, bearing hard and inflexible against one of my thighs, which I had not yet opened, from a true principle of modesty, reviv'd by a passion too sincere to suffer any aiming at the false merit of difficulty, or my putting on an impertinent mock coyness.

I have, I believe, somewhere before remark'd that the feel of that favourite piece of manhood has, in the very nature of it, something inimitably pathetic. Nothing can be dearer to the touch, nor can affect it with a more delicious sensation. Think then! as a love thinks, what must be the consummate transport of that quickest of our senses, in their central seat too! when, after so long a deprival, it felt itself reinflam'd under the pressure of that peculiar sceptre-member, which commands us all: but especially, my darling, elect from the face of the whole earth. And now, at its mightiest point of stiffness, it felt to me something so subduing, so active, so solid and agreeable, that I know not what name to give its singular impression: but the sentiment of consciousness of its belonging to my supremely beloved youth gave me so pleasing an agitation, and work'd so strongly on my soul, that it sent all its sensitive spirits to that organ of bliss in me, dedicated to its reception. There, cencentring to a point, like rays in a burning glass, they glow'd, they burnt with the intensest heat; the springs of pleasure were, in short, wound up to such a pitch, I panted now with so exquisitely keen an appetite for the eminent enjoyment, that I was even sick with desire, and unequal to support the combination of two distinct ideas, that delightfully distracted me: for all the thought I was capable of, was that I was now in touch at once with the instrument of pleasure and the great seal of love. Ideas that, mingling streams, pour'd such an ocean of intoxicating bliss on a weak vessel, all too narrow to contain it, that I lay overwhelm'd, absorb'd, lost in an abyss of joy, and dying of nothing but immoderate delight.

Charles then rous'd me somewhat out of this ecstatic distraction, with a complaint softly murmured, amidst a crowd of kisses, at the position, not so favourable to his desires, in which I receiv'd his urgent insistence for admission, where that insistence was alone so engrossing a pleasure, that it made me inconsistently suffer a much dearer one to be kept out; but how sweet to correct such a mistake! My thighs, now obedient to the intimations of love and nature, gladly disclose, and with a ready submission, resign up the soft gateway to the entrance of pleasure: I see, I feel the delicious velvet tip! . . . he enters me might and main, with . . . oh! my pen drops from me here in the ecstasy now present to my faithful memory! Description too deserts me, and delivers over a task, above its strength of wing, to the imagination: but it must be an imagination exalted by such a flame as mine that can do justice to that sweetest, noblest of all sensations, that hailed and accompany'd the stiff insinuation all the way up, till it was at the end of its penetration, sending up, through my eyes, the sparks of the love-fire that ran all over me and blaz'd in every vein and every pore of me; a system incarnate of joy all over.

I had now totally taken in love's true arrow from the point up to the feather, in that part, where making no new wound, the lips of the original one of nature, which had owed its first breathing to this dear instrument, clung, as if sensible of gratitude, in eager suction round it, whilst all its inwards embrac'd it tenderly, with a warmth of passion, a compressive energy, that gave it, in its way, the heartiest welcome in nature; every fibre there gathering right round it, and straining ambitiously to come in for its share of the blissful touch.

As we were giving then a few moments of pause to the

delectation of the senses, dwelling with the highest relish on this intimatest point of reunion, and chewing the cud of enjoyment, the impatience natural to the pleasure soon drove us into action. Then began the driving tumult on his side, and the responsive heaves on mine, which kept me up to him; whilst, as our joys grew too great for utterance, the organs of our voices, voluptuously intermixing, became organs of the touch . . . and oh, that touch! how delicious! . . . how poignantly luscious! . . . And now! now I felt, to the heart of me! I felt the prodigious keen edge, with which love, presiding over this act, points the pleasure: love! that may be styled the Attic salt of enjoyment; and indeed, without it, the joy, great as it is, is still a vulgar one, whether in a king or a beggar; for it is, undoubtedly, love alone that refines, ennobles and exalts it.

Thus happy, then, by the heart, happy by the senses, it was beyond all power, even of thought, to form the conception of a greater delight than what I was now consummating the fruition of.

Charles, whose whole frame was convulsed with the agitation of his rapture, whilst the tenderest fires trembled in his eyes, all assured me of a perfect concord of joy, penetrated me so profoundly, touch'd me so vitally, took me so much out of my own possession, whilst he seem'd himself so much in mine, that in a delicious enthusiasm, I imagin'd such a transfusion of heart and spirit, as that coalescing, and making one body and soul with him, I was he, and he, me.

But all this pleasure tending, like life from its first instants, towards its own dissolution, liv'd too fast not to bring on upon the spur its delicious moment of mortality; for presently the approach of the tender agony discover'd itself by its usual signals, that were quickly follow'd by my dear love's emanation of himself, that spun out, and shot, feelingly indeed! up the ravish'd indraught: where the sweetly soothing balmy titillation opened all the juices of joy on my side, which ecstatically in flow, help'd to allay the prurient glow, and drown'd our pleasure for a while. Soon, however, to be on float again! for Charles, true to nature's laws, in one breath expiring and ejaculating, languish'd not long in the dissolving trance, but recovering spirit again, soon gave me to feel that the true-mettle springs of his instrument of pleasure were, by love, and perhaps, by a long vacation, wound up too high to be let down by a single explosion: his stiffness still stood my friend. Resuming then the action afresh, without dislodging, or giving me the trouble of parting from my sweet tenant, we play'd over again the same opera, with the same delightful harmony and concert: our ardours, like our love, knew no remission; and, all as the tide serv'd my lover, lavish of his stores, and pleasure-milked, overflowed me once more from the fulness of his oval reservoirs of the genial emulsion: whilst, on my side, a convulsive grasp, in the instant of my giving down the liquid contribution, render'd me sweetly subservient at once to the increase of his joy, and of its effusions: moving me so, as to make me exert all those springs of the compressive suction, with which the sensitive mechanism of that part thirstily draws and drains the nipple of Love; with much such an instinctive eagerness and attachment, as, to compare great with less, kind nature engages infants at the breast, by the pleasure they find in the motion of their little mouths and cheeks, to extract the milky stream prepar'd for their nourishment.

But still there was no end of his vigour: this double discharge had so far from extinguish'd his desires, for that time, that it had not even calm'd them; and at his age, desires are power. He was proceeding then amazingly to push it to a third triumph, still without uncasing, if a tenderness, natural to true love, had not inspir'd me with self denial enough to spare, and not overstrain him: and accordingly, entreating him to give himself and me quarter, I obtain'd, at length, a short suspension of arms, but not before he had exultingly satisfy'd me that he gave out standing.

The remainder of the night, with what we borrow'd upon the day, we employ'd with unweary'd fervour in celebrating thus the festival of our re-meeting; and got up pretty late in the morning, gay, brisk and alert, though rest had been a stranger to us: but the pleasures of love had been to us, what the joy of victory is to an army: repose, refreshment, everything.

The journey into the country being now entirely out of the question, and orders having been given overnight for turning the horses' heads towards London, we left the inn as soon as we had breakfasted, not without a liberal distribution of the tokens of my grateful sense of the happiness I had met with in it.

Charles and I were in my coach; the captain and my companion in a chaise hir'd purposely for them, to leave us the conveniency of a *tête-à-tête*.

Here, on the road, as the tumult of my senses was tolerably compos'd, I had command enough of head to break properly to him the course of life that the consequences of my separation from him had driven me into; which, at the same time that he tenderly deplor'd with me, he was the less shocked at; as, on reflecting how he had left me circumstanc'd, he could not be entirely unprepar'd for it.

But when I revealed the state of my fortune to him, and with that sincerity which, from me to him, was so much a nature in me, I begg'd of him his acceptance of it, on his own terms. I should appear to you perhaps too partial to my passion were I to attempt doing his delicacy justice. I shall content myself then with assuring you, that after his flatly refusing the unreserv'd, unconditional donation that I long persecuted him in vain to accept, it was at length, in obedience to his serious commands (for I stood out unaffectedly, till he exerted the sovereign authority which love had given him over me), that I yielded my consent to wave the remonstrance I did not fail of making strongly to him, against his degrading himself, and incurring the reflection, however unjust, of having, for respects of fortune, barter'd his honour for infamy and prostitution, in making one his wife, who thought herself too much honour'd in being but his mistress.

The plea of love then over-ruling all objections, Charles, entirely won with the merit of my sentiments for him, which he could not but read the sincerity of in a heart ever open to him, oblig'd me to receive his hand, by which means I was able, among other innumerable blessings, to bestow a legal parentage on those fine children you have seen by this happiest of matches.

Thus, at length, I got snug into port, where, in the bosom of virtue, I gather'd the only uncorrupt sweets: where, looking back on the course of vice I had run, and comparing its infamous blandishments with the infinitely superior joys of innocence, I could not help pitying, even in point of taste, those who, immers'd in gross sensuality, are insensible to the so delicate charms of VIRTUE, than which even PLEASURE has not a greater friend, nor than VICE a greater enemy. Thus temperance makes men lords over those pleasures that intemperance enslaves them to: the one, parent of health, vigour, fertility, cheerfulness, and every other desirable good of life; the other, of diseases, debility, barrenness, self-loathing, with only every evil incident to human nature.

You laugh, perhaps, at this tailpiece of morality, extracted from me by the force of truth, resulting from compar'd experiences: you think it, no doubt, out of place, out of character; possibly too you may look on it as the paltry finesse of one who seeks to mask a devotee to Vice under a rag of a veil, impudently smuggled from the shrine of Virtue: just as if one was to fancy one's self completely disguised at a masquerade, with no other change of dress than turning one's shoes into slippers; or as if a writer should think to shield a treasonable libel by concluding it with a formal prayer for the King. But, independent of my flattering myself that you have a juster opinion of my sense and sincerity, give me leave to represent to you, that such a supposition is even more injurious to Virtue than to me: since, consistently with candour and good-nature, it can have no foundation but in the falsest of fears, that its pleasures cannot stand in comparison with those of Vice; but let truth dare to hold it up its most alluring light: then mark how spurious, how low of taste, how comparatively inferior its joys are to those which Virtue gives sanction to, and whose sentiments are not above making even a sauce for the senses, but a sauce of the highest relish; whilst Vices are the harpies that infect and foul the feast. The paths of Vice are sometimes strew'd with roses, but then they are for ever infamous for many a thorn, for many a canker-worm: those of Virtue are strew'd with roses purely, and those eternally unfading ones.

If you do me then justice, you will esteem me perfectly consistent in the incense I burn to Virtue. If I have painted Vice in all its gayest colours, if I have deck'd it with flowers, it has been solely in order to make the worthier, the solemner sacrifice of it to Virtue.

You know Mr. C*** O***, you know his estate, his worth, and good sense: can you, will you pronounce it ill meant, at least of him, when anxious for his son's morals, with a view to form him to virtue, and inspire him with a fix'd, a rational contempt for vice, he condescended to be his master of the ceremonies, and led him by the hand thro' the most noted bawdy-houses in town, where he took care he should be familiarized with all those scenes of debauchery so fit to nauseate a good taste? The experiment, you will cry, is dangerous. True, on a fool: but are fools worth so much attention?

I shall see you soon, and in the meantime think candidly of me, and believe me ever,

MADAM,

Yours, etc., etc., etc.

'Far more amusing, fantastic and enthralling
than, say, Frank Harris's *My Life and
Loves*'
Tribune

MONSIEUR NICOLAS 7/6

Restif de la Bretonne

Translated by Robert Baldick

De la Bretonne was a man who loved and
worshipped women, perhaps not wisely but
definitely extremely well. Despite the
writing of 240 books, he dedicated himself
tirelessly to their pursuit and conquest. This is
his sometimes-embarrassingly frank account
of his life and loves—of the two women he
worshipped, of the hundreds he enjoyed.

'Has been described as possibly the most
amazing and intimate biography ever printed.
And it is'
The Scotsman

Fully illustrated